Finesse da Game

Finesse da Game

PRELUDE

Her troubled moans wake me.

"Nooo... leave me alone... get offa' me."

"Nessa." I whisper her name and try to pull her away from her demons. The webs of sleep try to hold me back as my eyes adjust to the darkness. I see her small frame struggling beside me, trying to get free, fighting a ghost.

"Nessa, wake up." I try to shake her awake, but she only struggles harder.

"Stop it... somebody help me." The strength she fights with lets me know how terrified she is. "Nooo!" she screams then snaps awake. Her eyes look around wildly until they find me. "Dena?" I reach for her and she collapses into my arms trembling, sweating, breathing heavily.

The same thing happens almost every night; she relives the trauma that monster put her through. Twenty- one years old and Finesse still be having nightmares about what Lafu did to her.

"Shhh, it's okay baby. It's only a dream. Go back to sleep." I murmur softly as I hold and rock her. I feel the tension leave her body as she starts to relax, but I know she isn't going back to sleep.

I wait.

Her breathing returns to normal and the trembling stops. Then her hands start to explore; one moves slowly up my thigh between my legs, the other eases my shirt up as her mouth finds my breast. I know what's coming next.

I was eighteen when Finesse first told me what Lafu was doing to her. We went to the movies together to see the new Ice Cube movie 'Players Club' starring Lisa Raye.

Right after the part when the character Diamond's younger cousin Ebony gets raped while getting ready to strip for a bachelor party, Finesse got up out of her seat.

"I'm ready to go."

"What? Why? This movie good as hell."

"You stay and watch it then." She shuffled past me and out of the movie theater. Already deep into the movie and wanting to see how it ended, I was reluctant to follow.

I kicked the back of the seat in front of me.

"Damn, damn, damn!" The guy sitting in it turned around. "Whatchu' lookin' at." I said before getting up and following.

Finesse was already halfway across the parking lot when I came out.

"Wait up girl." I said catching up. "Why you leave?"

"I didn't like the movie."

"That movie was good as hell and you know it. "

"I didn't like it."

"Come on now, what about the part when Ice Cube hit that big ole dude in the back with that chair? Tell me you didn't like that part. You say you like thug niggas."

"I just didn't like the movie that's all."

Finesse is just like that sometimes. She'll close up on you and go inside her own head. Other times she's her wild, crazy, fun-loving-self. I always figured it had something to do with her being in foster care when she was younger. Something bad must have happened because she was shellshock when she first came to live with us. Whenever my mother would try to dress or touch her, she would either flinch or run away. For a while, I was the only person she would respond to. Over time I got her to open up. I became her best friend.

"Finesse, sometimes I don't understand you."

"Sometimes I don't understand myself."

That night my bladder woke me in the wee hours screaming for release. After going to the bathroom, I stumbled half asleep back towards my room. That's when I heard Finesse cry out. Her voice came through the bedroom door clearly.

"Leave me alone...getcho' hands offa' me.

Thinking that someone had broken in and was attacking her, I ran back to my room like Lisa Raye in the movie and got my chrome Barretta out of the closet. After jacking a bullet into the chamber, I ran back to Finesse's room ready to blow somebody away. When I burst through the door, all I found was Finesse in the bed by herself fighting the covers. Disappointed that I wouldn't be getting a chance to test my shooting skills, I went and woke her up.

Finesse came out of her nightmare shaking and shedding tears. She looked up at me and instantly began scooting away and shaking her head.

"Nooo...please no..."

"Finesse, it's me Dena. Girl you alright?"

For a moment she seemed confused, but I could tell that my voice had triggered something. Then she relaxed and sat up on the side of the bed. Dropping her forehead in the palm of her hand, she blew out a breath.

"Stupid dreams."

I sat down next to her. "What the hell was you dreaming about that gotchu' so scared?"

"Oh girl... it wasn't nothing. Just a big ole coojo-looking- dog chasing me all over the place." She gave me a fake laugh. I knew she was lying, just didn't know why.

"Coojo had you screaming getcho' hands offa' me?" I challenged giving her direct eye contact. Her eyes dropped away from mine and landed on the gun in my hand.

"And what was you gone do with that?"

"Whatchu' think I was gone do with it. Shit, I thought somebody was in here witchu' the way you was screaming." We both laughed. "For real though, what was you dreaming about?"

"Just let it go Dena."

"Come on Nessa, this me. You know you can talk to me about anything."

"Just let it go Dena, damn!" Guess she felt bad for snapping at me because she said, "Look, I don't wanna see nothing happen to you."

"Something happen to me. Girl whatchu' talking about?"

That's when the tears came. That's when she finally broke down and told me.

It all started when she was five years old, not long after my mother adopted her and she came to live with us. Lafu use to go into her room at night and read her bedtime stories until she fell asleep. She told me that she used to love listening to his funny accent. Then he told her that he knew a trick that would make her sleep better than any bedtime story there was. When she asked him what it was, he pulled down her underwear and used his mouth on her. Thinking that it tickled a little and not really understanding what was happening, she let him do it. Every chance he got after that, Lafu would go into her room, read her stories, and do the "bedtime trick." Eventually she began looking forward to it just as much as the bedtime stories.

One night he went into her room after she was already asleep and woke her up. He told her that he had read a whole bunch of bedtime stories, but still couldn't go to sleep. Being the sweet innocent little girl that she was and not knowing any better, she asked did he want her to try the bedtime trick on him. So he showed her how. Lafu told her that she had to keep it a secret because little girls weren't supposed to know how to do grownup tricks and if anyone ever found out, she could get into trouble. So she never told anyone.

Over the years he showed her all kinds of "bedtime tricks" using her hands and mouth, but when she felt the pain of him trying to penetrate her young body at eleven years old. That's when she told him that she didn't want to do it anymore. That's when he turned mean. That's when he told her that she wasn't a little girl anymore and she'd better be quiet and deal with it. That's when he forced himself inside of her and stole the last of her innocence.

"He told me that if I ever told anyone he was gone hurt you."

I couldn't stop my tears from falling. Sympathy and outrage couldn't even begin to describe the emotions I was feeling. Finesse was sixteen years old. That meant that she had been dealing with this by herself for eleven years.

"Does anyone else know about this?" She shook her head.

"And you can't tell anyone either. Promise me you won't say anything." I thought about the suffering and fear she must have been going through all those years with no one to come to her rescue.

"I'm gone kill that muthafucka!"

"No Dena, you can't. Promise me you won't say nothing." I wasn't trying to hear her. "See that's why I didn't want to tell you. I couldn't take it if something happened to you." I turned on the bed to face her.

"You see this?" I asked holding up my Barretta. "I know how to use it. Ain't nothin' gone happen to me."

"Dena..." she struggled to find the right words. "You don't know what he's capable of. Yo daddy a monster."

The fear that I saw in her eyes was real. Finesse believed what she was saying.

I promised her that I wouldn't say anything.

I made a promise that I knew I couldn't keep.

Ever since I was seven years old, I had Finesse, who mama said was my responsibility to take care of and set a good example for. Coming from the foster home at five years old, she was a broken child who had suffered unimaginable physical and mental abuse. Taking care of her was a full-time job that I took pride in doing. She didn't talk. She didn't respond to anyone or anything. Over time, with a lot of patience and persistence, I was rewarded with her smile, then her words, and eventually her trust. I was the only one she accepted love from. By the time she was ten years old, Finesse was happy, animated, and functioning like any other normal ten year old girl. But there were still those moments when she would close up and go back inside of herself.

Moments that not even I could reach her.

CHAPTER 1

Me and Finesse didn't grow up like your average everyday American kids. Our family had money. Lots of it. I don't mean just wealthy, I'm talking rich.

Filthy rich.

Our financial status kept the other kids jealous and us from making friends. Guess that's how Finesse and I grew to be so close. The money along with how much we moved around made it to where we had to be home schooled. We never stayed in one place too long. First we lived in Miami Florida. Then it was Tampa. Then Atlanta Georgia, then New York, then Los Angeles, then Las Vegas, and a whole bunch of small cities and towns in between. Now it's Forrest City Arkansas, a small town not far from the Arkansas and Tennessee state line.

We were used to living in luxury, but nothing as extensive as the mansion we moved into when we first came to Arkansas. As big as the White House and sitting on a hundred and fifty acres of land, it looks like something straight off of MTV Cribs. Mama said that Lafu had it built from the ground up so we wouldn't have to worry about moving around anymore. This is home and has been for the past going on five years now. The inside is amazing. The garage itself is a site to see with its rows and rows of expensive and foreign cars. Then there's the indoor pool, the gymnasium with the basketball court and exercise room, the tennis court, movie theater, but of all of the amazing places inside of the mansion, my favorite by far is the Rain Forest Room. A man-made tropical paradise, it's beauty is breath taking. With all kinds of exotic birds and trees that grow exotic fruits, it has real waterfalls the flow over real rock cliffs down into a big Bahama-blue lake. On January third, 2003, the day before my twenty- third birthday, that's where I was, chilling alone, trying to get some me time in.

"Deeena...Dena." Finesse's voice broke in on my solitude interrupting the flow of words going through my head. "Where you at hooker cause I know you in here hiding somewhere."

From my spot posted under a mango tree, I see her before she sees me.

"Ain't nobody hiding." I say drawing her eyes in my direction.

"There you go. I should have known. Here I am looking all over for you and you in here ducked off writing in this damn poetry book."

"And what's wrong with that?"

"What's wrong is, while you in here tryna' be Poetic Justice, I'm tryna' be like Smokey smoke smoke! Girl I'm gone getchu' high today, cuz you ain't got no job... and you ain't got shit to do!" she says holding up a freshly rolled blunt and imitating the character that Chris Tucker played in the movie 'Friday'.

I can't help but laugh at her silly antics. This girl watch way too much TV.

"Alright, just let me finish these last few lines."

"Girl, put that thing down and come on here." She grabs my hand and pulls me to my feet.

Finesse has said the magic words because although I don't drink or indulge in any other medicated forms of extracurricular activity, I loves to get my smoke on. Finesse and I walk through the foliage until we find a comfortable spot in the most secluded part of the trees.

After stretching out on the ground and lighting up, Finesse says, "Sing something for me D."

I sit with my legs crossed and back resting against the trunk of a tree. "What you wanna hear?"

"How about some Mary J." she says passing me the blunt.

"Which one?" I suck in a lung full of the potent smoke.

"The one where she had on all black and wearing the dark shades."

I blow it out and catch an instant head rush.

"Not Gone Cry?"

"Yeah that's it. Sing that one."

After hitting it a few more times, I pass the blunt back to Finesse, then close my eyes and let the euphoric feeling from the weed take me away as Mary J's words flow off of my tongue. Finesse loves to hear me sing. Every time we're alone together somewhere getting high, she asks me to sing something from one of her favorite music videos. She says that I can out sing any of those women on B.E.T and MTV put together.

After I finish she says, "Damn D, I wish I could blow like you. Girl you got some skills." She looks at me like I'm a star and she's my biggest fan. Her admiration feels good.

"One of these days I'm gone go on Apollo and sing those people right outta' they seats."

"Ooh yea, and I can be yo' manager." Finesse says falling right in with my fantasy. "You be like Biggie rockin' the crowd. I'm gone be Puffy up there doing the Harlem Shake." She gets up and starts doing the crazy New York dance. I fall out laughing. "Then I'm gone get sanctified wit it." Finesse starts imitating the dances that Puffy did on the 'Missing You' tribute to Biggie video. She dances and sings. "Every step I take/ every move I make..." I jump up and join in singing with her. "Every single day/ every time I pray/ I'll be missing you..." We dance, sing, and kick it amongst the birds and trees in the Rainforest Room.

Then my mother's voice echoes from the intercom system and fills the room.

"Nessa! Dena! Where y'all at babies?"

"Mama!" Our fantasy instantly dissipates as we race towards the exit of the Rainforest Room.

It had been two weeks since we'd seen her last. Before that, a whole month with only a three day stop through in between. We find her and Uncle Fresh standing in the foyer at the entrance of the mansion both surrounded by several shopping bags.

Uncle Fresh, known to others as Johnny Ray or Mr. Make- It- Happen, is Lafu's right hand man and has been around since before I can remember. I gave him the nickname Uncle Fresh when I was just a little girl because that's how he always smells when he comes around; like a breath of fresh air or a tropical- blue- wave- breeze on a sunny beach. That plus the fact that he's always dressed fresh to death whenever you see him. Rather it's night or day, early morning or late night, you won't ever catch him in nothing less than some creased up slacks with a nice button down or some kind of tailor made suit. And never without a sharp brimmed Dob Hat on his head. When it comes to any dealing pertaining to the family business, Uncle Fresh is the one you need to see. While Lafu was playing the shadows, living it up, and hardly ever leaving the mansion, Uncle Fresh and Mama were both out taking trips, going state to state, maintaining things, and managing the clubs.

From the time I can remember, Finesse and I have always had any and everything our hearts desired. Gucci, Prada, Chanel, Dolce and Gabbana, Gianfranco Ferre you name it we had it. Hell, I was driving a Bentley at the age of sixteen. There was never a time that we were uncomfortable. But the one thing we wanted and needed most was never there. Our mother. Don't get it twisted, I loved my mother and I know she loved us, it's just that she was never around. Her and Uncle Fresh were always gone on some kind of trip or other keeping the family business going. Either that or she was out hosting one of her many charity events and donating money. She could never really know how much we needed her home.

Mama stood with her arms outstretched.

"There go my babies!" Just like when we were younger, we ran into them giving her a big hug. "I missed y'all so much."

Although I was turning twenty- three the next day and Finesse was twenty- one, we loved the fact that she still called us her babies; something she'd been doing since we were little girls.

"Don't I get some love?" Uncle Fresh asked.

"You know we can't forget about you Uncle Fresh." I say wrapping my arms around him and inhaling the masculine scent of his Escada cologne. "Cause I know you didn't forget about us while you were up in the Windy City." I say eyeballing the shopping bags on the floor.

"I think I mighta' found a thang or two with Nessa name on it, but I couldn't find anything in Chicago that I thought was to yo liking."

"What!?!" I gasp pulling away in alarm.

"Johnny Ray, quit teasing that girl before she has a stroke." My mother laughs displaying her deep-dimpled, Colgate smile that I'd inherited from her.

"Alright alright, let me see what I got here." he says kneeling down and digging through the bags. "Okay here we go." He pulls out a long wide, flat box. "This one here is for you Nessa."

"Hey now, let me see." Finesse says as Uncle Fresh hands her the box and she anxiously begins to open it. "Ooh we this is too fly." she says pulling out a black and gold, open back, wrap around summer dress by Versace. "Thank you Johnny Ray. I'm gone rock this bad boy to the Avant concert next week."

Uncle Fresh pulls out another box, this one short and wide. He gives it a couple of twist and turns like he's trying to figure out what's inside.

"Oh yea, this one here is yours too Nessa." Inside is a Versace clutch purse that matches her dress. Then she gets a pair of Manolo Blahniks with the gold heel and ankle strap.

Although Finesse and I are close and share everything, I feel myself getting jealous. After all, it's my birthday tomorrow not hers.

"What about me? Where my gifts?"

"Be patient, " Uncle Fresh says "I gotta' figure out where I put it." He digs around some more until he finds a large gift wrapped box that's bigger than all the rest. My eyes grow big with excitement until he says, "Nope, this one's Theresa's." and hands it to my mother.

"Uncle Fresh!" I say stomping my feet like a spoiled little girl.

My mother laughs again then walks over, puts her arm around my shoulders, and whispers in my ear.

"Don't worry baby, I got something special just for you later on. Plus I got a secret to tell you." Although my eyes are still on Uncle Fresh and the shopping bags, I smile because her words make me feel special and I know they're only for me.

"I just remembered..." Uncle Fresh says standing up and reaching into his inside jacket pocket. "Aah here we go." He pulls out a scroll of paper wrapped with a bright red bow and hands them to me.

"What's this?" I ask with confusion before opening and reading them. "It's some kind of deed. I don't understand."

Mama and Uncle Fresh both smile and share a look between each other.

"Well Babygirl, we know how much you love ya poetry and how you always writing in that little book of yours, so me and ya mama figured it 'a be a good idea to open ya own club."

"What, you mean like a poetry club?"

"Yea baby," mama says stepping up to me and placing her hands on my cheeks "God didn't give you that gift with words to keep to yourself. You gotta 'share it with the rest of the world. Let em hear how you express yourself."

"And speaking of gifts," Uncle Fresh says joining in "that voice of yours needs to be heard too."

"Yea Dena, people would love to hear you sing. I know I do." Finesse says.

"I could have an open-mic-night so other people can come out and display their talents too. Then I could use social media to advertise and scout for poets... and I could hire a live band..." I could see it all in my head. The possibilities were endless. "Aw you guys, thanks." I grab Uncle Fresh and Mama both at the same time and pull them in for one big hug. "It's a great idea. I love it. I couldn't have asked for a more perfect gift."

Uncle Fresh rubs my back and says, "Glad you like it Babygirl."

"Happy birthday baby." Mama says and kisses my cheek.

The smell of ganja announces his presence before he even comes into view. Wearing black Arabian silk pajamas, unbuttoned down the front with no shirt, one hand deep in his pocket, the other holding a gold-tipped cigarillo blunt, Lafu walks into the room and the jovial vibe instantly shifts.

"Johnny Ray, Tar-eee-sa," he says stretching out my mother's name with his thick Jamaican accent "welcome bak' ta' da' 'ome front." He kisses my mother's cheek then turns to Uncle Fresh and shakes his hand. "Any problems?"

"Nothing I couldn't handle." Uncle Fresh answers with his natural swag.

"Dats wat me wan 'ere."

Despite living in the mansion together, Lafu and I rarely come face to face with each other. With pupils as red as blood from either years of marijuana smoke or simply because of the evil that lay behind them, Lafu's eyes land on mine.

"And wat g'wan wit' da birfday gal?"

"Just happy to have my mother home for a change." I say, never losing eye contact and wondering, not for the first time, how I could have been created from someone who I despise so much. Long seconds tic by with me looking into those evil red eyes.

"Johnny Ray, come, we tak' bizness." Then with a final puff of his gold-tipped blunt, Lafu turns and walks back out of the room leaving behind a trail of smoke.

Mama, Finesse, and I spend the rest of the day in Memphis going shopping, out to eat, and to the spa. It's the most fun we've had together in a long time. Although forty-three years old, Mama still had that natural youthful glamour about her that still turned plenty of heads. Several times throughout the day, she and I were mistaken for sisters. We even stopped in West Memphis on the way back home to check out the site of my new club. Though it was no more than just an empty building, the vision I had in my head for it was clear.

That night, around one a.m., my mother poked her head through my bedroom door.

"Knock knock... baby you still woke?"

"Yea ma, come on in." I say placing my poem book face down across my lap.

She came in wearing a satin, peach nightgown with her long, dark hair falling in silky waves across her shoulders.

"What are you still doing up?"

"I could be asking you the same question." I look into her beautiful face and notice the worry lines etched across her forehead.

"I was waiting up for Nessa. I been trying to get her alone all day so we could talk but..." Her words trail off as she shakes her head.

"We've been together all day, why didn't you just talk to her then?"

"Well, I wanted to get her alone, just me and her so we could talk. I mean really talk." She looks deep into my eyes and at that moment I can't help but to wonder if she somehow knows.

"She went out on a date with some supposedly cute guy she met at the club the other night." I say rolling my eyes. "She should be back soon though."

My mother looks at me endearingly and runs her hand across my hair down to the side of my face.

"I know I haven't been a good mother to you girls."

"Aw ma you..."

"No, nooo Dena..." she says cutting me off." I know I haven't been there. I let what Lafu wanted become more important than what you guys needed. You girls have had to grow up without me and for that, I'm sorry. There's no way that I can make up for lost time, but I promise you from here on out, things are going to different. I'm giving up the family business."

I can't even pretend that those aren't the words that I've been waiting my whole life to hear.

"Mama are you serious? "

"Yes baby. Me and Johnny Ray already talked about it and he said that we're as established as we could possibly be. Outside of needing my signature here and there, he can handle the rest on his own."

"Oh mama!" I grab and hug her with all of my might as words evade me and my emotions take over. Just the thought of having her around all the time is enough to bring tears to my eyes. Then a thought hits me.

"What about Lafu?" I ask pulling away and looking into her eyes.

"Don't worry about Lafu, I can handle him. He's only the big bad wolf to you guys." She smiles and uses her thumb to wipe away my tears. "Ooh..." she says reaching into the pocket of her robe and pulling out a square, flat, gift wrapped box "I got something for you."

"What is it?"

"Open it and see."

I take the box from her and quickly open it. Inside is a uniquely designed, princess cut, diamond necklace with the wrist and ankle bracelets to match.

"Oh my gosh, these are beautiful!"

"They were your grandmothers. She gave them to me on my wedding day. They were my something new. The day I walked down the aisle with Lafu was the proudest day of her life. To her, I couldn't have picked a more suitable mate."

"You mean to tell me, she actually liked Lafu." I ask surprised.

"Believe it or not, Lafu was once a very charming man."

I give her a look. "I find that hard very hard to believe."

"Believe it. Before all of the big money and trouble came, he was actually a pretty good guy. But once the hundreds of thousands started turning to millions... he started to change. The man I fell in love with disappeared." Then she turned serious. "Dena, I want you to promise me something."

"Okay, what is it?"

"That no matter where you go or what you accomplish in life, you'll always remember that there's someone out there in a less fortunate situation than you who needs some of what you got more than you do."

I digest her words and let them take root in my heart.

"I promise."

Then she takes the jewelry pieces out of the box and starts putting them on me.

"Let these be your reminder. Money ain't everything. Too much of anything can be bad for you." I finger the diamonds on my neck.

"I'll never take them off."

"I know you won't baby." She looks at her watch. "Where is Nessa."

"You know how she gets when she finds a new conquest."

"Actually I don't, but oh well. I was saving this for her." She reaches in her robe pocket and pulls out a skinny joint.

"And what is that?!?" I ask not believing my eyes.

"Whatchu' think it is?" she answers laughing.

"If it is what I think it is, where's the rest of it?"

"Girl, that's for y'all youngsters. This here is enough to get the job I need done."

"And since when did you start smoking weed?" I ask still not believing what I'm seeing.

"I take a toke every now and then."

"I'm scared of you." I say laughing.

She pulls a lighter out of her pocket and lights up.

"Girl I've been married to Lafu for over twenty-five years. How could I not indulge?" She has a point.

"So is this the secret you whispered to me about earlier?"

"Not quite." she says and takes a deep toke before passing it to me.

That night, my mother and I lay in my bed together getting high as the midnight stars and talked like long lost buddies until we fell asleep. When I awoke the next morning, she was gone. That was the last time I saw my mother alive.

I woke on my birthday, January fourth, 2003, and received the most devastating news of my life. My mother had been found stabbed to death in a motel room out in the country. Forty-six times she was stabbed in her head, neck, and back. What I couldn't seem to make sense out of was how she went from sleeping in the bed beside me to ending up in a rundown roach motel out in the country.

Police investigation concluded that my mother had a secret lover who she'd met for a middle of the night rendezvous that ended in a jealous crime of passion. The police put an APB out on the guy who'd rented the room under a false name fitting the description of an older African Male between the ages of sixty and sixty-five, six feet in height, sporting dreadlocks and a long salt and pepper colored beard. A guy they would never find.

The guy who'd worked the graveyard shift at the motel the night of my mother's murder who'd given the police the description told Uncle Fresh the same thing. But once Uncle Fresh pulled out ten thousand dollars cash and promised to keep it between just the two of them, he remembered a few minor details that he'd failed to tell the police. He remembered that the man was kind of strange and the only word he spoke throughout the entire transaction was the word "single" before placing ten crisp one hundred dollar bills on the counter. He also remembered that the guy had eyes that he would never forget.

CHAPTER 2

Six months after my mother's death

As soon as I walk through those club doors everything changes.

I'm no longer just plain ole Dena.
I'm Dena the Don Diva.
The Boss Lady.
I run shit.

The Hot Spot Gentleman's Club is where I spend most of my time and conduct most of my business. Since my mother's murder six months ago, I've had to fill her shoes as the sole owner of this and forty-nine other clubs across the United States; not to mention the other five in Jamaica. This is where it all goes down.

Wearing my signature snakeskin thigh-high stiletto boots and black body dress by Donna Karen that barely covers the bottom curve of my ass cheeks, I step past the low whistles and lustful stares like I don't have a care in the world. Mojo and Pitbull, my two trusted bodyguards who escort me to and from my car every night, walk close by my side making sure none of these fools get out of line by copping a free feel of my ass or grabbing my hand trying to spit their weak game; something that's encouraged in here, just not with me. My diva stroll carries me past the stage where Cherie, one of my dancers is heating it up with her dildo and whipped cream routine. Adena Howard's 'T shirt and Panties' bump through the speakers.

It's after eleven on a Wednesday night, which is one of the busiest nights for my girls, so the place is jumping. Wednesday through Sunday between the hours of eight and four in the morning, it's all about my girls getting down for their crown. Grinding for their findings. Working that pole for a bankroll.

Behind the tint of my Chloe Glasses, my eyes take in the room. I see Miesha, Lolita, Butta, Na-Na, and the rest of my girls working the floor giving lap dances, hustling drinks, and working tricks for their chips. The house is packed with plenty of so-called ballers so there's definitely money to be made.

Then I see her.

Across the room sitting at a table full of niggas. Perched on one of their laps. One hand in the air. Drink in the other. Animated. Being everything that I'm not.

Finesse doesn't notice me when I walk up, but the guys at the table do.

"Damn Dena baby, how you doing? You sho' looking good tonight." says the one who's lap Finesse is sitting on.

"Hey Big Fitty." I say with a smile, but my eyes are looking at Finesse, who finally looks up and sees me.

"Deeennaaa!" she screeches melodramatically as she jumps up and throws her arms around my neck. Unlike mine, her ass does pop out from under the Jersey Dress she's wearing and the guys at the table get an eye full. She smells like a liquor still.

I'm pissed.

I pull her arms from around my neck, grab her wrist, and say, "Let's go." Before we can take a step, Big Fitty is on his feet holding on to her other wrist.

"Hold on Dena, slow ya roll love. Yo' girl alright, she with me."

"Yea Dena, why you trippin'?" Finesse slurs trying to snatch her arm away.

"You know why I'm trippin" I say ignoring Big Fitty. "You supposed to be in here watching the girls and making sure they handling they business and you ain't even handling yours." Big Fitty tries again.

"Come on now Dena, you too pretty to be actin' all ugly. We just tryna' kick it and spend a lil money." He pulls out a large wad of cash. "Have a seat and kick it wit' ya boy for a minute."

"Maybe next time Fitty. Right now, I need to talk to her." Finesse smacks her lips and rolls her eyes.

"Aw that's fucked up. We yo' customers in here spending money tryna' have a good time and this how you gone treat us." I'm trying to be nice, but my patience is wearing thin. I take a deep breath and force a smile.

"Tell you what, I'm gone send a couple of my girls over here to keep y'all company and the next coupla' bottle is on me. How's that sound?" Another guy sitting at the table speaks up.

"Sounds like a plan to me. Shiid, that's wassup!" Big Fitty finally releases Finesse's wrist and I drag her away from the table through the club. When we reach the bottom of the stairs that lead to my upstairs office, I turn to Mojo and Pitbull.

"Have Keita send a couple bottles of Moet and a few of the girls over to kick it wit' those guys and make sure no one comes up these stairs unless you check with me first."

"Aiight Boss Lady. Anything else?" I look at Finesse in disgust.

"Yea. Make me a pot of coffee for this drunk ass bitch."

I slam the door so hard when we make it into the upstairs office that the tropical fish inside the large, thirty foot aquarium that dominates the room take off swimming in a frenzied blur of color.

"Why you always gotta' show yo ass Finesse? Why you can't just do right?"

"Come on D," she says easing up to me with her inebriated smile trying to wrap her arms around my neck "don't be like that. I was just having a coupla' drinks with the guys." I slap her arms down and point my finger in her face.

"That's just it Finesse, you ain't supposed to be drinking and you know it. Or was all those promises you made me just a bunch of bullshit to get in my panties?" She seems unaffected by my words and that pisses me off even more. "So what, you back using too?"

Although she steps away from me rolling her eyes, her smile never wavers.

"You always overreacting." Finesse dismisses what I'm saying with a wave of her hand, turns, and heads towards the canopy bed sitting on the raised platform across the room.

"Oh am I? Was I overreacting when I came in here and caught you and Lafu fucking?"

Seems like my words sober her up she spins back around to face me so quickly. But I'm not finished yet.

Walking towards her I say, "Was I overreacting when I traded my life to Lafu so that he would leave you alone. Huh, was I? Was I overreacting when I spent all those long days and nights helping you kick yo cocaine habit when that muthafucka had you strung out?" Then so close in her face that her warm liquored breath heats my skin. "Am I overreacting when I have to wake up and comfort yo ass because you having another nightmare about that monster raping you?"

The slap comes so quick and hard that I don't even see it, only feel the sting when it lands and knocks my glasses across the room.

Just as quickly and twice as hard, I return the favor.

The sting from another slap hits my cheek.

I retaliate with one of my own.

We stand starring at each other. Nose flaring, mouth set in a tight line, I feel my hand itching for another slap. Finesse has fire in her eyes. Then her whole disposition changes. Her fiery look softens to sultriness. A smile teases the corners of her lips.

"I don't want to fight with you D. Let me make you feel good." Her lips press against mine.

I push her off of me. She does it again, this time with more intensity.

I can't stop my body from reacting. My heartbeat does a two-step inside my chest. Another pulse percolates inside my thong. My juices start to flow. I'm powerless against her, the only human being that has ever come in contact with my body sexually.

My best friend.

My lover.

My adopted sister.

If sex was liquified, Finesse would drown in her own essence. The walking personification of the word, she knows no boundaries. A pint-size, five-four goddess with enough curves, fireworks, and sexuality to cause a gay man to go straight. I can't begin to count the number of people, male and female, that I've seen left lost and broken behind Finesse's femininity, chasing something they'd never catch. The things that Lafu did to her body and mind growing up left her so twisted that the only peace she finds is in pleasure. Physical pleasure. Pleasure that inevitably leads to pain. Rather giving or receiving, her desire is to indulge. No one is immune.

Not even me.

Her hands grip the back of my thighs right on the exposed flesh between the bottom of my dress and the top of my boots. They hold me tightly as she walks me backward towards the bed. Her tongue caresses the inside of my mouth.

"Nessa stop." My weak protest is in vain and we both know it. Still, I press my hands against both of her shoulders breaking the kiss and say, "What if somebody comes?"

"Don't worry, one of us will." Knowing that I just told Mojo not to let anyone up the stairs and we won't be interrupted; Finesse gets more aggressive.

My back bumps against the canopy post of the bed. Her mouth against mine wills me to reciprocate. A hand squeezes my breast then pinches my aching nipple. Another eases up the front of my dress and massages the silk triangle of my thong. My center melts. I'm soaked. Finesse has explored my body repeatedly and knows exactly what buttons to push. With a mind of their own, my hips move against the pressure of her fingers.

"Shit Nessa...ooh... you make me sick." What I'm feeling is too good to deny. I can't help it, I'm past the point of no return. My teeth sink into the flesh of her bottom lip hard enough to make her whimper. Then I suck it into my mouth as I become the aggressor.

Moving off of pure instinct, I grab a hand full of hair at the back of her head and pull until she drops to her knees at the foot of the bed in front of me. I straddle her face. Our eyes meet. Without words we communicate our desires to each other.

She needs to taste my nectar.

I need her tongue.

My dress gets pushed up over my hips, my thong pulled to the side. The contact of her tongue on my clit sends electricity through my body causing me to inhale deeply.

"Sssss...uhnnssshiiit." I can't control my moans. With Finesse's head resting backwards on the bed and my hand gripping a hand full of her hair, I close my eyes and work my hips with abandonment. "Eat this pussy."

The pressure inside my honeypot builds, consumes me. Holding onto my thighs, Finesse does magic tricks with her tongue that cause me to double my movements. I ride her face like a jockey on a horse spreading my juices across her nose, mouth, and chin. An orgasm creeps up from my toes and sends my entire body into a seizure. It's powerful.

"Fuuuck...sssooohhshiit...aaahhdamn...Nessa! Damn Nessa!" I cum so hard that it feels like I'm about to pass out. For the past three years, Finesse and I have been getting down like this.

Lovers.

Ever since I made a deal with the devil.

In the beginning, I guess it was guilt that made me give in to her sexual advances. Guilt because I'm the one who was supposed to be taking care of her, her big sister, the one who she looked up to, had failed to protect her. I failed to protect her when that monster was abusing her. And even after confronting him that first time, I still let him pull the wool over my eyes and lure her back in by using liquor and cocaine. By the time I discovered what was going on the second time, my baby was no more than a nymphomaniac junkie. So yea, I laid in bed and held her at night as she went through withdrawals trying to help her kick her cocaine habit. And no I didn't move my hand when she would place it between her legs and use it to rub herself to orgasm every night before she went to sleep. I can even blame my inexperience and naivete for me letting her fondle my young virgin body into the first orgasm that I ever experienced. But in the end, I'll just call it what it really is.

Love.
I love Finesse.
More than I love myself.
Love her so much that I'll do anything to protect her.
Even kill.

****

"Hey Babygirl, what's going on?"
"Just another long busy day." I say from the backseat of the limo that's parked outside of the club at three O clock in the morning.
"You all studied up and prepared for the mission tomorrow?"
"As ready as I'll ever be."
"So what's on your mind?"
"Nothing much, just thinking."
"About?"

I blow out a breath of frustration and debate whether or not to share my true feelings with him. Although Uncle Fresh has always been there and is the only other person besides, Finesse I trust, things are just too complicated right now.

"Finesse." I say putting it simply.
"What about Nessa? She ain't thinking bout backin' out on us is she?"
"No nothing like that. It's just..." I hesitate.
"Come on now Babygirl, you know there ain't no such problem that you and I can't figure out together."
"I know... it's just... ever since we found out that Lafu was the one behind Mama's murder, she been trippin."
"Trippin how? You don't think she's back out there on that stuff again do you?"
"I don't know, but tonight when I went to the club, she was in there drunk."

He lets my words sink in before saying, "Maybe she's just taking Theresa's death harder than you think."

"Or maybe Lafu is up to his old tricks again. I mean, come on, it's been six months since Mama's death.

"Has six months been enough time for you to heal?" My silence is all the answer he needs. Uncle Fresh says, "Everybody's got their own way of dealing with things Babygirl. Death ain't easy, but there's one thing I know fa sho... everything done in the dark...will always come to light." His words marinate in my thoughts as I climb out of the limo and head back inside the club to refocus on the business at hand.

Finesse da Game — Roger Hill

Sex.

Rather it's being emulated up on the stage or stripper pole, stimulated through a lap dance, or actual penetration is taking place in the back rooms, that's what we're selling, pure unadulterated sex. But that's not the only commodity being bargained for in the 'The Hot Spot Gentleman's Club'. You see, when it's all said and done, although I've inherited everything from my mother and all of the ownership papers now carry the name Dena Simone Givens, the family business is actually owned by Lafu. And Lafu's business was built and revolves solely around cocaine.

As for my role in it and unbeknownst to my mother and three years prior to her death, 'The Hot Spot' had already taken ownership over me. In order to save Finesse, I'd sold my soul to the devil, became a slave within the same walls that I dwell every day. My life no longer my own. Had my mother of known that the very clubs that named her as the owner were all major drug distribution centers, she would have given them up a long time ago. But she didn't. And as long as she never found out and I managed the dealings going on within 'The Hot Spot ', Lafu promised to never bother Finesse again.

Lafu came up in the ghetto slums of Kingston Jamaica. Son of a whore with a father who was a junky that was murdered before he was born, he was forced to raise himself. Pulling petty crimes just to get by was an everyday way of life for him. That is until, at the age of eighteen, his older brother Jamar, who lived in the States, came and rescued him from his predicament.

Jamar was a club owner in Miami Florida who not only owned a couple of clubs but had access to some of the best cocaine to ever come through the state of Florida. After taking Lafu in to live with him, exposing him to Miami's addictive night life, and schooling him to the clubbing business, Jamar turned him on to the dope game. With a natural ruthlessness and a hunger like no other, Lafu took to the dope game like a crackhead to the pipe.

The driving force behind Jamar's drug business was none other than Uncle Fresh. Mr.-Make-It-Happen. The two met back when Jamar was only twenty three years old and had just opened his first club. They were introduced through a mutual acquaintance when Jamar noticed the large amounts of cocaine moving through his club and inquired about its source. A deal was arranged and soon Jamar was seeing more money than he ever imagined thanks to Mr.-Make-It-Happen. There was one problem though. Uncle Fresh didn't like Jamar's flamboyant lifestyle. He had all the swagger and finesse of a true ladies man but lacked the ruthlessness and mentality it took to really be successful in the drug business. The answer to that problem came when Jamar brought his younger brother Lafu on the scene. Uncle Fresh saw in Lafu all the qualities and potential it took to take his business to the next level. He took him under his wing and molded him into a money-making-machine and Lafu exceeded all of his expectations.

By the time he was twenty-five years old, Lafu owned ten clubs of his own and was moving fifty kilos of cocaine a month. With a natural business mind and low-key disposition, his gangsta spoke for itself; competition got squashed, opposition switches sides, and enemies disappeared. The streets of Miami knew Lafu was not to be fucked with.

Uncle Fresh and Lafu became thick as thieves and went on to make millions together while Lafu's brother Jamar stayed behind and was content with his financial status and playboy lifestyle. Uncle Fresh stood proudly behind his protege allowing him to bask in limelight of their shared success while he played the position of a silent partner. Eventually the two branched out extending their business to other cities and states. With each new territory they concurred came a new resistance; crews, families, and mobs who'd already claimed the area and weren't willing to relinquished control of it without a fight. And Lafu gladly annihilated them all. His reputation preceded him so greatly that some just gracefully bowed out when he came to their area. But when they came upon Las Vegas, a city with ties and connection to almost every mob family across the stretch of globe, Uncle Fresh warned that they should pass it by. But Lafu was relentless. Each new successful takeover made his team grow stronger, his money longer, and him that much more ruthless and power hungry. Ignoring Uncle Fresh's warning, Lafu began to make blood flow throughout the goldmine of a town. But with the mob families came F.B.I. surveillance, D.E.A. attention, I.R.S., and a few more agencies. It wasn't long before they had Lafu in their sights. Being his right-hand man, Uncle Fresh backed him in every conflict, but when Lafu put it in mind and began murdering and blowing up the houses of F.B.I. agents, Uncle Fresh knew that he was out of control. By 1993, Lafu had become public enemy number one. Every agency in America had a target on his head forcing him into hiding. That's when Uncle Fresh stepped out of the shadows and handled things.

Uncle Fresh adopted the name Mr.-Make-It-Happen from his ability to make the impossible possible. With him having connections everywhere from inside The White House down to the ghetto gangstas of the hood and money as long as the Mississippi, nothing was outside of the realm of probability. Since all of Lafu's clubs were being raided and harassed on the regular in an attempt to bring him out of hiding, Uncle Fresh's first order of business was to put a stop to all drug transactions going on inside the clubs to stop loss and to prevent the government from seizing any of them. Next he needed a fall guy, someone who matched Lafu in appearance all the way down to his eyelashes. For you to hear about Lafu's reputation without ever laying eyes on him, you would definitely be surprised by his appearance. 5'10 with a medium build, light skin complexion, short naturally curly hair, and boyish good looks, he has the ability to fool any unsuspecting victim.

Once Uncle Fresh found the sacrificial lamb he was looking for, it was only a matter of switching around a few medical and dental records, making sure the F.B.I. and other agencies were tipped off to his whereabouts, then letting them witness his demise, which Uncle Fresh chose to have done by car bomb. Once the charred remains of the fall guy were pulled from the burnt car and a full autopsy was performed, Lafu was officially pronounced dead bringing all investigations and manhunts to an end. My mother being his wife inherited his entire estate.

After a reasonable amount of time passed, Uncle Fresh and Lafu continued the cocaine flow throughout the clubs and business resumed as usual. Only difference was, now Lafu's intimidating presence was missing. With Lafu believed to be dead, his opposition tried to move in on his territory, but soon found that although he was missing in the physical, Lafu's power and influence still lived on. If anything, his foes were being destroyed with more malice than ever.

Slowly but surely, more and more territories continued to be invaded. The once powerful man known as Lafu was now an entity that had taken on a life of its own. A ghost. Fear was felt whenever his name was mentioned, and whispered rumors of his existence spread throughout the underworld.

CHAPTER 3

February 2004

'Enchanting Voices'.

My sanctuary. My refuge. My place of peace. The only place I can come to escape the ills of my life.

As I walk through the front entrance of my poetry club, the now familiar feeling of tranquility washes over me completing my transformation from the craziness of the world outside these doors to the calmness inside. The aroma of herbal essence greets me along with the soothing voice of my multi-talented emcee, Dejhoun.

"There she is ladies and gentlemen, the heartbeat of this here fine establishment." he says pointing from the stage and directing all the attention towards me. "In the flesh, Miss Dena Givens."

The genuine applause touch me as I move through the tables full of faithful patrons who have claimed 'Enchanting Voices' as their own personal place of refuge just as much as I have.

"Hey Dena."

"How you doing sista?"

"I know you got something good in store for us tonight." Some touch my arm, others shake my hand, a few even stand and embrace me in warm hugs. The love I get when I come in here is so powerful that it feels like I'm in the presence of real family making me regret that I only get a chance to come once or twice a week. No matter what though, I always try to make it on Wednesdays; open-mic-night.

It only took three months to get this place up and running. Once the idea took root inside my mind, I put all of my energy into manifesting it to reality. It also gave me something to do besides dwell on my mother's death. I intentionally gave the club an Afrocentric theme signifying the unification of our own kind. Contrary to the outside world where we're divided and hurting and killing each other, we come here to uplift and celebrate the history of our heritage together.

"Why do you always do that?" I say against Dejhoun's ear as he and I embrace when I make it upon the stage.

"Because they love to see you come. We all do. We just hate to see you go."

Dejhoun, a fifty-two year old Nigerian brotha with a natural aura so powerful and soulful that people are naturally drawn to him, was the first to respond to the internet post that I set up requesting to hear from any neo-soul, renaissance type who were looking for a place to let their voices be heard and be around like-minded individuals. He contacted me and we hit it off instantly sharing our mutual desire to share our gifts with others. A deep brotha who does everything from play instruments to sing and spill poetic words of ebullience, he was the one who came up with the name 'Enchanting Voices'. From the time the club was in its infancy stages up until opening night, he was here helping build it up to what it is now.

"Thank y'all so much." I say grabbing the microphone "but he's the real heartbeat of 'Enchanting Voices'. Without him being here six nights a week with this talented band behind me creating an atmosphere of peace and relaxation, wouldn't none of us be able to come and let our lights shine." The audience applauds in agreement.

Then a lone voice yell, "Let us hear something Dena!"

"Aw I... I just got here; I'm not even prepared yet.

"Come on now, we know you got something!"

"Yea Dena, give us something!"

"So y'all just gone put me on the spot like that?"

"Dena! Dena! Dena!" they chant in union.

"See what you did?" I ask directing my question at Dejhoun. He only shrugs his shoulders and smiles. "Alright, " I say knowing there's no point in protesting further. "I've got this piece I've been working on called 'Breathe'. I'm gone try and do it for you guys. Dejhoun, can I get a little melody?"

"Sure thing." He goes over and grabs his favorite brass instrument from the side of the piano then returns to my side.

The therapeutic harmony of his saxophone comes to life and spreads throughout the room like a cloud giving my words something to float on. I feel the vibe in my body.

"I can't... breathe breathe breathe...I can't... breathe breathe breathe...I can't... breathe breathe breathe...I can't...

If everyday way special the way it should be,
Then time would never put space between you and me.
Because a part of me is gone whenever you can't stay,
Cause every time you leave; you take my breathe away.
And every time you return, I breathe life anew,
Absorbing fresh oxygen through the gift of you.
Your presence is like heavens breath setting my ship a sail,
Then you depart leaving my heart waiting to exhale...and I can't... breathe breathe breathe...I can't...breathe breathe breathe.... I can't breathe breathe breathe...I can't...

If every day was like today, then toast would be served with old mold for dinner,
And I'd be unclothed in the cold of winter.

Misconstrued, confused, face turning blue,
Suffocating, waiting for your face to come into view.
Ice feeling, trembling, yet trying to be strong,
Can't remember a time you've ever been gone this long.
Still you haven't come, I'm numb and can't feel my toes,
The lungs in my chest close and my whole world is froze...and I can't... breathe breathe breathe...

Words that came together in my brain while reminiscing on the memory of my mother.

The finger snapping applause I get is overwhelming.

"Thank you. Thank you very much." I say with a bow.

Dejhoun accepts the mic from my hand and says, "One more time ladies and gentlemen, Miss Dena Givens." With more enthusiasm, the applauds returns. I smile and let that good feeling carry me down the four steps on the side of the stage into the crowd of fellow writers waiting to have a word with me.

Shaleitha, a sista from Jersey who just recently moved here and began to frequent the club, approaches me showcasing her beautiful smile.

"That was soulful sista. Real nice. I connect with you every time I hear you bring your expressions to life."

"Well thank you, I'm glad you liked it. But hey, you ain't short-stopping yourself when you get up there you know."

"Yea but Dena, you glow." Her eyes drop down to the swollen bulge of my belly. "The essence of your spirit is radiating through your pregnancy."

My hands instinctively rub my stomach.

My baby.

The equilibrium of my sanity and the only good thing to come out of the nightmare that's been my life since my mother's murder fourteen months ago.

As I stand there rubbing my bundle of joy and listening to Shaleitha go on and on about how much of a blessing the life growing inside of me is, a feeling passes through me. A feeling that I haven't felt in over four months. A feeling that only one person has the ability to give me. I can feel his presence.

My eyes search the crowd although I know the impossibility of him being here. The feeling is so strong that even the baby seems to be having a reaction as the movement inside my womb goes crazy. I try to refocus on what Shaleitha is saying, but my eyes stray, scanning each face until...

He's standing in the midst of the writers. Looking directly at me.

Click.

The father of my unborn child.

Back from the dead.

When Uncle Fresh first revealed to me that Lafu was the one behind my mother's murder, I made myself a promise that I wouldn't rest until he was dead. Uncle Fresh told me to be patient and stay ready, that whenever opportunity presented itself, we would make our move. That opportunity came six months later. Apparently, Lafu's older brother

Jamar was killed during a carjacking. The person charged and sent to prison for his murder was a guy named Deshawn Fevers, also known as Click. And he was due to come up for parole.

Lafu, by way of Uncle Fresh, wanted me and Finesse to help him set this guy Click up. Crazy as it sounds, the plan was for us to be waiting at the bus station for him when he was released from prison so we could get acquainted and talk him into coming to the mansion and robbing Lafu. How him robbing Lafu was gone help Lafu get back at him for killing his brother was beyond me. But that part wasn't Important. What was important was us using Lafu's plan against him. Instead of asking Click to rob Lafu, we offered him a truckload of cocaine and millions of dollars in exchange for him taking Lafu's life. But things went terribly wrong.

He started out as just a mark, the target of a mission that Finesse and I were on that was supposed to serve a much greater purpose. He swaggered past without noticing me to a payphone sitting next to the bus station entrance. After pulling out a card and dialing some numbers from it, he turned in my direction and for the first time, we locked eyes. Something that I can't explain passed through my body.

His gaze was intense.

Right there in that moment, I was more aware of myself than ever. The way the black Wife Beater I was wearing enhanced the swell of my breast. How my tight Apple Bottoms embrace the curves of my hips. How exposed my feet felt in my black stilettoes. I played it off by looking his frame over from head to toe and dismissing him with a turn of my head in the other direction. But I could still feel his eyes on me, probing, taking in my every imperfection.

Just then, Finesse screeched into the parking lot driving like a mad woman. In typical scene-stealing-Finesse-fashion, she pulled up in front of me, music bumping, rims spinning, sunlight reflecting off of the flakes in the white paint job of her brand new 2003 Escalade, rolled down the tinted window, and said, "What's up bitch?!? Come on and get yo ass in here. I know you burning up out there in that hot ass sun."

"Girl you ain't never lied." *I say grabbing my luggage and rounding the truck to the passenger side. After putting my luggage in the backseat, I climbed up front and adjusted the air vents so that the A.C. was blowing directly on my face and cleavage.*

"Whew, damn it's hot out there. What the hell took you so long?"

"I had to stop and get something to roll up. I knew you was gone want something to smoke after taking that long ass ride on a stanky bus." *she said holding up a single cigar and a bag of sticky light-green. I couldn't help but to smile.*

"Ooh bitch, I could kiss you right now."

"I know, I know, but you can thank me later. Where ole boy at?" *she asked looking around. I pointed out the mark who was still using the pay phone with his eyes focused on the Escalade.*

"Damn, that muthafucka fine. And he buff. Ooh girl watch this." *Finesse made quick work of breaking down the cigar and filling it with weed then she backed the truck up into a parking space a few spaces away from where he was standing. After making sure both windows were cracked about two inches, she lit up and started blowing smoke out the window.*

"What the hell you doing?"

"What hood nigga you know can resist the smell of some good weed"

"Girl you stupid." I said laughing before taking the blunt and getting a few tokes myself. We passed it back and forth a few times and waited while grooving to the sounds of R. Kelly. Sure enough the mark started to ease our way.

"Look, here he comes." Finesse said sitting the half smoked blunt in the ashtray. "Now it's time for the shock treatment. Watch the master at work." I didn't know what she was up to, but it looked like she'd lost her damn mind when she jumped out of the truck and started jumping around and screaming.

"Ooh shit...shit it's burning Dena! It's burning girl!"

'This bitch is crazy', I thought to myself as I burst out laughing. Her timing couldn't have been more perfect. The mark was just rounding the back bumper of the truck when Finesse jumped out catching him off guard. He stood right in front of her shocked as she put on the performance of her life jumping around, screaming, and running her hand in and out of her thong, all the while pulling the waistband of her shorts away from her body showing the mark all of her business. When it hit me that she was acting as if she dropped the cherry from the blunt down her shorts all in the name of getting his attention, I couldn't help but to laugh harder. Only a fool like Finesse would think of some shit like that. I opened the door to get out of the truck but was so caught up in the grips of laughter that I could only roll out of my seat.

Finesse, still in her role said, "Damn girl, I almost set my pussy on fire and you over there laughing!" That bought on a whole new wave of laughter along with a few tears. "Fuck you bitch, that shit ain't that funny." Then Finesse started laughing too.

Her laughter along with the effects of the weed had us both looking like giggling idiots. Even the mark started laughing which made it all the funnier.

"Ooh ooh, I gotta pee...I'm gone pee on myself!" Finesse cried out before turning and running into the liquor store.

Seeing that Finesse had managed to draw the mark in with her little shenanigans, I had to get a grip on myself and get back focused on the mission. With some effort, I finally got control of myself and started wiping the tears from my face. It was my turn to become the actress.

"And what you laughing at?" I asked the mark.

"Man I'm just tripping off y'all. I wish I had a camcorder or something so I could show yo' friend how she looked."

"Okay! That shit was too funny." knowing that I had his full attention, I sat back down in the truck, grabbed the half blunt out of the ashtray, and puffed it back to life. Once the smoke was flowing good, I held it out to him.

"You smoke?"

"Fa sho!" he said.

Just as he reached for the blunt, I snatched my hand back and said, "First, you have to tell me yo' name and something shocking about you." He was totally caught off guard and stuck on pause until I hit him with my best flirtatious smile. His lips curled into a sexy smirk in return.

Seeing him up close and personal for the first time, I couldn't deny his attractiveness; Tall, cinnamon complexion, muscular build, his dark intense eyes staring into mine. That feeling passed through my body again.

"Aiight," he said as I lifted the blunt to my lips for another toke. "My name is Deshawn, but everyone calls me Click….and I ain't had no pussy in ten years."

Not expecting such a strong comeback, I choked on the smoke I was inhaling. It settled uncomfortably in my chest and I fell into a coughing fit.

"You aiight?" he asked as he came over and patted me on the back. All I could do was pass him the blunt and try to clear my lungs.

"Dang boy...What you tryna do...choke me...choke me to death?"

"Naw shorty, I just did what you asked me to. You wanted something shocking right?" he asked with an amused look on his face before taking a deep pull of the blunt.

"I asked but damn, ten years. I couldn't do that, uh-un."

"What about ten years?" Finesse asked coming out of the liquor store carrying what I knew was some kind of alcoholic beverage in a brown paper bag.

My first instinct was to say something about the drink. Instead I said, "Girl can you imagine not having no dick for ten years?"

"Ten years?!? Uh-un girl, I be done hurt my lil stuff from playing with it so much." We all laughed. My laughter was because I knew Finesse was telling the truth and not just acting.

"So..." Click said "it's your turn. Tell me your name and something shocking about you."

"Okay, but first let's get in the truck. We standing out here smoking like it's legal or something."

Click didn't hesitate to climb in with us. Guess he figured he'd hit the jackpot by hooking up with two pretty females after only being out of prison a few hours, but he just didn't know what he was getting himself into.

Not only did Lafu survive, but Finesse ended up taking a bullet in the neck and fell into a coma. On top of that, Lafu knew that we were on to him about my mother's murder and knew we wanted him dead. So he threatened to pull the plug on Finesse while she lay in a coma unless I helped him and finished what we started. In the end, I was forced to set Click up and Lafu had him killed. The bad part about it, he had Uncle Fresh be the one to do it.

But not before he and I fell in love.

Not before I gave him the gift of my virginity and in return, he left me with the gift growing inside of me.

i"Dena, girl you alright? You look like you just seen a ghost." Shaleitha says bringing me back to the moment. If only she knew the accuracy of her words.

"Um yea...Can you excuse me. I gotta...I gotta go." I find myself moving through the crowd towards him, never taking my eyes off of him, scared that if I look away or even blink, he might disappear. I move until I'm standing face to face with the man who's death I had been mourning for the past four months.

"I can't believe it's really you." Before I can think about it or stop myself, I wrap my arms around his neck tightly and bury my face in the crook of his neck. Just touching him and inhaling his scent, something that I thought I'd never be able to do again, causes my emotions to spill down my cheeks.

"Oh Click, it's really you. I thought you were dead." Beside myself with happiness, I kiss all over his neck and face. I kiss his lips. I kiss until I finally notice how tense his body is. That's when I notice that his arms are still at his sides and not wrapped around me.

Slowly, I withdraw myself from him so that I can look into his eyes. What I see causes me to take an involuntary step backwards. The truth rushes me like a defensive end does a quarterback.

I betrayed the man I love.
I set him up.
I'm no longer his Suabo.
I'm the enemy.

CHAPTER 4

Click

Her shocked hazel eyes meet the dark brewing rage of my pupils.

With slightly parted lips, Dena's breath catches in her throat as a look of fear mixed with regret takes over her face. Long moments of us staring into each other's eyes pass. The zealous admirers surrounding us are oblivious to the moment. If she had any inclination that things between us were still the same, it quickly disappears. The look I give her lets her know to miss me with the sentimental gesture; love don't live here anymore.

"Click, I..." she struggles to find the right words but coming up short. Finally, with a defeated sigh she says, "Come with me, we need to talk." Then without waiting for a response, she grabs my wrist, turns, and leads me towards a closed door at the end of the short hallway.

Curious glances follow us as she leads me to the door, takes out a key, and begins to open it. Dena steps inside what I can now see is a large plush office and stands waiting for me to enter behind her. As soon as she closes the door and turns back around to face me, my hands close around her throat as I slam her against the door with all of my might and begin chocking. The sound of her body crashing into the hard wood sounds out as her hands come up and wrap around my wrist in an effort to relieve the pressure I'm putting on her larynx. Only vaguely aware of her struggling, thoughts of my beautiful cousin, my last remaining family member, taken away from me, dead because of Dena and her lies consume me.

I squeeze so hard that both of my arms begin to shake.

Panic fills Dena's eyes as she realizes that she may have already taken her last breath. But then I think about the seed growing inside of her. My seed. By killing her, I may also be inadvertently killing all hopes of the Fever legacy being carried on. That thought causes me to let go.

Dena instantly slides down the door gasping for air.

Bad as I want to take her life, I know I can't. Me being the last living member of my family, it's up to me to resurrect our bloodline. For that reason alone, I'm gone do everything in my power to make sure that this child makes it into this world alive and well. Once that mission is complete, then I can kill this bitch.

A loud knock comes at the door.

"Dena, are you alright in there? What was that noise...Dena?" A concerned female voice comes through the door.

Seeing that we've drawn attention, Dena pulls herself together and rises up from the floor holding her throat still trying to catch her breath. Muffled voices come from the other side of the door. Then a couple more knocks before the door opens and in walks the emcee who played the saxophone during Dena's poem followed by two other gentlemen and the sista dressed in the kente cloth.

The emcee with the peanut shaped bald head says, "What's going in here?"

"Everything is fine." Dena manages to say while still holding her throat.

"It don't look that way to me." he says giving me the evil eye. "This guy bothering you Dena?"

"No, it's okay. Thank you Dejhoun, but I can handle it."

He turns to me. "I think you need to leave."

"And I think you need to listen to the lady and mind your own business before you fuck around and get hurt." He and the other two guys exchange looks before their eyes all come back and settle on me. I can see the shift in their demeanor, the aggression in their body language. They're ready to drop the positive black man role and take it to the streets.

The sista in the kente cloth goes over and makes a big fuss over Dena guiding her to an expensive looking leather sofa sitting against the wall and helping her sit down. Then she turns on me in anger.

"Brotha, it's bad enough for a man to put his hands on a woman out of anger, but I know you didn't put yo hands on this sista while she's pregnant?!"

It's blowing my mind how all of these people are coming to Dena's defense like she's some kind of angel or something when I know she's rotten to core. But then again, she once had me fooled too.

"Shaleitha, Dejhoun listen." Dena who has finally regained her full composure speaks up "I appreciate your concern, but I'm fine. Really. Things just got outta hand for a minute but I'm fine." She looks at me. "Click and I have some unfinished business that we need to discuss, but if I need any assistance, I'll call you. I promise."

"Sorry Dena, but I ain't leaving you in here alone with this... brotha." Dejhoun spits the word brotha with contempt.

"Me neither." Shaleitha says with finality.

The weight of the pistol in my waistline coupled with the anger and frustration I'm feeling lets me know that it's time for me to get up outta here before I end up catching another case. I reach into my jacket pocket, pull out a small prepaid phone, and toss it into Dena's lap.

"Make sure Johnny Ray gets that. Let him know he'll be hearing from me within twenty-four hours." Then I walk out. Leaving the animosity inside the room, I move down the hallway and out of the club. Once I make it back outside behind the wheel of my car, I pull out my phone and call Lil-Eighty.

"Click, what's good my nigga?"

"It's time. Put everything in motion."

"Enough said. I'm on it." I hang up and sit there for a moment thinking about the things I got in store for Dena and her Jamaican boyfriend. For the first time in a long time, a small smile creeps across my lips. I crank up the music in my ride and pull off.

****

"Hello."
"Whatchu doing?"
"Nothing much. Just sitting here watching 'Martin' and wondering why you haven't called me."
"I'm calling you now."
"Damn Click, it's almost midnight. Is that the only time you call; when you want a late-night booty call?"
"Come on ma, miss me with all the extra shit. You tryna see a nigga or what?" Her voice softens to a purr.
"You know I wanna see you."
"That's what's up then. Unlock the door. I'm out front." I hang up. With my buzz going strong but not quite drunk, I try to get myself together before I head inside to kick it with my lil piece Niesha.

After leaving from seeing Dena at her poetry club in West Memphis, I made the half hour drive back to Forrest City. Once there, the liquor store was my first destination. With a pint of Hen and a fat blunt to puff on, I rode around checking traps and collecting money while trying to escape the thoughts inside my head. I thought that I was ready, but the confrontation with Dena had left me rattled. Coming face to face with her for the first time since seeing her fly away in a helicopter with Lafu and leaving me for dead, I almost lost control. Putting my hands on Dena wasn't my intention when I first went to the club. I just needed her to see me and know that I was alive. Needed to look into her eyes. What I wasn't prepared for was her reaction to me. Her throwing her arms around me, crying and kissing all over me like she was happy to see me alive. Like she really loved me. I have to give it to the bitch though, she's a damn good actress. What really pissed me off, was how my body still responded to her touch. How I felt all tingly and shit after she let me go. How I couldn't help but to notice how good she still looked. Just finally seeing for the first time with my own eyes, this pretty muthafucka carrying my baby inside her.

I make sure to leave my phone in the car before getting out and heading up towards Niesha's house. Before I'm halfway up the sidewalk, the front door opens, and she appears holding the screen door open.

"Hurry up it's cold out there." I walk into the warmth of her lil cozy two bedroom house carrying my car keys, a fresh pint of Hen, and a small basket of strawberries.

"Here you go." I say handing her the strawberries after she closes and locks the door behind us. She takes them and gives me a quick peck on the lips.

"Guess you planning on having strawberries and cream tonight?"

"And you know it." I say wrapping my arms around her waist and palming the round globes of her ass while burying my face in the crook of her neck.

"Umm, you smell good."

"And you smell like a liquor store." she says scrunching up her nose and pushing back out of my embrace. I watch the way her ass cheeks jiggle in the pink lace boy shorts she's wearing as she walks away.

Standing fifty-seven with a caramel complexion and enough hips and ass to cause a person to go blind from looking too hard, Niesha is the closest thing I have or want to a girlfriend. I met her back when I first moved out of Reece's apartment and went searching for a place of my own. She's the real estate agent who spent the entire day taking me around showing me different properties. Me being the guy that I am, once I saw how attractive she was, it was only natural for me to get my flirt on by lacing her with compartments and keeping her laughing throughout the day. In the end, my flirting paid off because before we parted ways, I had her phone number with plans to take her out the following weekend. Now months later we still kick it on a regular basis, but lately she's been letting me know that she wants more. If I ever decided to settle down and get serious, she'd be the one I'd do it with. Unfortunately for her, until I finish this thing with Dena and Lafu, that isn't even a possibility.

"Where my Lil Queen Bee at?" I ask heading for Niesha's daughters room.

"Uh-un, no you don't." She jumps in front of me planting a firm hand on my chest. "Nadia is where all four year old little girls need to be at this time of night. In the bed sleep and don't go in there waking her up." I grab her around the waist and pull her body flush against mine.

"Well how about you and I go in yo room and do what all grown folks do at this time of night."

"Uh-un now Click, you stink. Ain't no way you coming nowhere near my bedroom until you get in the shower. And yo toothbrush is still in the bathroom. You need to hit yo grill while you at it partna." She smiles and pats my stomach twice before walking off a leaving me hanging.

"Aw that's cold. Least you could do is come get in wit me."

"Already took one." she throws over her shoulder before disappearing into the kitchen.

I grab my bottle of Hen and take a healthy swig before going into the bathroom and handling my business. When I come out twenty minutes later wrapped in a towel, Niesha is sitting Indian style in the middle of the couch rolling a blunt. She has the tv turned to videos with the volume muted and a Tyrese CD playing softly from the stereo system. Besides the T.V. screen, all other lights in the house are off and a couple of inscents are burning around the living room. I climb on the couch behind her and get comfortable wrapping my body around hers. She turns her head to the side and leans back for a quick kiss. I oblige.

"Ummm, so fresh and so clean clean." She sparks up the blunt and takes a few puffs before asking, "So what you been up to today?"

"The usual, getting money." I take the blunt from her hand. "What about you?"

"Well, I didn't get off work until late because I finally closed the deal on that big property that I've been telling you about."

"Oh, so you finally pulled it off." I ask while releasing smoke from my mouth.

"Yup, finally. The commission is going to be lovely, but the paperwork was a bitch." I pass the blunt back to her then run both of my hands up under her sports bra cupping her breast and playing with her nipples as she continues to talk and smoke.

"I didn't make it to pick up Nadia from Mama's until after five and as usual, she talked shit. Then I came home and did the mommy thing; cleaned house, washed clothes, cooked me and Nadia something to eat, then spent the rest of the night watching tv with my baby until she fell asleep. And yes, she's been asking about you all day."

"Why didn't she call me?"

"She did. Of course you would've known that if you ever check your voicemails. Where yo phone at anyway?"

"Huh? I'on know. Probably left it in the car."

"Um-huh. You think you so slick. I bet you left it out in the car on purpose so I wouldn't be able to see all the hoes you got calling you."

"You ain't got no business going through my phone no way." Her nipples turn to pebbles between my fingers as I fondle them while kissing her neck. A soft moan escapes her lips.

"Click, what are you doing?"

"I'm waiting on you to finish telling me about your day." My right hand slips down inside the front of her boy shorts.

"Click you better...uummm... "

More intoxicated by her body than the Hen, I take the blunt out of her hand, place it in the ashtray, and flip her on her back. Reaching under her ass and grabbing her waistband, I peel the boy shorts from her body and place a couple kisses on the inside of her thighs. The aroma of her essence fills my nose. I can't resist a couple of long licks from the bottom to the top of her treasure box before coming up and settling my weight on top of her curvy frame.

"Click, why are you teasing me?" I don't answer. Instead, I remove her sports bra then place my hardness in the crease between her lower lips. Planting my legs on the outside of hers, I use them to hold hers closed. Filling my mouth with her apple-size breast, my hips rotate in a motion that causes my pole to slide up and down between her folds. The friction on her clitoris is driving her crazy. Her sexual moans caress my ears and fuel the fire that's burning between us.

"... put it in." Her legs push against mine trying to open. I hold them closed and continue my assault on her body.

It's not working.

I'm trying everything in my power to get lost in this moment with Niesha, but thoughts of Dena keep tickling the corner of my consciousness. Her arms around me. Her smell. Her kisses. I can't understand how I can still desire her after all she's done to me, everything that I've lost because of her. It's pissing me off. That desire is what caused me to wrap my hands around her neck and begin squeezing. I was trying to kill my desire for her. The same desire that has me wishing that it was her beneath me right now instead of Niesha.

Suddenly angry, I grab my manhood and slide it deeply inside of Niesha's wetness all in one stroke.

"Uhhhhn baaaabbby...Click!" Without holding back, I rock every inch of my anger in and out of her. Stroking. Stabbing. Trying to kill all thoughts of Dena with my nature. Niesha's body beneath mines squirm as she tries to escape from my leg-lock. My long strokes are relentless. With her body trapped beneath me, my six one frame dominates her completely. Her moans loud and constant. When I feel her trembles come and her teeth sink into my shoulder, I know it's time.

I reach my arm towards the table sitting in front of the couch and grab two strawberry from the basket sitting on top of it. Then, I release her legs allowing her to open them wide and wrap around me. I sink deeper into her heat, hips rolling and long stroking. Just as her love begins to come down and her juices start to flow, I place one of the strawberries in her mouth and bite into the other one. Removing my manhood, I replace it with my tongue. Her center melts into my mouth and I savor the taste of strawberries and cream. The quick flick of my tongue takes her over the edge. Her orgasm has her lost in a world of praises and curses. Grabbing my head, squeezing my face between her legs, she's outside of her body.

Fueled with liquor and driven by anger, I flip her onto her stomach and slide a couple pillows underneath her hips. Then I submerge myself back inside of her center. From top to bottom, my pole disappears repeatedly.

Dena's face won't leave my mind.

I want to make her pay.

I want her to hurt.

My pace quickens as my hips slam into Niesha's ass cheeks. One hand gripping a fist full of hair, the other holding one of her rounded hips tightly, I pound away at her body. Looking back at me with that it-hurt-so-good-face, ass in the air, juices running down the inside of her thighs, Niesha takes all I have to offer. Over the next couple of hours and through many more positions, I rotate between slow lovin and ruff fucking taking all of my frustrations out on Niesha's sex.

"Mommy, Deshawn, wake up!" her little cute voice sings from the bottom of the bed before I feel the weight of her small body climbing up and between us. Niesha, lying beside me, rolls over and groans into the pillow.

"Nadia, nooo. Not this morning, I need sleep."

"But mommy, it's five- thirty. You got to get up for work and get me ready for day care." She never misses a beat. Every morning since the first time I ever slept over, like a baby alarm clock, Nadia comes into the bedroom at five-thirty on the dot and wakes us up. Even on weekends. Niesha told me that she use to wake her up at five o clock. As a single parent beginning a career in real estate, that was the scheduled start time that she'd set for herself to begin her days. But after a year of Nadia's punctuality, Niesha had to convince her that they'd established the routine enough to sleep in an extra half an hour.

"Mommy, you and Deshawn have to get up. I want some Capt'n Crunch and you told me not to fix it all by myself because I'm not big enough and the last time..."

"Okay! Okay Nadia... I'm getting up. Just... go brush your teeth and wash up. I'll be in there in a minute to fix you some Capt'n Crunch. Okay baby? I just need another few minutes...."

"Alright Mommy, but If you don't come, I'll be back." We both know she means it. If I wasn't so tired myself, I'd probably laugh knowing how wore out Niesha must feel after the workout I put on her ass last night. Then Nadia uses her small hands to give my body a good shove.

"And you get up too Deshawn. I'm mad at you. You didn't call me back yesterday."

"I'm getting up Queen Bee." I mumble knowing she won't give up until she gets a response. Satisfied that she's performed her morning duty, Nadia climbs down out of the bed and skips out of the room. Seconds after her tiny footsteps fade, I begin drifting back into slumber. I'm too exhausted to dream. No red-eyed deranged Jamaicans come visit me in my sleep. No pretty deep-dimpled angel of deception interrupt my peace. Just plain sleep.

A loud thunderous BOOM jars me awake.

Niesha and I both sit up at the same time eyes frantically searching the room looking for anything out of place. The unmistakable sound of a gunshot is followed by an eerie silence. Then a low wail begins that gradually grows into all out bawling.

"What the...Nadia!" Niesha jumps out of the bed and races out of the room. Still somewhat discombobulated, I stumble around looking for my underwear before remembering that I left them in the bathroom with the rest of my clothes last night when I took a shower. Then another sickening thought hits me.

"Oh shit!" Now fully awake, I grab a sheet from the bed, wrap it around my waist, and head towards the bathroom.

"Shhh, it's okay baby. You alright. You alright."

Niesha on the bathroom floor with her daughter wrapped safely in her arms rocking, rubbing and kissing her hair, comforting, thanking the Lord that her baby is alright. A few feet away laying menacingly on the floor is my fully loaded, seventeen-shot, black and grey nine millimeter.

Niesha's accusing eyes land on mine. "Get out."

"Look baby, I..."

"Get out!" Although I know there is nothing I can do or say to fix this, I still don't want to leave like this.

"Hey lil Queen Bee, you alright?" I reach for Nadia, but she turns her face away from me and buries it in her mother's bosom. That hurt.

Then with finality, Niesha says, "Get. Out."

Without another word, I get dressed, gather all of my shit, and leave.

CHAPTER 5

I walk into Uncle Fresh's study a little after midnight. The sound of B.B. Kings powerful raspy voice moaning in the background and the sixty and seventies paraphernalia lacing the room pulls me into Uncle Fresh's retro vibe.

Large photos of him with some of the greatest blues legends of all time are framed on the wall behind him; Bobby Blue Bland, John Lee Hooker, B.B. King and his famous guitar Lucille, Muddy Waters, younger versions of Uncle Fresh in all those memorable moments stare down at me.

I collapse into a tired heap on the sofa sitting across from him more mentally exhausted than physically. He's sitting behind his desk in a high-wing back chair playing a game of chess against himself no doubt in one of his deep analytical zones plotting on a level of intricacy that surpasses the understanding of us mere mortals. After staring at the chess board for a moment, he takes a white knight and places it in front of a black pawn putting the black king in check. My eyes are trained on him and the board watching for his next move. Several minutes of contented silence go by as he works through whatever is going on in his head. Finally, he grabs the black king and moves it out of check.

"Uncle Fresh, why didn't you just take the knight with that pawn?"

"Because, " he says demonstrating "had I of done that, the next move would have been checkmate." I look closely at the board, but still can't see what he sees. Once again demonstrating, he moves a white pawn forward securing the two places that the black king would have otherwise been able to escape to, at the same time, clearing the lane between the black king and white bishop causing an automatic checkmate.

"Everything ain't always what it seems Babygirl." he says, a statement that he's recited to me on more than a few occasions. "Sometimes the weakest and most expendable looking player in the game is the strongest and most powerful." I digest his wisdom with a silent nod understanding the message. Then my thoughts drift back to Click and what happened earlier tonight. Uncle Fresh leans back in his chair giving me his full attention.

"So what's on yo mind?"

Gathering my strength, I get up and go stands in front of Uncle Fresh's desk. Then I reach down and remove the little black phone from inside of my stiletto boot where I had it hidden and set it down in front of him.

"Click says you'll be hearing from him within twenty-four hours." Without another word, I return to my position on the couch. When my eyes look into Uncle Fresh's face, all I see is calm. Sitting here looking at my father, the first man that I ever loved, I experience my first heartbreak ever. How can he sit there so calm knowing that he lied to me? Knowing that he told me out of his own mouth that he killed Click and even comforted me as I mourned his death.

In a voice as smooth as a neo-soul melody, Uncle Fresh says, "There's a difference between lying to you and protecting you so don't be looking at me like that with those accusing eyes." I hold onto my silence.

"Lafu is not a fool." he continues. "He's much more intelligent and perceptive than you could imagine. He's been watching you, studying your every move and emotion. I wouldn't even be surprised if he was having you followed. One indication of anything false from you and we would have both been dead by now. He had to see you grieve. He needed to witness the depression you fell into when you first thought Click was dead. It was scary, especially when it became unhealthy for the baby, but it was necessary." Then he falls silent and let B.B. King and his guitar take over the sound in the room.

The truth of his words hit home.

Truth don't need no explanation.

Uncle Fresh being my father is the truth that my mother revealed to me the night of my birthday before she was murdered. Now that I look back on it, it only made sense. I remember the joy that erupted inside of me when she told me, like the relief of something being confirmed that I already knew.

"Why didn't you ever tell me?" The words come out of my mouth without my permission. Uncle Fresh takes his time in answering. Enough time for B.B. King to go off and be replaced by the smooth-silky sounds of Sir Charles asking, 'Is anybody lonely?'.

Finally he says, I did. I told you every day." I had switched subjects without warning or explanation yet Uncle Fresh still knew exactly what I was talking about.

"Every day of your life, I've made it my business to show you that you are the apple of my eye. My Babygirl. I've protected you. Comforted you. Shielded you. Taught you. Loved you with everything that I have inside of me for any child of mine rather it be a daughter or son. You didn't need to hear the words because I showed you." Pregnant and already filled with emotion, a tear threatens to spill from my eye. My hurt at feeling deceived and lied to earlier fades away. The warm glow of affection that I have for this man grows stronger.

Then he burst my bubble by saying, "Now go pack up all of your things and be ready. Your catching a flight out of here first thing in the morning."

"Flight to where?" I ask with raised eyebrows.

"What day is the baby due to be born?"

"April 24th." I say rubbing my belly and wishing it would hurry up and get here already. Extra weight and swollen feet is not idea of cute.

"Well until that time comes, and our little soldier decides to make an appearance, your new residence will be Atlanta Georgia."

"And who's making this decision about my life without my permission? "I ask giving him my best disappointed daughter look.

"The one who's been showing you since the day you were born that you are the apple of his eye. The one who loves and protects you and would never forgive himself if he ever let anything happen to you."

"But Uncle Fresh I..."

"Dena, this is not up for discussion." he says before standing up and heading towards the office door. I know there is nothing further I can say. When Uncle Fresh gets like this, there is no moving him. Plus, he called me Dena instead of Babygirl something he only does when he's upset with me or being firm letting me know that my pouting and tears won't work.

Still I say, "And why am I being sent away again?"

Standing with his hand on the doorknob, Uncle Fresh turns to me with a serious look on his face and says, "Because it's game time Babygirl and your boy is ready to make a play. So until I get a chance to see where his head is at and what he's got planned, I'm not letting him nowhere near you. And don't think I didn't notice those marks on your neck either." Then he walks out the office leaving me once again with the realization that the father of my unborn child is still alive and probably wants nothing more than to see me dead.

****

Knowing that I won't be able to sleep, I go into the garage and climb into the first vehicle that suits me for the moment, which happens to be one of Lafu's newest toys, a midnight-black 2004 Mercedes Benz S 500. Floating out of the garage into the darkness of the night at thirty miles per hour with nothing but the glow from the dash and no headlights, I maneuver onto the familiar terrain of the mansions rocky driveway with ease. By the time I navigate to the end of the quarter mile of tricky curves and turns, I've got my blunt lit and Fantasia's 'Free Yourself' bumping from the speakers. Spinning a sharp right onto the dark pavement and flipping on the headlights, I take a long, deep puff of the blunt and press down hard on the gas pedal. The Benz races down the deserted highway as quick as the thoughts begin racing through my mind.

I can't believe that Click is still alive.

That one thought sends my emotions all over the place. I saw him with my own eyes, I touched his face, can still feel the impression of his body against my skin. His scent still in my nose. How is this even possible? No one survives against the monster known as Lafu. For Uncle Fresh to deceive the devil and become Click's angel of mercy, he definitely has something big planned. Oh my god, shit is about to get so crazy and Uncle Fresh is trying to send me away in the morning! There's no way I'm leaving here without talking to Click first.

The determination in that thought causes me to put more pressure on the gas pedal and pull on my blunt harder.

"What the hell you doing here?" is the first words out of her mouth when she opens the door. The scowl on her face and body language tells me that whatever reason I have for showing up at her door after one in the morning, it better be good.

"I need to talk to Click and I know if no one else on this earth knows where to find him, you do." Her reaction is instant.

"Bitch... you gotta lotta muthafuckin nerves showing up at my door in the middle of the night. Even if I did know where Click was, I wouldn't tell yo snake ass!" Her facial expression is appalled, mouth hanging open in disbelief.

"I know you and I have never really seen eye to eye but..."

"No bitch, I don't like you." I keep my attitude in check because I knew before I got here that there was a chance that this would be a confrontational encounter, even thought about turning around a couple of times but the shortage of time made me come anyway. Now I kinda wish I would have just followed my first mind.

"Look Reece, I didn't come here for all that. It's some serious shit going on and if you care anything about Click you would help me find him. I'm trying to make sure nothing bad happens to him."

"Bitch you already happened to him. Didn't you set him up? Ain't you the reason he showed up at my door all beat up and barely breathing a few months ago? I wouldn't help you find him if you had a court order. Now get away from my door." She attempts to slam the door in my face, but my quick reflexes has my foot in the way before she makes it that far. Her eyes drop down to my stiletto boot that's wedged in the door then come back up to meet mine. A couple of seconds of her looking crazy before she opens the door all the way and her and I are standing face to face. I'm a couple of inches taller and outweigh her by at least ten pounds, but our difference in physical stature is not what has me shocked. It's our physical similarity.

Her pregnant belly poking out as far as mine.

She as far along and as impregnated as I am.

I think back to the first time I ever laid eyes on Reece. It was the night I watched her husband get killed in the Jackpot Projects. I ended up rescuing Click and her husband's brother from a shootout and rushed them to the hospital. Since Click had taken a couple of bullets and was in surgery, I stayed in the hospital waiting room with the husbands brother whose name is Mechi. From the moment we walked through the hospital doors, Mechi had been raising hell, cursing out, and threatening anyone who couldn't come up with some type of information about his homeboy and brother. When a doctor did finally come out and inform him with his deepest apologies that his brother, Travis Aaron Bell was dead on arrival, Mechi snapped and punched the doctor in the face. Although he said it over and over in the truck on the way to the hospital, it's like actually hearing someone else confirm that his brother was dead made the reality of it sink in. Before leaving the hospital in a rage, Mechi screamed at the top of his lungs.

"On everything I live, ride, and die for, Nutcase and the rest of those bitches over in the JP's is dead! They muthafuckin dead!!!" Then he punched his fist through and shattered the glass door in the emergency room and walked out.

After he left, I sat alone with my thoughts hoping and praying that Click would pull through when a pretty brown-skinned sista wearing sweats and a scarf on her head rushed into the emergency room and up to the front desk.

I heard her say, "Yes my husband was shot."

"What's your husband's name ma'am?" asked the nurse behind the desk.

"Travis. Travis Bell." That's the name of the person that I heard the doctor tell Mechi was dead. Travis Bell was Mechi's brother. This had to be Mechi's brother's wife.

The nurse says, "Okay and what's your name ma'am?"

"Reece Bell."

"Okay Mrs. Bell, have a seat and I'll see what I can find out for you."

"Is he alright? Can you at least tell me that?"

"I can't tell you anything until I go check it out. Just go have a seat and I'll call you as soon as I find out something." Looking anxious and worried, Reece came over and sat in the empty seat next to me.

"Please God please God please. Please just let him be alright." Seeing her with her hands together under her chin praying in earnest pulled at my heartstrings. Knowing that her prayers are in vain, knowing that her husband is dead and gone I can't help myself.

"Excuse me." She looked over at me as if she didn't realize that anyone was sitting next to her.

"Yeah?" Looking in her face and trying to find words, I realize that I don't know what to say to her, don't know how to say what I'm trying to say.

"Do you know a guy named Click?" I blurt out.

"Yeah that's my husband's friend. What about him?"

"Well I saw him and... I'm the one who gave him a ride here. He was shot."

With her hand to her chest in alarm she asks, "Who was shot, Click? Click got shot too?"

"Yeah, he was with another guy."

"Was it my husband?"

"No, I don't think so. The guy's name was Mechi."

"Mechi? That's my husband's brother. Where was my husband?"

"I don't know." I say on the verge of tears.

"Well, where is Mechi?"

"He left after...I saw him talking to one of the doctors and... look girl I'm sorry."

The word "No" comes out on a strangled cry. The top half of her body folds over and with her face down by her knees, her heartbreaking sobs come out. Her pain so strong it's almost tangible. The same kind of pain that was living inside of me. Her cries serenade my tears into a full flow.

Unexpectedly, she sits back up and faces me. With a tear-stained face, she looks directly at me.

"Is he dead?" Her mouth asks for one thing, but her eyes beg for another. "Tell me."

I nod my head.

Her eyes close as she leans toward me with a silent cry.

Stranger or not, I wrap my arms around her body and give her comfort. Her emotions resurrect the feelings that ran through me the night Finesse shot herself in the neck. For long moments us two strangers shared pain.

The last thing I want to happen is for us two pregnant black women to be out here fighting in the middle of the night, so I take a deep breath and let it out slowly before trying to reason with her.

"Listen Reece, this is Click's child that I'm carrying inside of me." I emphasize my words by holding my stomach with both hands and looking deeply into her eyes. "I know you have every reason not to believe me, but I would never willingly put myself in a position to have to one day explain to him that I'm the reason why his daddy ain't here. I admit that what I did before was fucked up, but there's nothing I can do to change what happened. The important thing is that Click is still alive and I'm trying to do whatever it takes to keep him that way. All I'm asking you to do is at least get him on the phone for me." For a split second, I think my words have penetrated her anger, that maybe she being a widow and expecting mother herself, we could put our differences to the side for a moment and help each other. Boy was I wrong.

With enough animosity to raise the temperature in the room she says, "Oh you think I'm playing? Bitch I said..." With more speed and strength than I would have expected, Reece pushes me in my chest hard enough to make me fly backwards into the apartment door directly across the narrow hallway from hers. "... get the fuck away from my door!"

My taekwondo training kicks in instantly causing me to grab ahold of her wrist and pull her with the momentum of my fall. My natural instinct is to kick up at her midsection, but I'm too conscious of her baby. Instead, I pull her in for a sharp elbow to the face to slow her down.

"You stupid bitch!" she screeches touching her face and pulling back to find blood on her hands. "I think you broke my nose!" Now fully enraged, she rushes me with a barrage of wild swings and punches that mostly get blocked. A few get through, but not enough to do any real damage.

Again, my back slams into the apartment door across the hall as I step backwards dodging blows. I sidestep and circle out into the middle of the hallway, giving myself more room. I don't want to hurt her, but I definitely ain't gone let her hurt me either.

"Would you stop!" I try to rationalize. "What we look like out here fighting and we both pregnant?" Guess her killer instincts are stronger than her maternal instincts because Reece is relentless in her attack, screaming and swinging.

Staying relaxed and timing it just like Uncle Fresh taught me, I use her weight against her by simply sidestepping and grabbing her arms and using them as a steering wheel to direct her body where I want it to go. I follow up with a swift right hook to the jaw that sends her tumbling to the carpeted hallway floor with a dull thump.

"Look, I'm out of here. I don't have time for this." I say backing away ready to make my exit. No point in sticking around and letting a bad situation become worse. Just as I'm turning to leave out the same way I came in, Reece looks up at me clutching her stomach.

"Wait... somethings wrong." I can hear the panic in her voice, see the fear mixed with pain written across her face. "My baby."

"What, are you serious?" I'm by her side within seconds. "Tell me your kidding."

"No bitch, I'm not fucking kidding! Something is wrong with my baby!" Now more than ever, I'm wishing I would have never come here.

"Okay, tell me what you need me to do." I say kneeling down next to her.

"Help me up. I need to get to the hospital." I wrap one arm around her waist and let her use my shoulder to hold on to as I pull her up. Suddenly this dirty bitch catches me off guard by grabbing two handfuls of my long pretty hair and dropping all of her weight down backwards onto the floor. Headfirst on my hands and knees, I land between her legs. Her legs come up and wrap around my midsection. Her fist punch all over my face and head. I remain calm and reach up with both hands until I find her face.

My nails dig in deep.

She releases a painful cry and her punches stop landing. Desperately she tries to get my nails out of her face.

"Aaah, let my face go you snake ass bitch!" Sitting on top of her, I get my feet planted up under me firmly before I remove my nails and stand up over her.

"I keep telling you to chill. I'm trying not to fuck you up!" I back up dodging her kicking feet and putting plenty of space between us.

"Fuck you bitch. You lucky I'm pregnant." Moving slow and winded, Reece climbs to her feet mumbling. "Got me out here fighting in the middle of the night." I can only shake my head to myself. Not sure if she's given up or not, I watch her every move. With one arm braced against the wall, Reece stands there catching her breath.

The door across the hallway opens and out steps a bare-chested, short, husky, brown-skinned brotha rocking deep waves in his hair with a temp fade and a full beard that's trimmed to perfection.

"Reece what's up, you good?" His eyes take in her bloody nose then moves back and forth between her and I.

"Yeah Jay, I'm good. Just dealing with this fucking snake." She moves in my direction again.

"Whoa whoa..." he says stepping in between us and holding his arms out. "Y'all chill out."

"I'm cool. " I say holding up my hands. "She's the one you need to be talking to."

"You came to my house bitch!"

"You know what, I ain't gone be too many more bitches."

"What you gone do about it?" she says trying to get around him. "Bitch, bitch, bitch!"

"Come on Reece, " the guy uses his body to block and steer her small body back into his apartment "let me get you something to clean your nose with."

"Nah, fuck that, I'm finna kick this bitches ass!" She struggles to get away from him and continue to scream and curse. One by one, more apartment doors open up and down the hallway as nosey neighbors poke their head out trying to see what all the commotion is about. The guy gives me one final look back before he and Reece disappear into his apartment and the door slams shut behind them. Just that quickly, the chaotic atmosphere becomes still and silent.

I stand for a few seconds contemplating my next move before the uncomfortable feeling of all eyes on me cause my feet to start moving towards the exit. The thought of one of the neighbors possibly calling the police and reporting the disturbance makes me put a little more pep in my step. Back behind the wheel of the Benz, I chastise myself out loud.

"That wasn't very smart." I knew coming here was a long shot, but I was hoping that Click still lived here and would emerge out of her apartment and come break us up. I was hoping that he would want me to find him. I was hoping that he would want to hear what I had to say. I was hoping against hope.

Just as I'm putting the car in reverse to back out of the parking space, my cell phone rings. I wait until I'm driving away from Reese's before I answer.

"Where you at hooker?" It's Finesse. I can hear loud music playing in the background.

"On my way to find Click."

"Click?"

"Yes, Click."

"Wait a minute. Let me go into the bathroom, I'm having a hard time hearing you." A long pause as I hear a bunch of shuffling. The background music fades all together. "Ok now, what did you say? It sounded like you said you were on yo way to find Click."

"I did."

"Click? You mean Click Click?"

"Yup."

"You mean yo unborn child's dead father Click?"

"Yes my child father Click, but he's not dead."

"Wait a minute D, you losing me. What do you mean he ain't dead?" She's having a hard time wrapping her mind around the fact that one of Lafu's victims survived.

"Just what I said, he ain't dead."

Still sounding skeptical, she asks "Well, do you know he's alive for sure? "

"He came to the club tonight. I saw him with my own eyes."

Another long pause before she says "Shut the front door! Bitch... what did he say?"

Knowing how she'll react if I tell her that he put his hands on me, I simply say, "Let's just say he isn't very happy with me."

"Well duh, I bet he ain't. If I was him, yo ass wouldn't even be breathing right now. I would have... wait a minute... that means that Johnny Ray crossed Lafu?"

"Yes. So now you know I'm really worried. Plus, Uncle Fresh is sending me to Atlanta in the morning."

"Atlanta, what?"

"He says I can't come back until after the baby is born."

"Damn D, so what we gone do?"

"I don't know Nessa." I say with an exasperated sigh. "You know how Uncle Fresh is once he's made his mind up. All I know is, I can't leave here without talking to Click first. And what's all this we stuff? "

"Yes bitch, we! I know you don't think I'm letting you leave here without me so you might as well come pick me up right now. You already know where I'm at." I can't help but smile. That's one thing I love about Finesse; she has my back and is down for me no matter what.

CHAPTER 6

Dena

"I still say we should go back and whoop that bitch ass." Finesse says as we ride down the street.

"What part of she's pregnant don't you get?"

"What part of I don't give two fucks don't you get? She wasn't thinking bout yo baby when she swung on you so why you worried about hers?"

"Because unlike her, I happen to care about human life. And besides, I went looking for Click not a fight."

"Well you sure found one." Finesse cracks. "Now if it was up to me, we would go back and whoop that baby up outta her ass *and* make her tell us where Click at."

"Well thank God it ain't up to you. Let's stick to the plan."

Truth of the matter is, we really don't have a plan nor the slightest idea where to begin looking for Click. When he and I were a couple, we spent every waking moment together. The only time we were apart is when he decided that he wanted to go spend time with Reece, which I didn't and still don't understand; not like he was her man or something. Other than Reece, Click would go and hang with Lil-Eighty and the rest of the fellas in his old neighborhood so that's where we're headed to now.

"Girl these muthafuckas out here like zombies." Finesse says as we cruise slowly through the run-down neighborhood looking at all the junkies scrambling in and out of the shadows of the late night hours. It's after three in the morning and the only thing out moving besides the junkies is the dope boys.

Still amazed at the powerful effect that crack cocaine has on people; I wonder out loud "What would make a person use that stuff knowing what it does to them?"

"Dena, I don't think no one knows what that stuff is going to do to them until it's already done."

Realizing that Finesse is speaking from her own personal experience with cocaine, I don't comment on it any further. Instead I say, "Well I'm gonna stick to using this." and pull out my stash of sticky light-green. "Nobody I know has ever acted like that from smoking this."

"Yes girl, now you talking"

"Only problem is, I don't have anything to roll in."

"Hold up, I might have something. "Finesse begins looking through her Gucci bag. I keep my eyes on our surroundings as we come to a stop sign. Halfway up the block to our right is the house that Lil-Eighty and the rest of the young wild boys that Click ran with sell drugs out of.

"Yes!" Finesse says pulling out a pack of rolling papers.

"What the hell is that? We can't roll no blunt in those."

"I said I might have something. I didn't say nothing about no cigar. Then she pulls out a little one-hitter. "It's either those or this."

"Nah, I think I'd rather go with the papers, but we gone have to stick a few of them together and roll a spliff or something because a little bitty joint ain't gone be able to do nothing for me right now."

"Yea, it's gone take a big joint to give me what I need too." Finesse says gyrating her hips in her seat with sex on the brain as usual.

"Bitch you need help." I laugh. She only giggles and commences to licking and sticking papers together.

"Damn, business must really be good." So much traffic of cars and people running in and out of the house that it looks like a fast food restaurant.

"Must be." Finesse says. "I say we just park somewhere and stop one of these lil niggas out here and ask for ya boy. Either that or act like we're one of these junkies trying to buy some drugs."

"They definitely ain't gone believe that. They'll think we're the police before they think we're junkies." We both laugh.

"Yea you right. Fuck it, just pull over and I'll go up to the front door and ask for the nigga. They know who you is, they don't know shit about me." I know Finesse's ass is crazy enough to do just that. Then it hits me.

"Wait a minute Nessa, you just might be on to something." I find the nearest spot and pull over and park. "You were already in a coma before I even met Lil-Eighty and his crew and only a short time passed between you waking up and Lafu making his move on Click. That means they don't have no way of connecting you to me." I think about it for a few seconds more. "It just might work."

"Duh, that's what I'm trying to tell you." Finesse says victoriously while putting the finishing licks on a perfectly rolled spliff. "Who's yo bitch?"

"You are but, bitch you betta be careful."

She reaches inside her Gucci bag again and pulls out a little twenty-five automatic with a pearl-pink handle.

"Girl you know I never leave home without it. I got this."

"Okay good, but I don't want you to go inside Nessa. Just go to the front door and ask for Click. If he ain't there, see if you can get his phone number or get one of them to contact him for you. Make up something to make it seem like it's an emergency and you have to find him now."

She puts some fire to the spliff and asks, "What you want me to do if he is in there or they get him on the phone?" I hadn't thought that far so I have to pause for a second before the answer comes to mind.

"That's when you tell him I'm outside."

We go over our little readymade plan some more while finishing up our spliff before Finesse tucks her piece and gets out of the car.

"Okay remember what I said Finesse. Under no circumstances are you to go inside that house."

"How many times you gone tell me? I told you I got this." She closes the car door and heads toward the house. As I watch her walk away, I get a bad feeling.

The Benz is actually parked four car lengths past and across the street from the house, so I have to use my side and rearview mirrors to keep my eyes on Finesse as she walks onto the front porch and knock on the door. Again, I survey my surroundings. There's a lot of activity going on for this to be the middle of the night. I see a lighter flame flickering in the darkness as a couple squats between two houses smoking what I can only assume is crack. A group of young boys walk pass my driver side window arguing loudly about something. Cars coming and going. One car carrying two people pulls over and parks directly in front of me. Moments later the passengers head disappears into the lap of the driver.

I make sure my car doors are locked then look around for my trusty 380 that I keep with me at all times only to realize that I left it at home; something that I never do. This thing with Click has really got me trippin. My eyes go back to my mirrors just in time to see someone open the door for Finesse. I watch her exchange words with the person before a dark-skinned, heavy-set guy wearing glasses and carrying a Hennessy bottle steps out onto the porch followed by two more guys. From my viewpoint, none of them appear to be familiar. Definitely not Click or Lil-Eighty. I feel myself get nervous and have to pee at the same time.

Although I know Finesse knows how to handle herself, especially with men, I also know how these niggas act. Managing a strip club has shown me firsthand how reckless a group of niggas drinking liquor and lusting over the ladies can be. Had I been thinking clearly, I would have gotten my two bodyguards, Mojo and Pitbull to come with us when I picked Finesse up from the club. Guess it's too late to be thinking about that now.

My phone rings.

It's Uncle Fresh.

I let the call roll over to voicemail.

Uncle Fresh would never understand what would cause me to be out here in the middle of the night not only putting myself, but also Finesse in harm's way. He would never understand the love that I have for Click and how important it is for me to make him understand that I didn't set him up because I'm just some grimy bitch. I did it because I didn't have a choice.

When I look back towards the house, my heart drops down into my stomach.

"What are you doing Nessa? No." I say out loud although she obviously can't hear me. After all of my pep-talking, I watch as the heavy-set guy with the Hennessy bottle holds the door open for Finesse and she leads the way inside. They all follow her movements with their eyes, two of them even slaps hands behind her back before they step in after her and the door closes shut.

"Shit shit shit." I feel myself begin to panic as my options start running through my head. I can't go in behind her or it'll defeat the whole purpose of me not going in the first place. All it takes is for one person to recognize me and we'll sure enough be in trouble. I could call the club and have Mojo and Pitbull come and go in after her. But nah, anything could happen by the time they get here. I pick up my celly and call Nessa's phone. After several rings, it rolls over to voicemail. I hang up and call right back.

A loud knock on the car window distracts me from my call. I look up to see a face pressed against the glass peering inside at me.

"What the hell?!?"

"Who you looking for?"

"I um.... I'm waiting for someone."

"Huh?"

A little louder I say, "I'm waiting for someone." He does a motion with his hand.

"Roll the window down." Yea right. Like that's really going to happen. I try to look back towards the house that Finesse went inside only to find several more faces pressed against my windows. The one on my driver-side taps my window again.

"You lookin for some work? I got some fat ass twenties." To prove his point, he spits something out of his mouth into his hand and tries to hold it up where I can see. "Roll the window down." My hand is on the key ignition starting the car so fast.

"No, no, I'm good. I'm waiting on my friend." I want to pull off but there is no way I'm leaving Finesse out here by herself.

"Man fuck yo friend. I got the best dope out here."

From the other side of the car, I hear "Nigga you a lie. I got that Butta!" Then these fools literally start arguing back and forth about who has the best drugs. For the second time tonight, I'm kicking myself in the ass for making such a dumb, impulsive decision. And on top of everything else, my bladder feels like it's about to burst I have to pee so bad.

"Y'all niggas back up. What the fuck is y'all doing? She don't want no damn dope." Finesse's voice is like music to my ears. "Get the fuck outta my way." Then a male voice.

"Y'all muthafuckas heard her. Get the fuck on." All at once, the young boys surrounding the car dispersed. Then Finesse is at the passenger side pulling on the door handle.

"Open the door bitch." I pop the locks so she can get in.

"Where the hell you been? I thought I told you not to go inside. Finesse what were you thinking?" I ramble out all in one breath.

"Girl chill out. I told you I got this." she says leaning inside the car giving me a wink. "I ran into an old friend of mine."

"A friend?"

Before she has a chance to respond, the guy bends down and leans inside giving me a clear view of his familiar face and offering me his prosthetic hand to shake.

"Mane what's happenin Shawty? Long time no see." It's none other than Mechi, Click's dead best friend's brother.

Chapter 7

Click

It's barely six o'clock in the morning and here I am out here riding around half sleep and irritated with myself for fucking up the way I did.

I was so caught up in my thoughts with Dena last night and focused on getting in between Niesha's legs that I totally forgot about my pistol being in the bathroom with the rest of my clothes. No matter how distracted I was, I still shouldn't have been so careless knowing Nadia was in the house. Niesha ain't gone never let me live this one down as much as she stresses the importance of watching what we say and do around Nadia. Even when you think she ain't paying attention, Nadia is tuned in. At four years old, she's like a human recorder remembering and repeating everything she sees and hears. Thank God she didn't get hurt though. I gotta come up with something special to make it up to my lil queen bee and Niesha, but right now, it's time to shake off yesterday and get my mind focused on what's about to go down today.

The 454 engine in my new old-school vert, a midnight black 72 Chevelle, rumbles powerfully as I pull into the Waffle House looking for a place to park. It feels good to see the shinning chrome twenty-four inch Davins on my ride reflecting off the building as I pass by. Knowing that I grinded for this whip and it's a result of my own hustle gives me the satisfaction that I never felt while driving the Range Rover that Dena bought for me. Thanks to Lil-Eighty, the money is flowing real lovely right now. He was smart and resourceful enough to stack the dough he made off the plug he had with me and the 'Hot Spot' and go find his own connect. Whoever Lil-Eighty fuckin with must be giving him the cotton candy treatment because he's been dropping it in my lap with the sweetest prices since I healed up and got back on my feet.

For the past four months the only thing that's been on my mind is stacking my paper and plotting my revenge. Now that my pockets are right, it's time to make my move on Lafu and hit that Jamaican muthafucka where it hurts.

After finding a place to park, I dig my phone out of the console of my ride where it's been all night and see that I have seven missed calls. Three of them are from cats who buy weight from me on the regular, probably calling to let me know that they're all out of work and ready to re-up. Another call came from Reece at two this morning. The last two calls came from Mechi at three something. Curious to know what all of the middle of the night calls are about; I don't even bother listening to my voicemail. Instead, I began making call-backs. The first one I make is to Reece, but she doesn't answer so I hit Mechi's line.

"Click, what up my nig!" he answers sounding way too energized for it to be six in the morning.

"I don't know, you tell me."

"You already out and about?"

"Yea unfortunately."

"Where you at?"

"What's up with all the questions bra? You the feds or something?"

"Nah mane, I got a lil sum-sum up here with me that I know you don't want to miss out on."

"Up where?"

"I'm at the Ramada. How soon can you get here?"

"Whoa, slow down playboy. If you trying to hook me up with some of them chickens you be messing with, I'm good."

"Nah mane, it ain't nothing like that. Trust me, not only is you gone be thanking me, but you gone owe me big time for this one." I can't even front, the nigga got me curious now.

"Mechi, it's too early for the bullshit. You gone spit it out or what?"

"It ain't nothing I want to talk about over the phone. Just come up here. I'm in room145." then he hangs up.

I sit there for a moment contemplating what he could be up to. Ain't no telling with this nigga. Mechi is an old-school vet in the game who's known for keeping one up his sleeve, especially since he's been off the dope and back on his hustle. I figure it's probably a money move or something.

Inside, the Waffle House is buzzing with the early morning work force traffic. The same every day nine to fivers getting their morning fix and doing whatever mentally motivating ritual they do to prepare themselves to make it through another day. I duck off into one of the back booths away from everybody else, but still in position to keep my eyes on my ride.

A short, petite, co-co puff brown female with a cute face and tired smile comes over and takes my order of hash browns and coffee with a Mexican cheese omelet. I use the time waiting for my food to make the rest of the calls I need to line up my plays for the day. By the time she comes back with my food, I've got money on my mind and ready to get to it.

"I'm sorry Miss um...." I look at her name tag. "Miss Charity, but can you bag that up for me?"

"You leaving already?"

"Yea, I changed my mind. Think I'll take it to go."

"Don't tell me I took that long bringing your food back."

"No, not at all." I say giving her a reassuring smile. "I just got some things that I need to hurry up and get to."

"Oh okay just making sure, although you really don't strike me as the type of guy who changes his mind a lot. You seem pretty sure of yourself."

"I am, but you know what they say about time and money. You never seem to have enough of either one of em."

"I can definitely feel you on that one. At the same time, you should never be in a rush cause you know what they say about patience right?"

"What, that it's a virtue?"

"No. Patience is life and without it you rush death." She flashes that tired smile again and says, "I'll be right back with your order." then walks away. I follow her with my eyes until she disappears into the back behind the counter.

For long moments, I sit there trying to convince myself that it's just a coincidence, that there is no way that this random female working for tips at the Waffle House is somehow connected to Lafu. Then again, anything is possible when it comes to this crazy Jamaican. A master at playing head games, Lafu is never to be underestimated. I made that mistake once before and almost didn't live to tell about it. This time around things are going to be different. Today he's going to find out that he ain't the only one that knows how to finesse the game.

I go straight home after leaving the Waffle House, shower, and get fresh dressed from head to toe in my Akedimic gear. With my glamour on point and a full stomach, I pack a duffle bag with everything I'm going to need for today's mission, throw it in the trunk, and head out. My first stop is to pick Lil-Eighty up from some new chick's house that he met out in Marianna. When I finally find the spot, Lil-Eighty comes out the front door puffing on a blunt and walking like he's the ding-a-ling king or something. I laugh to myself knowing how it is when you first hook up with a new female and feel like you put your thang down.

"What's up my guy?" I greet him with some dap when he climbs in the car.

"I can't call it." He closes the door and hands me the blunt.

"You know you slippin right?"

"Slippin how?"

"How you gone let some chick pick you up and drive you way out here without having your own whip to get back?"

"Aw man, shorty a lame to the game. She don't do nothing but work and read the Bible. A real church girl."

"Yea aiight. When Deacon Dynamite pop up at the door talkin about some what the fuck you doing in my house nigga! and you find yoself running down the backstreets in nothing but ya draws, don't call me." He cracks up laughing.

"No doubt, but good as shorty pussy is, I think it's worth the risk."

"Trust me my nigga, ain't no pussy worth that kind of risk." I hit the blunt a few times while reflecting to myself how us as men always seem to let women put us in positions to fall victim to other men. Pussy has been man's greatest weakness and downfall since the dawn of humanity; from the Garden of Eden all the way to the Kobe Bryant rape scandal.

"So what's up, you got everything ready to go?" I ask passing the blunt back to him and changing the subject.

"Yea, I put everybody on point last night. All we need now is Mechi's inside plug."

"Speaking of that fool, I talked to him this morning."

"Oh yea? What he on?"

"I don't know bra. He want me to come up to his hotel room. Talkin bout he got something up there that I don't want to miss out on."

"Sounds to me like he probably got a couple of freaks or something."

"Yea, that's what I said, but he say it ain't nothing like that."

"Shid, ain't no telling with that nigga."

"I know right. I'm bout to slide up there now. You tryna slide up there with me or you want me to drop you off?"

"Take me to my ride. I still gotta get my shit together and make sure everybody in position and know they role. We can't afford no fumbling and bumbling today. Too much at stake."

"Who you telling? I got everything ridin on this."

"No doubt. Don't worry tho, my team gone be ready to perform. You just make sure you take care of that old slick ass nigga Johnny Ray."

"Oh you bes believe, I got something in store fa his ass. He the captain of the ship so you know he gone sink with the rest of em."

"No doubt." I drop Eighty off, pull into the Ramada Inn parking lot, and dial Mechi's number.

"Click?"

"Yea man, I'm pulling up now. What room you say you were in?"

"145, but I ain't in the room right now. I'm sitting out in the parking lot. Matter of fact I see yo Vert pulling up now. You got that bitch clean don'tcha bra."

"Yea he aiight, where you at?"

"Keep coming down. I'm in the black Benz to ya right."

The Benz he's sitting in is parked backwards, so I pull forward into the space next to him. When he rolls the tinted window down, I can't believe my eyes. Sitting next to him in the passenger seat is none other than Finesse. She gives me a finger wave and a devilish smile.

"Heeey Click." I don't even bother responding. Instead, I look back at Mechi with a 'what-the-fuck-is-you-doing-look'. He opens the car door.

"Let me holla atchu for a minute bra." We both get out and stroll towards the hotel. Finesse's voice follows us.

"I see that body still lookin tight Click. Ass fat too." Mechi shakes his head and snickers. I flip her the bird over my shoulder. I notice how fresh Mechi is dressed in an orange, black, and green Nautica Army fatigue outfit with the all black Tim's and matching scarf around his head.

"Look my nigga, before you start buggin out let me give you the full run down. I haven't really told you or Eighty nem the business because I didn't want none of y'all second guessing my judgment. But shorty the one who been feeding me the info on Lafu."

"Who Finesse?"

"Yea. She got it out bad for that nigga. How you think we found out about all of his out of town spots?" So that explains it. Ever since Mechi found out that Lafu was the one behind his hand being cut off, he's been just as obsessed with getting back at Lafu as I have. Shit got real when Mechi came to me a couple months back and told me he had a line on a club that Lafu owns in Memphis. He had the whole layout; the security setup, money drops, when and where the drugs came in, everything. After scoping it out, we ran up in the spot and came off with almost half a mil in money and drugs. Since then Mechi has led us on four more licks at some of Lafu's other out of town clubs and all of them have paid off. None of them has been as big of a lick as the one we're about to hit today, which happens to be the one that Dena manages in town. 'The Hot Spot' is Lafu's main distribution center and a club that I personally know generates over five million a month in drug money alone. Not only are we going to rob 'The Hot Spot', but today is the day that Lafu's new shipment of cocaine comes in and Mechi has the inside scoop on the whole play. Now I know how.

"Man you know you still can't trust this broad right?"

"Come on playa, I'm the one who taught y'all lil niggas the game. Never let yo guards down, especially when it comes to a bitch."

"No doubt." We dap it up on that piece of knowledge. "So how you end up linking with her anyways."

"I was at a club across the bridge one night partying with some strip hoes and she was with em. That was back when I was indulging you know." He thumbs his nose letting me know he's talking about snorting cocaine. "Shorty was the life of the party. She was setting out big dope, getting everybody up in that muthafucka high so shiid...I worked my show and slid up under her. We ended up partying and freaking all night."

"Did she know who you was?"

"How could she? This was before you even got out the joint. Matter of fact, I didn't put two and two together until that night in the Jackpot when you and my brother got shot. Yo shorty pulled up and saved our ass driving that same White Escalade trimmed in gold that Finesse use to drive back when me and her was kickin it."

"Man watch yo mouth nigga. That bitch ain't none of my shorty."

"Whatever nigga. Anyway, I thought it was just a coincidence at first until I thought back to the one time that Finesse and I spent the night together."

"Damn, y'all use to kick it like that."

"Oh yea, we use to get it in. Funny thing is, she would never go to sleep around me. No matter how hard we use to freak and get high together, when the party was over, she would always dip out. Then one night out of the blue, she called me up on some vulnerable shit. Said she didn't want to get high or fuck, she wanted me to come and make love to her. She had a room, so I slid up there and put it down. Sexed her so good that she fell asleep curled up in my arms like a baby. Then shorty just wigged out, woke up screaming and shit like somebody was tryna get her in her sleep. Guess she was having a nightmare or something. She kept hollering for Dena. She wouldn't tell me what she was dreaming about, but when I asked her who Dena was, she told me that was her sister's name. That's how I figured out that yo shorty and my shorty sisters."

"Man how many times I gotta tell you that ain't my shorty." Mechi only laughs at my irritation.

"She might not be yo shorty, but she definitely carrying yo shorty."

"Say what? Where you get that from?" That's not a topic that I've discussed with anyone. Not even Reece.

"Why you think I was calling yo phone last night? They came to the hood looking for you."

"Who came looking for me?"

"Dena and Finesse nigga. Who you think driving that Benz? Know you didn't think it was mine." I look back at the car in time to see Finesse getting out and walking towards us. I can't even front, despite what I feel towards her personally, Finesse is the true definition of a bad bitch. From the swivel of her hips all the way down to her French manicured fingertips, her whole style has a way of casting a spell on a person. I can't help but to remember all the sexual encounters I've had with her and how skilled she is in the bedroom.

Turning back to Mechi, I ask, "Where Dena at now?"

"Upstairs in the room asleep."

Finesse comes up behind me and bodaciously walks her little body in between us, runs her finger across my lips, and says, "And she has no idea what's going on so I would appreciate it if you keep that sexy mouth of yours closed." With her other hand she cuffs Mechi's groin area then keeps walking. "Now I'm going to get something to eat so you boys can finish sharing y'all lil pussy stories." Mechi and I are both left standing speechless watching her sexy ass switch off.

CHAPTER 8

Dena

Water drops fall close by.

Don't know if my eyes are closed or the lights are out, but I can't see. A gentle breeze against my flesh exposes my nakedness. Goosebumps gather across the surface of my skin. I can hear Finesse moaning my name in the distance. My feet take unsure steps in the darkness towards her sound, her moans echoing in my ears.

The sudden touch of a warm hand on my thigh causes me to stand frozen in place. Another one touches my neck. Then another on my stomach. And another one. Hands touch me everywhere at once. I feel exposed. Cold, naked, and alone. I stand in the darkness being possessed by a thousand hands.

Fingertips brush lightly across my most intimate part. My nipples harden painfully as I'm being caressed, torn between the sensations flowing through my body and finding my Nessa. I'm aroused yet afraid.

A hard body presses me from behind. A man. His skin heated next to mine, his nature pressed tightly against my back. Powerful arms wrap around me. I feel safe in his embrace. Finesse moans loudly in my ear. Sounds like she's in pain. She needs me. I need to find my Nessa. I struggle to get free but am held hostage by the pleasure he's giving me with his fingers. Suddenly I'm alone again. No one is behind me. No one is touching me. I'm alone but I can see. My mother is standing in front of me illuminated in light. Her bright smile so beautiful as she reaches for me. Her lips moving, but no sound coming out. I try to read her lips but a rush of fluid from between my legs distracts me. I look down to see myself standing in a puddle. My water has broken. When I look back up, my mother is gone. Again, Finesse moans my name. I see her silhouette moving away from me. I call out to her.

"Finesse." My own voice wakes me.

"Nah, Not Finesse." A Male voice says. I open my eyes to see Click sitting in a chair near the bed watching me. I'm conscious of the moisture between my legs. Wispy images from my dream flash and fade. I try to remember but can only recall my mother's face.

"Huh?" I'm lying in a bed alone, on top of the covers, fully clothed. I remember that I'm in a hotel. "Click...how long have you been there?"

"Long enough to know that I'm not the man of your dreams."
"I can't... I can't remember what I was dreaming about."
"Finesse. You called her name in your sleep." For some reason I'm embarrassed.
"Where is she? Her and Mechi were both here when I fell asleep."
"They're down in the cafeteria. They didn't want to disturb you."
"Why didn't you wake me?"
"I didn't want to disturb you either." His face is expressionless, eyes dark and focused in on me. His gaze uncomfortable, like he's trying to see through me. I wish he would look away.

"I have to pee." Is all I manage to say before making my way off the bed and into the bathroom. The intense beat of my own heart becomes noticeable as soon as the door closes shut behind me. I have to remind myself to breathe. What is it about this man that makes me react this way? And why am I so nervous when I'm the one who came looking for him? Okay Dena pull it together. I look at my reflection in the mirror and can see a disaster. Not only is my hair all over the place, but there's a two inch spot of dried saliva on the side of my mouth from where I've been slobbing in my sleep. I wonder was I snoring too. Finger combing my hair into something close to order, I decide that the best thing for me to do right now is to take a quick shower to get my thoughts together. Quickly, I splash water on my face, use the restroom, then step back out into the room to find Click talking on the phone. It was still dark out when I dozed off shortly after five in the morning when we checked in. Now the curtains sit wide open letting the sunlight in to highlight every corner of our unimpressive ninety dollar room. There was no way that I was waiting for Click in some trap house, mouse trap, or whatever Mechi called it last night when he suggested that we stay and wait. The only way Finesse got me to agree to come to the hotel was by stopping at Walmart with me first, so I could put together an overnight bag to carry with me, since stopping at the mansion was out of the question. Uncle Fresh called so many times last night that I eventually just cut my phone off.

Click's eyes seem to capture my every movement as I scoop my bag up from the side of the bed and return to the bathroom. When I come back out thirty minutes later he's still on the phone.

I hear him say, "Don't worry, I'll take care of it. Aiight ma, holla atcha later." before hanging up. 'Ma?' An instant streak of jealousy runs through me, knowing how much I love it when he calls me that and how it makes me feel. Wondering who she is and if it makes her feel the same way. Guess it never crossed my mind until now that he might have found someone else. Just the thought of him touching another woman causes my stomach to hurt.

"Wassup, you trying to get some breakfast?" He looks at the watch on his wrist. "It's eleven thirty. If we hurry we can still make it."

"Um yea, I am kinda hungry." Now that I think about it, I haven't eaten since sometime around yesterday afternoon."

"Cool. The room comes with complimentary a breakfast, but we can go somewhere else if you ain't feeling the hotel food."

"No, the hotel breakfast is fine."

"Aiight cool." He stands up and I can't help but to admire how good he looks in his beige, baggy, Akedimic pants on top of peanut butter Tim's with the matching peanut butter and yellow Akedimic button down. His hair, which I noticed has grown a lot in four months, is neatly parted and braided to the side hanging down to his shoulders. A small diamond blinging in each ear with a Chrome Exclusive Fossil watch on his wrist has his swag on point.

I don't know what I expected from Click after him choking me at the club, but it definitely isn't the cool, cordial, laid back person that he's displaying right now. Under normal circumstances this is his everyday demeanor, but these circumstances are anything but normal. Yet and still, as we make our way down to the lobby, Click does all the normal gentlemanly gestures he use to do when he and I were together. Opening doors for me, hand on the small of my back, he even remembers what food I do and didn't like when we make it to the dining area.

"Know you love these." he says using the prongs to put a freshly baked bagel on my plate as we move down the breakfast cart.

"Ooh yes. And some of that cream cheese too please."

"Definitely can't have the bagel without the cream cheese. Okay let's see now, fruits. I know you don't like cantaloupe or green apples, but you love pineapples, grapes, and bananas." He fills a large bowl up with my favorite fruits.

"Aww you remembered, but why you getting so much?"

"Because you're eating for two now and I want my son to come out as healthy as possible."

"Son?" I give him a look. "How do you know it's going to be a boy when I haven't even had the doctor confirm the baby's sex yet."

"I just know." He answers with a shrug and enough confidence to make me think that he knows something that I don't.

"Well, I say it's going to be a girl and I'm going to name her after my mother. Princess Theresa."

"Wrong. No disrespect to your mother, but it's going to be a boy and he gone be named after his father. Deshawn Jr."

"Girl."

"Boy."

"Whatever, you don't know what you talkin bout." I turn to walk off but am stopped in my tracks by what he says next.

"You wanna make a bet?" I turn to face him.

"We can bet whatever you want to Mr.-Know-It-All."

He only smirks and says, "Okay tell you what, whoever wins gets a full twenty-four hour period where the loser can't say no to nothing the winner asks." I have to stop and think about it for a minute.

"Let me get this straight. Basically you gone have to give me anything I want and do whatever I say for a whole twenty- four hours?"

"If you win, yea. I'm your Shazam for a day. But just know..." He takes an intimidating step closer, close enough for my baby bump to press into his body as he towers over me. "If you lose, you're my genie in a bottle for a whole day and I plan on making every second count."

Not backing down, I say, " You got a bet. Hope you ain't no sore loser." then I walk off. Although having Click at my mercy for twenty-four hours is a thrilling thought, I'm more excited by the fact that he's open to spending any time with me at all.

"You sure you not the one eating for two?" I ask once we get settled at a table and I notice how much food is piled in front of him.

"Naw, I'm just a grown man with a grown man appetite."

"And the grown man munchies too nigga. Don't think I can't tell when you been smokin.'' I laugh and for the first time in a long time, Click gives me a real smile.

In this moment sitting here with him, laughing, talking, acting as if the bad things between us never happened, I'm reminded of all the things about him that I fell in love with. His personality, always charming but challenging me at the same time. How attentive and aware he is of me when I'm in his presence. Definitely that too cool swag of his, but when he smiles at me like he's doing now, something inside of me shifts. I lose all sense of what's going on around me; nothing or no one else matters. It's just me, him, and that smile.

"Dena?"

"Huh?"

"I was asking if you want some sausage." He has a link stuck to the end of his fork holding it out to me.

"Oh...yea it do look good." I lean forward to take a bite but Click pulls his fork back before I get a chance to sink my teeth in.

"Who said I was talkin about my food?" My eyes meet his and the look on his face helps the full understanding of what he's saying sinks in. Suddenly, my panties are moist thinking about how good he use to feel inside me.

In a trance I say, "I would love for you to take me back to the room and remind me over and over again how good it is."

"Ummm... I wasn't talking about that either. I was just offering to get up and go get you some sausage from the breakfast cart."

"Oh." I say feeling completely embarrassed. That is until I notice how hard he's trying not to laugh. "You know what, forget you punk." I punch him in the arm then grab ahold of his wrist pulling his fork to my mouth. "Give me some of this damn sausage." I bite down and take the whole link. Click is beside himself with laughter, slapping the table, tears rolling down his face, the whole nine.

"You make me sick." I say around a mouth full of meat. He only laughs harder.

"Aww...look at y'all two over here getting along. " Finesse says as her and Mechi walk up.

"We was until Click started acting like an asshole."

Finally sobering up and wiping his eyes, Click says, "You have to admit, I got you good."

"Whatever."

"What the hell is so funny my nigga?" Mechi asks.

"Aw nothing man, just a little inside thang." Finesse comes over and sits beside me.

"How you feeling hooker?"
"I'm good."
"Did you get enough rest?"
"Girl yes, and it was much needed too."
"Everything good?" She cuts her eyes to Click. I nod my head and answer with a slight smile.

"Well, you might as well turn this back on." Finesse says reaching in her Gucci bag and handing me my phone. "You know who has been blowing my phone up all morning and he definitely ain't looking for me." There's no doubt in my mind that she's talking about Uncle Fresh.

"Did you answer?"

"Hell nah! I ain't trying to get in the middle of that." Damn, for a while there, I actually tricked myself into believing that this was just an ordinary day that I was out spending with my child's father and we were still in love. But the reality is, I ran off in the middle of the night to find him so that I could explain the reason for my deception. The reality is, I intentionally disobeyed Uncle Fresh and he's probably beside himself with worry looking for me.

I take the phone from Finesse but decide against turning it on.

Mechi says, "Aiight Dena, let me find out you got some nigga stalking my shorty phone looking for you."

"For your information Mechi, I don't get down like that. I've only dealt with one man in my whole life and right now he's being an asshole."

"Say word? You mean to tell me that Click is the only nigga to ever hit that?" Finesse frowns at Mechi.

"Damn nigga, can she have her business back."

"What?" Mechi asks sounding all innocent. Finesse only ignores him. I look over at Click who is now just listening with that expressionless poker face of his back in place.

"Anyway, speaking of business, Click wassup my nigga? You ready to make that move?" Click looks at his watch and stands up.

"Yea it's about that time."

"Where y'all going?" Finesse asks.

"Damn, can we have our business back?" Mechi mocks before he and Click turn to walk off.

I can't hide the disappointment in my voice when I ask Click, "You leaving already?"

"Yea, I got a lil something I need to go take care of."

"But we still haven't had a chance to talk yet."

"Be cool ma, I'm coming back. Unless you got something else you need to do. We can just hook up later."

"No, she'll be here waiting when you get done." Finesse answers for me. "Plus, Mechi just paid the room up for another day."

"The same room?" I frown my disapproval.

"Yes, the same room." Finesse throws her arm around my shoulders. "We can order take out and spend the afternoon stuffing our faces and giving each other mani's and pedi's until they come back. Come on girl it'll be fun."

"I guess." I'm not really feeling the idea but, I'll go along if it means that I get to spend time with Click later. But I do say, "Least y'all can do is go get us something to smoke since we gone be stuck here all day waiting for y'all."

" Something to smoke?" Click looks at me like I'm crazy. "You must already be smoking crack if you think I'm gone not only go get you something to smoke, but even allow you to smoke it around me knowing you carrying my seed. Come on ma, you trippin."

"Allow?" I want to tell him so bad that no he's the one trippin if he thinks he's about to start trying to control my life just because I'm pregnant, but instead I roll my eyes at his retreating back as he and Mechi walk away.

With my arms folded across my chest and lips twisted up, I make a "Hmp" sound.

"Don't even sweat it D. We still got this." Finesse says holding up the remainder of the bag we were smoking on last night. My facial expression quickly changes to a smile.

****

"Didn't you tell me you left your pistol at home?" Finesse asks as she passes me the remainder of our last blunt.

"Uh-huh."

"So make me understand how you managed to
remember to grab yo poem book but forgot to grab yo lifeline."

"This is my lifeline."

"Those words on paper ain't gone have yo back or save yo life if some shit pop off."

"Yea, but you will." I say offhandedly while puffing the blunt and trying to focus in on the words playing around in my head.

"I ain't gone always be around D. You gotta always play fa keeps. And you know rule number one in this game."

"Yea, yea, rather be caught with than without, I
know." I say laying my poem book down and puffing the blunt one more time before passing it back to her. "But why you always trying to wreck my flow when you see me trying to get my zone on?"

"Cuz D, I'm bored. Plus, you always get all quiet and weird when you writing. It's like being alone in a room with Hannibal Lecter or some shit. I be scared you gone just bust out and say, 'Give me yo kidneys bitch!'"

I can't stop myself from cracking up laughing.

"Nessa you are so fucking silly."

" Fa real tho, Dena yo ass is crazy."

"I gotta be something to let you talk me into staying in this damn hotel room all day. And what happened to you going to the store to get the stuff so we can do our toes and nails?" I look at the time and see it's after two in the afternoon.

"Girl my ass done got lazy. I ain't trying to do nothing but lay here and get my booty rubbed." She rolls onto her stomach and looks back at me with the puppy dog eyes.

"You must plan on rubbing it yourself, cuz I ain't doing nothing until I get a manicure and pedicure."

"I got you D, just sing to me and rub my booty for a little while. Please."

"No Finesse. You not getting me like that again. Last time we got high and you asked me to rub yo booty and sing, yo ass fell asleep on me." She laughs.

"Because girl, yo ass got some magic fingers. You know how to get deep down in there. Then listening to you blow while you do it. Ooh..." She shivers like she's getting the chills.

"See now, you laying it on too thick."

"Please D.?" I give her a look. "Ok look," she sits up on the side of the bed and starts putting her shoes on "I'm gone get up, cuz we gone need something else to smoke anyway. While I'm out, I can stop at the Chinese store and get the stuff for our feet and toes, but you gotta promise to give me a good long booty rub when I get back."

I give her another look.

"Bitch, you make me sick. You bet not take all day either."

"I won't, I promise." She says triumphantly as she grabs the keys to the Benz and heads for the door. "I'll be back before you even realize I'm gone."

I can't do nothing but shake my head and laugh to myself once she's gone. I pick my poem book back up and try to recapture the flow I had going on inside my head, but it's useless. My momentum is gone. Finesse does it to me every time. She doesn't understand how much writing helps me cope, how important those introverted moments are for me. Writing is truly my lifeline.

Without Finesse here to distract me, thoughts of Uncle Fresh creep inside my head. Not being able to put off the inevitable any longer, I pick up my phone and power it back on. There are so many voicemails and text messages, that it takes a whole two minutes before my phone stops vibrating. Besides the messages from Uncle Fresh asking where I am, there are several texts from different employees at the club. The more messages I read, the further my stomach drops down into the bottom of my feet. I can't believe I forgot. Today is the day that our monthly shipment of cocaine comes into the club. A day I would normally never forget. A day that Uncle Fresh usually depends on me to be there to make sure everything is taken care of correctly.

The shipment comes in at a different time every month. In one of the texts from Keita, who is my head security at the club and has been for over five years, she informs me that this month it's scheduled to come in at three-thirty. I look at the time and see that it's a quarter till three. I have forty-five minutes to make it to the club. My first mind is to call Finesse and tell her to hurry back, but my phone rings in my hand before I can dial her number.

"Hello." I answer.

"Boss lady, I've been trying to get in touch with you all day." It's my bodyguard Mojo.

"Yea I know. My phone has been off. Where you at?"

"At the club."

"Is Uncle Fresh there?"

"You know he is. He's been going crazy looking for you. Did you forget what today is?"

"No, I've just been caught up with a situation."

"Man everybody been asking about you, wondering where you are."

"I know, I know." I say feeling bad knowing how much everyone depends on me. "I need you to come and get me"

"No problem Boss Lady. Where you at?"

"I'm at the Ramada Inn off of Highway One."

"Okay, I'm on my way."

I hang up and take a deep breath to gather my thoughts. That one phone call takes all thoughts of Click away and leaves me feeling lower than low knowing that I'm letting my whole team down. I let that feeling motivate my mind back into Boss lady mode. One by one, I start calling all the top employees at the club letting them know personally I'm on my way. By the time I'm finished making my calls, Mojo is pulling up outside. Its ten minutes after three when I climb into his car.

CHAPTER 9

Click

It feels like deja vu.

Sitting in 'The Hot Spot Gentleman's Club at three something in the afternoon, looking around at all the patrons scattered throughout the room sipping drinks, getting lap dances, and enjoying the live entertainment on the stage; I'm reminded of the first time that I ever stepped foot off in this place. It was the day after I came home from doing a ten year bid, the day after I met Dena and Finesse for the first time and had the course of my life changed forever.

I look across the table at Johnny Ray, Mr.-Make-It-Happen himself and have to use every ounce of energy within me to keep my game face on, as I pick up my drink and take a sip.

"So, what's good old man? "

"Life is good young brotha. As you can see, business is booming as usual. Ain't nothing changed but the days."

"So I see, Seems like you got more action going on in here than usual for this time of day."

"Yea, I reckon so."

"More security too." I throw in casually to check his reaction. All around the club are muscle bound bouncers all posted up in groups of threes, each with weapons hanging from their hips or tucked in holsters under their arms.

Johnny Ray is smoother than ever, as he takes his time sipping his own drink before saying, "Yea, we've been running into a few minor complications lately. Seems like someone has taken a special interest in the Givens family business." His eyes come up to meet mine. "You wouldn't know anything about that would you?"

"Can't say that I do, I am interested in getting my hands on that Jamaican fuck Lafu tho."

"I'm guessing that's the reason you decided to finally contact me."

"If memory serves me correctly, I ain't the only one at this table who has a hard on for Lafu."

Johnny Ray doesn't confirm nor deny my statement, only leans back in his chair, adjust the Dob hat on his head, and flashes those pearly whites.

The Dee Jay gets on the microphone and says, "Okay all you pimps, hoes, playas and playetts, Ima need y'all to get up outta ya seats and empty those pockets for this next act. Coming to the stage is a bitch with mo pussy power than Paula Patton with a penis pump. Y'all give it up for Miss Nasty herself, Na-Na!"

I watch as a curvaceous, dark-skinned dancer covered in glitter and body paint rises up through the center floor of the stage by some kind of lift mechanism. She begins popping her hips to the beat, as the Dee Jay plays the old-school nineties banger 'Hot Spot' that comes on with Foxy Brown rapping, "You can catch me at the hot spot/ I fox...."

"So you really think you're ready to go up against Lafu huh?" Johnny Ray asks drawing my attention back to him.

"I'm more than ready. I wouldn't have called you if I wasn't."

"Well if my guess is correct and you're the one behind all the robberies at our clubs, then you're a long way from ready young brotha. You ain't did nothing but pissed off an already highly disturbed and pissed off man."

"What you tryna say old man?"

"Simple. If I was you, I'd get you and the rest of these little jokers that you brought here with you today the hell outta dodge before all hell breaks loose."

"Oh, we gone leave. Soon as we get what we came for and make this crazy Jamaican muthafucka feel
   us."

"Trust me young brotha, you thinking checkers against a chess master. Lafu may be crazy, but he's the smartest crazy person I know."

Johnny Ray's words cause me to scan the club with my eyes. They move until they land on Mechi, who's sitting next to White Cloud, an OG in our neighborhood who has been putting in work for years, and his nephew Mel G, a heavy-set dark-skinned youngsta who is just as radical as his uncle.

Thanks to Finesse, we know that the dope is coming through a liquor delivery truck, that should be pulling up behind the club at any minute now. Lil-Eighty and a mob of thirty of his young goons, all separated into three teams of ten, are strapped and posted up around the perimeter of the club waiting for the truck to come into view. As soon as they see it, Eighty is going to text Mechi's phone and give him the green light to cause a diversion inside the club to throw the security off. While that's happening, one of the teams outside is going to bumrush the front entrance of the club to further confuse the security at the same time giving us on the inside, an opportunity to get the drop on them while the other two teams led by Lil-Eighty, ambush the liquor truck in the back. To make things even sweeter, Finesse plugged us with Keita the club's head of security, who turned a blind eye and made it possible for me, Mechi, White Cloud, his nephew Mel G, and the other four goons who came in with us, to walk straight through the front doors with enough artillery to lay every soul in this place down.

When my eyes come back around to land on Johnny Ray, I can't help but to crack a small smile, knowing that this time around they underestimated me.

"Lafu only has one weakness?" Johnny Ray says. "To bring him down you're gonna have to..." he stops mid-sentence, looking somewhere past me.

I turn around to see what has stolen his attention and can't believe my eyes. The last person I expect or want to see right now, is walking towards us escorted by two bodyguards.

"What the fuck is she doing here?"

Dena walks up to our table with a confused expression on her face and asks, "Click, what are you doing here?" Her eyes travel back and forth between me and Johnny Ray.

At that moment, I see Mechi stand up and scream at the top of his lungs.

"Yeeeeaaa bitch, shake dat ass!" to the dancer up on the stage. Then he walks over to where she is and throws a large wad of cash in the air above her. "Whooohoo!" He reaches in his jacket pocket, pulls out another wad, and does it a second time.

Bills rain down all over her body as she backs that ass up in front of Mechi and shakes cheeks all in his face.

"Heeellll yea, that's what I'm talkin bout!" Using his prosthetic hand, Mechi begins slapping her on the ass.

Hard.

Too hard.

The dancer who was bent over on all fours, quickly turns around with a frown, and drops down on her stinging butt cheeks. Then she begins scooting away from Mechi towards the center of the stage, but he grabs one of her ankles before she has a chance to get too far.

"Oh no you don't, get back over here and finish shaking that ass." He pulls her to the edge of the stage where he's able to wrap both of his arms around her waist and pick her up by her ass cheeks.

One of the bodyguards standing with Dena makes a move to go intervene, but I stop him.

"No, stay here with her."

By now, White Cloud and Mel G are both on their feet, cheering Mechi on, along with half of the other patrons in the club.

The bouncers have seen enough. All at once, they begin closing in on Mechi, who is now bouncing the struggling dancer up and down in his arms chanting, "Don't stop, get it, get it!" All the while smacking her ass cheeks with his hard plastic hand.

I watch as it unfolds. The bouncers confront Mechi who instantly snaps, telling them to get the fuck outta his face, that he's a paying customer. They attempt to free the dancer from his embrace which leads to a struggle. Then without warning, Mel G creeps up behind the commotion, pulls out a nine, and dome shots three of the bouncers back to back.

Before the others have a chance to recover, White Cloud flips over a table, whips out a Tech nine, and begins spraying the rest of the bouncers.

Mechi tosses the dancer and drops to the floor and rolls out of sight.

The sudden gun fire puts an end to Foxy Brown's lyrics and causes everyone in the club to panic. Drinks flying, titties and ass bouncing everywhere, the patrons and strippers alike all run for cover.

By now, Dena has dropped to the floor between her two bodyguards, who are both squatting next to her brandishing weapons.

"Get her outta here!" I yell to them.

As soon as the shooting started, Johnny Ray pulled a pistol from a shoulder holster under his suit jacket, used his foot against the table to push himself over backwards out of the chair, rolled, and came up on one knee gripping his pistol with both hands. With surprising agility, that old man scrambled across the floor busting shots in Mel G and White Cloud's direction.

I pull one of my own pistols and try to find him in my sights so I can blow that Dob hat off of his head, but now he's nowhere to be found. Not being able to find Johnny Ray, I turn my attention towards Dena and my unborn child. The plan was for Finesse to keep her on ice, and out of harm's way until after the robbery went down. How she managed to fuck that up, I have no idea, but I've got to get Dena out of here ASAP!

I spot her and her two bodyguards over by the staircase leading to the upstairs office that overlooks the club and begin making my way towards them.

Suddenly a loud gun blast rocks the place as a security guard's body comes flying backwards into the club. Seconds later, Lil-Eighty's goons swarm in with shotguns gunning at the few remaining bouncers who are already retreating.

The bouncers don't know what hit them. One minute there were at least twenty-five of them surveying the club, confident that they had everything under control. Now there are less than ten, and that number seems to be diminishing quickly as the gunfire continues.

The whole club goes pitch black.

Feels like an eternity that I hold my position, waiting for my eyes to adjust to the darkness, listening to the panicking people scrambling trying to escape death, tho it couldn't have lasted no longer than sixty seconds.

Then I see red dots appear from everywhere at once, moving quickly across the walls, on the floor, seeming to be coming from somewhere above.

When the lights come back on, it's like waking into a nightmare.

Sliding down ropes from the ceiling, are a bunch of black clad female figures. The females use one arm and their legs to slide down the ropes while their other arm hold machine guns equipped with infrared beams. But they aren't the ones causing my heart to do a triple beat in my chest.

Rising up through the floor in the middle of the stage, dressed in all black, a gold-plated 44. magnum in each hand held at his shoulders pointing towards the ceiling, is the monster known as Lafu.

Chapter 10

Dena

A million questions race through my mind at the same time.

Like why was Click and Uncle Fresh here together? Did it have something to do with the phone that Click had me give Uncle Fresh and the call he was supposed to be making to him? And if that's case, why didn't Click just tell me he was on his way to meet Uncle Fresh instead of being secretive about it? And why did that dark-skinned guy, with the glasses, the one I recognize from the house last night who was on the porch talking to Finesse, why did he and that other guy who was with Mechi just start killing my bouncers for no reason? But most of all, why did I pick now of all times to leave my trusty 380 at home?

It's loud, at least seven different guns all shooting at once.

The sound of a single shotgun blast thunders throughout the club, causing me to turn around in time to see the security guard who works the front door at the club, Pierre's body slide across the floor, with his chest blown wide open.

"Oh my God, Pierre!"

"Keep moving Boss Lady!" Mojo yells from behind me as we climb the stairs leading to my upstairs office. Pitbull is a couple of steps up ahead of us covering me and Mojo as we continue to climb.

Several shotguns cocking and firing take over the sound of the other gunfire in the club.

This time I don't look back; not wanting to see another sight like the one I just witnessed. But I can't block out the sound, the sound of women screaming in terror or the men moaning in agony as bullets rip through their torsos. The thought of Uncle Fresh and Click being down there in the mist of all that chaos makes me wish I could rewind time and take us all away from this place.

As soon as we reach the door at the top of the stairs, all the lights in the club go out. Mojo, Pitbull, and I all pause momentarily in the darkness before one of them opens the door and we find our way inside the office. So familiar with the layout, I don't hesitate to move through the darkness towards the back where a closet is located, which is really an elevator that will take us downstairs to an emergency exit out the back side of the club.

"Boss Lady get down!" I hear Mojo scream seconds before I spot the red dot on the front of my shirt and feel the impact of his body crash into mine. I hit the ground hard with Mojo landing on top of me.

The lights come back on at the exact moment that I hear the rapid fire of machine guns and the thirty foot aquarium that dominated the room explodes spilling gallons of water into the office. Bullets spray everywhere above us. Then just as quickly as it started the shooting stops. Whoever had taken aim at the office is satisfied with the sudden damage they've caused because they've moved on and set their sights elsewhere.

I lay there for a few seconds in disbelief listening to the distant gunfire and wondering what the hell is going on. Everything happened so fast. The club went from a party zone to a war zone in a matter of minutes. But why?

The weight of Mojo's huge body pressing down on me causes me to become aware of my baby.

"Mojo, let me up." That's when I noticed how rugged his breathing is. That's when I notice how still and unresponsive he is. "Mojo? Oh my God, Mojo!?!" I struggle to move him, but he's too heavy.

I hear Pitbull say, " Hold on Boss Lady, I gotchu." before I feel him rolling Mojo off of me.

The entire front of his shirt is covered in blood and his eyes are already glazed over yet Mojo manages to ask, "B... Boss Lady...are you hit?'

"No. No Mojo, I'm okay."

"Good Boss Lady...that's real good..." then with a bloody smile, his eyes roll into the back of his head, he takes his final breath and fades off into eternity.

"Nooo....Mojo no...." I try to shake him awake, although I know he's gone on to the next life.

This is more than my poor heart can handle at one time. First the bouncers downstairs, then Pierre, now Mojo. I don't know what I'll do if I find out that Click or Uncle Fresh have also become victims of the madness going on downstairs.

As if on cue, Click bursts through the office doors.

"Come on, we gotta get up outta here. They're everywhere."

" Who's everywhere?" Pitbull asks standing up trying to see what Click is talking about.

"The ninja bitches!"

"Ninja bitches?" Even I snap out of my moment of sorrow, trying to figure out what he's talking about.

Then I see them.

Women wearing black body suits with black masks covering the bottom half of their faces. All carrying machine guns. All spraying and killing anything moving. Dancers, bouncers, security guards, the shot gun toting goons who were shooting the place up first, even the bartenders, they're not sparing anybody.

"What the..."

"I told you." Click says dropping the empty gun in his hand and pulling a mini mac 10 from a duffle bag he has strapped across his body and hanging from his hip.

That's when it hits me.

The drugs.

That's what this is all about and Click is somewhere in the middle of it all.

I see panic on Pitbull's face when he asks, "How the hell we gone get outta here cause ain't no way we going back down those stairs!"

Moving over next to him, I peek out the window and see what he sees; two of the black clad females with machine guns already coming up the stairs headed our way. My survival instincts kick in instantly.

"Come on, this way!" As fast as my feet will carry me, I race over to the closet, snatch it open, and begin dialing the secret code to activate the elevator. Seems like it takes forever for the doors to finally come open. As soon as they do, gunfire erupts outside of the office door right at the top of the stairs.

"Hurry!" I yell to Pitbull and Click who both seem to have been stuck in a trance watching all the murdering taking place down below. Now they turn and race inside the safety of the elevator with me. I press the button to close the doors and take us downstairs.

Everything after that seems to happen in slow motion.

The office door bursts open again and to my relief, it's Uncle Fresh.

"Over here Uncle Fresh!" I wave my arms excitedly at him.

With gun in hand, he hurries our way.

In the blink of an eye, a figure dressed in all black, using a rope, swings in through the opening where the fish tank glass once was.

"Behind you Uncle Fresh!" I warn, but it's too late.

Just as Uncle Fresh is spinning around, Lafu raises his gun and fires a single shot from his gold-plated 44. Magnum directly into his chest. The impact is so powerful that it lifts Uncle Fresh off his feet and throws him backwards across the room.

His body lands mere inches from us, so close that his grey dob hat comes off his head and rolls into the elevator beside my feet.

The high pitch of my own scream drowns out every other sound as the doors close and the elevator takes us down to where it all ends.

All of this began because I wanted to get revenge on Lafu for killing my mother. I wanted to make him pay for taking her away from me and all the twisted things he did to my Nessa. Instead, all I got was a broken heart. A broken heart from all the lives lost on my one track minded mission to kill the monster. All those people dead because of me. It's all my fault. Had I not have set Click up for Lafu over a year ago, Mojo wouldn't be dead right now. Click's best friend Travis and his cousin Shelly wouldn't have been murdered. Nor would Casey Myers and his crew in the Jackpot Projects. Or the three brothers from Omaha Nebraska. It's a never ending chain reaction. A deadly domino effect that fourteen months after my mother's murder, had caused seventy-two more people to lose their lives. So many children lost their mother and father, so many brothers and sisters, aunts and uncles, so many family and friends died that day in the Hot Spot Gentleman's Club. Sad to say, besides the three of us who made it to the elevator, only two other people survived what is now being called the "Mysterious Strip Club Massacre." Mysterious because by the time the police made it inside, they found a room full of dead bodies. Their killers, including Lafu, had mysteriously disappeared without a trace along with the surveillance camera video tapes.

I later found out that before Click and his friends tried to rob 'The Hot Spot', they had already successfully knocked off five of our other out of town locations. By Lafu knowing that whoever was behind the robberies had to be getting tipped off by an inside source and that they would be coming for 'The Hot Spot', being that it's his number one earning location, he made the ultimate chess move. He had set them up by having Uncle Fresh feed everyone on our team a bogus time that the shipment was coming in. And they had fallen right into his trap. Fools mated.

Uncle Fresh, as usual was ahead of the game. Him being the only one who knew that Click was still alive, had already put two and two together. That's why he was trying to send me away. That's why he was trying so hard to contact me the night I ran off; because he knew that once I found out that Click was still alive, I would go to him. Uncle Fresh was trying to stop me from getting caught up in the middle of what was about to go down.

I even believe that when I walked into the club on the day of the robbery and saw the two of them together, that Uncle Fresh was making one last attempt to warn Click off. Unfortunately for Click it was too late.

When the elevator doors opened on the bottom floor that day, Pitbull, Click, and I ran headfirst into a swat team of police officers pointing high powered weapons. So even tho Click made it out of there with his life, him being a felon caught with a duffle bag full of guns, found himself back locked up facing new federal charges.

Lafu had check mated the game. He had Uncle Fresh to send a regular liquor truck to the club, then tip the police off that there was a robbery in progress. But not even Uncle Fresh predicted that Lafu would show up at the club himself with a hired team of killers straight out of Jamaica and be waiting in the shadows.

Watching.

Seeing with his own eyes the deception taking place.

When Lafu saw his right hand man sitting at the table talking to the man who he was supposed to have killed, he snapped and came for my Uncle Fresh.

So here I stand in the cemetery, once again saying goodbye to another loved one. Black dress, black stilettos, black Chloe sunglasses, Pitbull and I watch as Mojo's casket is lowered into the ground.

"Bye Daddy." the oldest of the three little girls

standing with Mojo's wife says before throwing a single rose down onto the casket that's taking Mojo to his final resting place. One by one, the other mourners do the same.

Seeing Mojo's three beautiful daughters standing there, knowing they'll never see their father again because of me, is tearing me up inside. I drop my rose then go over to offer my condolences to the grieving family. When I make it to Mojo's pretty Puerto Rican and Black wife Shelena, I unfold the hundred thousand dollar check that I brought with me and hand it to her.

"I'm sorry for your loss and if there is anything I can do, please don't hesitate to call. Anything."

She looks down at the check in her hand then up at me. "You know what you can do for me? You can drop dead bitch!" she screams, then spits violently in my face.

So caught off guard by her anger, I can only stand in shock with her saliva sliding down my cheek as she rages on.

"My husband couldn't even stay home with his own family for trying to run behind you. Trying to protect you! Your highness! Well you finally got what you wanted your highness because he's dead. Dead! And no amount of money is going to bring him back!" she screams while tearing up the check I gave her.

Her outburst draws the attention of some of the other friends and family attending the burial and a few of them come over and try to contain her.

"If I ever catch you near me or my family again, so help me God...." Her threats continue on as they drag her away.

"Here you go Boss Lady." Pitbull says coming up beside me and handing me a handkerchief.

"Wow!" is all I can say as I remove my sunglasses and wipe my face.

"She didn't mean all that shit. She's just hurting right now and needs somebody to take it out on."

"Oh she meant it alright." Though I don't know her personally like that, her words still hurt.

"She can't blame you. I mean, Mojo was a bodyguard. He knew the risks of the job just like I do. It's what he chose to do, and you paid him well to do it."

"I still feel bad though. Here." I reach inside my clutch purse and find my checkbook. I write out a new check. "I want you to give this to her. She doesn't have to know where it came from. Just give her a little from time to time to help her out with the kids. She's gonna need it."

You have my word Boss Lady." He tucks the check into his inside jacket pocket, then gives me a look. "You're a beautiful person Boss Lady. They don't make em like you no mo." He just doesn't know how much I needed to hear those words.

"Come on Babygirl, it's time to get outta here and let the dead rest." Uncle Fresh says walking up and throwing his arm around my shoulder as Pitbull and I stand watching the departing mourners. "And quit always blaming yourself for everything" he says reading my mind as usual.

"How do you always know what I'm thinking?"

"It's called love Babygirl. When you love someone, you develop a special connection with them. When they worry, you worry. When they happy, you happy. When they hurt, you hurt."

"Like when I can tell you're thinking about and missing mama?"

He gives me a solemn look. Then nods his head up and down before saying "Yea, I reckon so."

I lean my head against my father's shoulder and deeply inhale the masculine scent of his Escada cologne. As he, Pitbull, and I begin heading toward the car, I find myself thanking the Lord that Uncle Fresh is a man who believes in taking his own advice. He always tells me to prepare for the worst and hope for the best. I guess him preparing for the worst is what made him wear a bullet proof vest to the club the day that everything went down. That bullet proof vest had saved his life, as well as made Lafu believe that he had killed him. At least it did for a little while.

Uncle Fresh being one of the two people that the police found alive inside the club, the news reporters and camera crews rushed him as he was being wheeled out on a gurney. Although he wouldn't answer any questions, the news played the clip of him saying, "Get that damn camera outta my face!" over and over again. That was enough within itself. No doubt, Lafu was somewhere watching and plotting how he was gone come back and finish the job.

CHAPTER 11

Click

"Fevers, you're up." the jailer standing at the entrance to our cell house calls out to me.

"Aiight, here I come. "I respond while checking my reflection in the blurry piece of metal that supplements as a mirror and wondering for the hundredth time since he'd came earlier and told me I had a visit, who has come to see me.

"Yo Click, tell yo baby mama to put some money on both our books so we can have some vittles to eat for the Superbowl. "this cat named Playboi cracks as I am heading out the door. He's the only one out of the other seven dudes in the pod with me that's even halfway on my level or worthy of having a conversation with. Fortunately, he's also my bunkmate. He and I just clicked from day one.

"Yea aiight, soon as you tell yo girl to pack that pussy and bring some of that good green up here so we can have something to smoke after we done eating."

"Nigga I don't even smoke." is the last words I hear him say before the cell house door slams shut and I'm headed up the hallway with the rest of the county jail inmates who are lucky enough to get a visit this week.

I got arrested on Thursday and here it is Saturday of the following week. The only person I've spoken with is a lawyer that Johnny Ray sent up here who'd told me that things weren't looking too good for me on the gun charges. He said that since they had a parole hold on me, there was no point in even trying to get a bond. Dena had tried to come visit me that first Saturday a couple days after I got locked up, but once I saw who she was, I turned around and denied her visit.

Fuck did me and her have to talk about.

The visitation is set up in a long narrow room, that's lined with several booths that are each equipped with telephone receivers so that we can sit and talk to our love ones who sit on the other side of the thick glass that separates us.

I spot Niesha as soon as I sit down. She's wearing a stylish red and black Roca-Wear outfit with her hair parted down the middle and hanging long just the way I like it. My little Queen Bee, who is standing next to her and holding her hand, spots me first and races over to the booth where I am.

"Hi Deshawn!" she exclaims with so much joy that I can't help but to smile.

"Hey Queen Bee, how you doing?"

"I'm fine. Look what I got." She says holding up her little arm so I can see. "A new Teletubby bracelet!"

"Aw man, where you get that from?" I ask matching her excitement and using the voice that I reserve only for her.

"My mommy bought it. She says every time I bring home a golden star from Preschool, I can get any Teletubby toy I want. Ain't that right mommy?" she turns around and asks Niesha, who is now standing directly behind her.

"It's isn't that right." Niesha corrects her child. "And yes baby, that's right." Niesha smiles and makes eye contact with me over Nadia's head.

Up until this point, I hadn't even realized how much I miss Niesha, but I'd give anything to get on the other side of this glass right now and wrap my arms around her. The look in her eyes says she feels the same way. The incident with the gun all but forgotten.

Nadia, who has been rambling non-stop asks, "Deshawn, are you listening to me?"

I shift my attention back to her and try to focus in on what she's saying. "Yes, Queen Bee I'm listening to you."

"Weeell?" I asked you why your wearing those funny looking orange clothes, and are you coming over our house with us?"

Not having the slightest idea how to answer the first question, I simply skip over it and say, "No I'm not going with y'all right now, but I will be coming over again soon."

"When?"

"Soon Queen Bee, real soon."

"How soon Deshawn?"

"I, uh..." I look up at Niesha hoping for some help.

Mercifully, she reaches in her pocket, finds a dollar bill, and says, "Nadia, don't you want to go get us some candy out of the vending machine?"

"Yaaay!" she explodes dropping the receiver and forgetting all about me. Anxiously she grabs the money and says, "I'll be right back Deshawn." before skipping off on her candy mission.

Niesha watches her daughter with a smile then picks up the receiver and says, "Hey baby."

"Wassup beautiful."

"She's been driving me crazy asking about you. Every day, "Is Deshawn coming over? Why hasn't he called ma? Mommy, Deshawn isn't answering his phone! So, I was like you know what, come on. Let me take you up here. Let's see if he can answer all these questions, cause I sure as hell don't have the answers." I look in her face and see the worry behind her smile.

"Is that the only reason you came up here, so Queen Bee could see me?"

"No." She answers with a blush. "I have questions too. Like why couldn't you call me and tell me something? Why did I have to see the news to find out where you were?" Her hurt is evident.

I had picked up the phone and dialed her number a million times in the past week, but just couldn't bring myself to put the call through. Couldn't find the energy to tell her how fucked up things really are.

"And tell you what, that I fucked up?"

"Something Click. I've been worried sick. You just up and disappear and I don't hear from you." I just sit there, cause nothing I say is going to make this any easier. After a few minutes she asks, "So are they trying to say that you had something to do with killing all those people?"

"Hell nah, nothing like that."

"Thank God." she exhales in relief. "So, what are they saying and what really happened in there? I've been hearing all kinds of crazy stuff."

"You wouldn't believe me if I told you, but I can't really talk about it right now." I use my eyes and head to indicate the two-way mirror tinted wall where the deputy dispatchers are monitoring all our conversations.

"Oh." she says looking that way, then back at me.

Then in a voice so soft and sweet, "Baby I miss you."

"I miss you too."

"I want you to come home."

Crazy how it takes for a person to be in a situation like this for their true feelings to become clear. I know right now that Niesha is someone I could settle down and think about spending forever with. She just has that something real feel to her and I know where her heart is. Though she's never said the words and we've never put a title on what we have, I know how she truly feels about me. Deep down, I know that I've been holding back from her because of Dena and the baby.

"There's a lot of things you don't know about me Niesha."

"Like the other women you got. I tried to put some money on your books just now and they said your account is filled."

"So that automatically means that I have other women?" I laugh. "You act like I'm a broke ass nigga or something."

"No, I'm not saying that." Now she's smiling too. "I just know you're a ladies man."

Nadia comes back skipping our way singing the words to the Barney song and sucking on a lollipop.

"Mommy, look what I got. I got the Jumbo Rainbow Pop. Want some?" Nadia holds it up next to Niesha's mouth who gets a taste and says,

"Umm, that's good. But where's mine? I thought you were going to get both of us some candy?"

"We can share." Nadia answers smartly.

"But I don't wanna share. I want my own." Niesha pulls out another dollar bill and gives it to her daughter. "Go and get mommy one."

"Oh alright." Nadia takes the dollar and begins to leave but stops to say, "I'll take my time coming back, because I know you and Deshawn want some grown up talk time." Without waiting for a response, she turns and goes on about her way.

Niesha and I both laugh.

I say, "She's way too advanced for her age, brain stay on a hundred."

"That's my baby." Niesha beams with pride.

"Yea, she had me wrapped after the first week."

Niesha looks at me long and hard. "You know that little girl loves you right?" I nod my head. "Her daddy died before she was born and you're the first and ONLY man that I've ever brought around my baby. So, all I'm saying is.... don't play with my daughter's feelings....and don't play with mines. If you have something to tell me Click, then I suggest you find a way to say it soon."

I sit for a moment thinking about what she's saying. Then I think about what I'm up against.

"Look Niesha, you already know that I'm on parole."

"Okay." She says listening intently.

"That's an automatic six month minimum that I gotta serve for parole violation alone." She doesn't blink. "Plus, I'm facing three counts of felony possession of firearm. Each one carries five years apiece. Fed time." She blinks. Twice. Three times. Ain't no faking when shit gets real. I lean back in my seat and let it marinate in her mind for a minute.

She blows out a breath. "The good news is, I already got you covered on a lawyer." My lips can't hold back a smile. "And I wouldn't care if you were facing the needle, I'm not going anywhere. We in this together." She points her finger at me to send her point home. "But like I said, if you got something to tell me...find a way to say it soon."

A deputy officer opens the door on the visitor's side. "Fevers, you have another visitor, but if wanna see em, you only have fifteen minutes left of your visit."

"Who is it?"

"A Demetrius Bell."

Mechi pops up behind the deputy with both of his hands in the air. "What up, nigga!"

I throw my hands up smiling and mimicking his gesture. "What up my nig!"

Mechi comes in and says, "Hey how you doing?" to Niesha before pressing his fist against the glass for a bump. I cover his fist with mine. "Mane, that's some bullshit you only get thirty minutes for a visit."

"I know right. Seems like I just got here." Niesha agrees with him before standing up. "Click, I'll be right back. I'm going to check on Nadia." She walks off giving us some room to talk.

"You keep a bad one on the team don'tcha?" Mechi asks eyeballing Niesha.

"You know how I do. But look at you Mr. Celebrity Survivor." Since Mechi was the only other survivor of the 'Mysterious Strip Club Massacre ' besides Johnny Ray, both of their stories and faces had been getting major air play on TV, even on World News.

"I'm tryna tell ya. All the hoes been at ya boy lately. But I ain't been out myself but about five or six days. They held me seventy-two hours talking about some questioning and pending investigation. I told those folks straight up; I don't know shit! All I know is when mafuckas started dropping, I dropped too. I climbed up under two corpses, put some of their blood on me, and played dead too."

I laugh. "You a fool."

"I ain't bullshittin. I ain't move until the police went to pulling bodies up off me. It was like Armageddon up in that bitch. They wouldn't have believed me about the ninja bitches anyway."

"Yo, that's because that shit was unbelievable. But what's good tho?" I ask not wanting to say too much more on the subject. "I ain't talked to nobody since I been up in here."

"Shit ain't right bra." he answers shaking his head.

"Mafuckas moving funny."

"Whatchu mean?"

"I mean eight ball in the corner pocket supposed to end the game, right? How about the eight ball ain't even roll with the play." I look in his face pretty much knowing what he's trying to tell me. Something that I've been thinking about myself; how did Lil-Eighty and twenty niggas not run into the S.W.A.T. team if they were supposed to be out back robbing the liquor truck. The news didn't say anything about no other arrests, no liquor truck robbery, or anything else besides what went on inside the club and that all the surveillance camera videos had been removed.

Then Mechi says "Plus mafuckas done got real brand new out here too. Like with the big head fa real." Now I know he's talking about Lil-Eighty. I had been noticing how puffed up and reckless he had been at the mouth lately. I just chalked it up as him acting the way typical niggas act when they start seeing real money for the first time in their life. Money does the same thing that liquor does to a nigga's ego. It has them feeling like they suddenly untouchable or some shit. Eighty has been getting plenty of it too.

"No shit?"

"Yea, but we gone chop it up later tho. Know we can't kick it like this with these crackers all in our video." We both look over at the mirror tinted wall.

"Right, right."

Mechi says, "A wassup tho, I just tried to put some money on yo books, but they said you got too much on there already. You doin it like that?"

"I think that bitch Dena did that shit. She came up here last week."

"Say word? What she talkin bout?"

"I'on know. I denied her visit."

"No shit?" he laughs.

"Yea man, I don't trust her or that old nigga Johnny Ray."

"I feel you mane. I wouldn't either if I was you.... oh, and by the way, Reece told me to tell you that if you don't hurry up and ring her line, y'all was gone be seriously beefing."

"I already know bra. I just been so messed up in the head about being locked back up that I ain't really been tryna talk to nobody. How she doing anyway?"

"She good bra, you know Reece's Piece's gone hold it down regardless. Her and the baby chillin. She wanted to come up here with me, but she couldn't find a babysitter and she said that she wasn't bringing her son up to no jailhouse."

"Whoa, whoa, whoa, slow down. Reece already had the baby?"

"Yea you ain't know? She said that her and yo shorty got to knockin because yo shorty came to her house looking for you."

"No shit? When did all of this happen?"

"Reece said that she showed up at her door in the middle of the night and they got to fighting and the next day she went into labor. Matter of fact, the same day that you got locked up."

"That's crazy." I had been so out of touch and caught up in my own world that it had totally slipped my mind that my best friend's baby was due to be born any day. And to find out that Reece had given birth to a boy, I'm definitely gone have to get in touch with her soon.

Mechi says, "Reece's still super-heated about the fight. She got scratches all over her face and shit. She said that next time she sees Dena it's going down."

"Ay yo, can you picture both of they pregnant asses out there tryna fight?" We sit for a couple moments laughing at that thought.

Then Mechi asks, "So what them folks talking about? You get a bond yet?"

"It ain't looking good. They been tryna question a playa for days trying to find out what went on inside the club since all the surveillance videos disappeared, but you know I ain't got no talk. They got me fucked up on the gun charges tho. Plus, I got a parole hold so ain't no bond."

He slowly shakes his head from side to side. "Damn playa."

"It's all good tho. You just keep ya eyes open out there and stay in tune with me."

"No doubt." We both spot Niesha and Nadia at the same time coming our way.

"Damn shorty nice." Mechi says eyeing Niesha again.

"You can take ya eyes off that one partna."

He laughs. "Aiight now Click, let me find out."

Mechi leaves and I spend the last few moments of my visit talking to Nadia and comforting Niesha, who can't hold back her tears when the deputy tells us our time is up. Especially when Nadia starts crying and asking why I can't come with them now and neither one of us has an answer. The hardest part about getting a visit while being locked up, is saying goodbye and watching your love ones walk back out that door knowing you can't go with them.

I make it back to my cell house feeling like I just took a half pint of Hennessy to the head and with a whole lot on my mind. I lay back on my bunk and think about how good of a girl Niesha is and how I've been cheating her out of what she truly deserves because of Dena. Thinking about how she'll react if I tell her that I got a baby on the way. I doze off thinking about all the time I'm facing and wondering what's really going on with this nigga Lil-Eighty.

When I awake a few hours later, it's nighttime and my bunk mate is in the cell with me sitting at the desk with his back to me.

Without turning around he says, "Had to sleep it off huh?"

"Huh? Sleep what off?"

"That drunk. I already know how it is coming off that first visit. Shit starts hittin a nigga hard fa real."

"Yea man you know.... " I say not even trying to deny it." What time is it anyway?"

"After seven." He turns around handing me something. "Here, light this and see if it helps you with that hangover."

Seeing that it's a blunt, I take it and say, "Damn nigga, I thought you didn't smoke. Where you get this?"

"I don't, that's you. This is my thang right here." He holds up a real pint of Hennessy. "And I got a couple of connections."

I sit up on the side of the bunk in disbelief. Not at the fact that he has weed and liquor, because I learned on my first bid that you can get your hands on just about anything behind these walls that you can get in the free world. It's just that normally it's a much smaller quantity for a much bigger price. And even if you are fortunate enough to get your hands on weed and liquor, the liquor is normally homemade and the weed is rolled in toilet paper wrapper, bible paper, or at best, cigarette rolling papers. It's very rare that you get to smoke a real blunt rolled in a real cigar wrap. Not only did he hand me a blunt rolled in a real cigar, but it's fatter than the ones I usually smoke on the streets.

I put the blunt up to my nose. "Smells like some of that good too. You got a light?"

"Oh yea, here you go." Thinking he's about to hand me a pack of the jailhouse issued matches, I'm surprised for a second time when he passes me a free world lighter.

I don't even question the lighter as I take it and fire up the blunt. The potent smoke enters my body and fills my lungs where I hold it for a few moments. When the pressure inside my chest becomes too much, I release it and feel an instant head change.

"Oh yea.... this that head bang boogie fa real."

He looks back at me and smiles. "I know. That's that Purp."

"Purp? Never heard of it."

Again, he says, "I know." He pours some Hen in a Styrofoam cup for me and we kick back and get our buzz on. The smell of good green in the air causes a couple of the other guys in the cell house with us to come over to our cell door asking bogus questions trying to be nosey. Playboi doesn't trip though. Although he knows the motive behind their conversation, he still listens then blesses them with a few joints when they finally get to the purpose of why they really pulled up in the first place. They leave our cell on a mission to get their smoke on.

"Every day is bullshit, niggas and flies." Playboi says rolling up what I can now see is about an ounce of weed in a plastic sandwich bag. "Everybody using fake smiles and handshakes to get what they want, seems like ain't nobody real no mo."

"No doubt bra, I see it every day."

"And every day I get better at maneuvering through em. Like Jay say, "knowing how to move in a room full of vultures."

That being one of my favorite quotes I say, "Exactly." Having already taken two good swigs from my cup and feeling the reefa smoke, I sit back and wonder, not for the first time, what's the story behind my bunkmate. Besides him telling me that he was born and raised right here in Forrest City Arkansas, our conversations have been limited to sports and women.

Now I ask him, "How long you been up in here?"

"A whole year mane. Crackers won't give me a bond, Niggas got bodies getting bonds and I can't get one for a damn arson."

"Arson?"

"You ever heard of 'Playboi's Palace'?"

"Yea, I think so. Ain't that the club that burned down a while back that.... oh, so you that Playboi huh? Yea, I heard about that."

"Bra, what I look like burning down my own club? They talkin bout insurance money and gambling debts. I don't even gamble mane, and my club was doing better than ever when it burned down." I could definitely believe that last part. His club burned down not long before I got out, so the hype and gossip was still in the air strong when I first came home. Word on the street was that the dude who owned 'Playboi's Palace', was also the plug on the best weed around. I heard the stories about guys going to his club getting package deals on pounds and pussy sold together for a playa price. That also explains how he gets his hands on the weed and liquor. Even behind these walls, Playboi's name and financial status carries enough weight to still make things happen.

I ask him, "So how they denying you a bond tho? They gotta have probable cause to do that right?"

"Yea but I skipped state on a Home Invasion charge back when I was a young nigga. Stayed on the run two years before they caught me. Even though I end up beating the charge, they still using it to label me as a flight risk."

"Damn, crackers play the game dirty." I say as I take another puff of the blunt. Him saying when he was a young nigga made me wonder how old he is because to me, he still looks like a young nigga. Standing about five-ten with long braids to the back and a round, brown-skinned baby face, he can't be no older than twenty-three.

"Even my lawyer told me how crooked the system is here. Everybody from the judge down to the District Attorney is in bed together. By him being from Little Rock and not in on the loop, every motion he file is being met with hostility and denied. That's how I know that whoever set me up is connected with somebody up high."

I can only imagine the amount of haters he's accumulated being a young playa getting money and owing his own club in a town like this. Being that we're talking about the clubbing business, my mind instantly thinks about Johnny Ray and Lafu. They're notoriously known for shutting shit down and squashing all competition.

I tell him, "Yea, I know how they work. This town is known as Railroad County. They sent me down on a ten-year bid. Just came home. Ain't even been out a year yet."

"Damn you did a dime?" What you go down for?"

"A body, one that wasn't even mine."

"Damn bra." He shakes his head and we both take a sip and sit in silence reflecting off the never-ending cycle called the system. It's a revolving door that once you walk thru, you seem to never find your way back out of.

"What you back locked up for?"
"Gun charge."
"What it's looking like, any chance of beating it?"
"Nah, I got caught in the raw."
"Damn, did you at least get a reasonable bond?"
"Parole hold."
"That's right you just got out."

"Yea and to make matters worse the gun charges are federal. Meaning I'm facing fed and state time." I take my last few hits of the blunt and flick the roach into the steel toilet as the sickening reality that I'm headed back to prison hits me like a ton of bricks.

Playboi and I sit up late into the night chopping it up about the different aspects of the game and how it's played. The more I talked to this kid the more I liked how his mind works. His perception of the game is a lot similar to mine.

I don't know what time I dozed off or how long I've been asleep, but I'm awakened by the sound of the lock to our cell house being opened. The echo of the jailors footsteps grows louder and louder as he nears our cell. Instead of walking past, he stops at our door.

"Fevers, wake up."

I lay there and play possum hoping he'll go away. This is the third middle of the night visits I've gotten since I've been here. Detectives wanting to interrogate me hoping I'll say something different about the club incident than the last time they questioned me. Fuck I look like, a snitch? My answer is going to remain the same; "I want my lawyer."

"Fevers wake up. You have an attorney visit."

This causes me to roll over. "Attorney visit? What time is it?"

"Time for you to get up and get dressed. You got five minutes."

After I brush my teeth and put on my jail issued uniform, I step out into the dayroom and see that it's a quarter past three in the morning. I've never heard of a middle of the night attorney visit, so my radar is on full alert as the jailor takes me out of the cell and leads me through the jail. You never know what to expect when dealing with these crooked crackers.

"Wait in there." the big racist jailor known as Sam says before pushing me into the small attorney-client room and slamming the door shut behind me.

Inside the room is a small wooden table with two chairs; no windows, no clocks on the wall, no way to tell if it's night or day. Nothing to look at but the four off-white walls and grey iron door that serves as the only entrance or exit to the room.

The only attorney visit I've had prior to this one was the lawyer that Johnny Ray sent who came about one in the afternoon so maybe this one is from the new lawyer that Niesha is supposed to be hooking me up with. My answer comes about twenty minutes later when I hear the door being unlocked from the outside. She walks in and the door closes and locks behind her.

"I know you didn't think I'd give up that easy, did you?" Dena asks standing in front of me wearing dark shades and a red designer dress covered by a black waist length leather jacket with the matching gloves. The scent of her expensive perfume fills the small room as she takes a seat across from me on the other side of the table.

"Why did you deny my visit?"

I remain silent and just look at her giving away no signs of how shocked I really am to see her here although my mind is racing a thousand miles a minute wondering how she managed to pull this off.

Dena takes her time removing her gloves then her shades before her hazel eyes lock into mine and she says, "I see you don't want to talk and that's fine.... I'd rather you just listen anyway. I need you to hear me out." Her presence in the room is powerful.

My senses experience a serious overload as the sound of her voice fills my ears and resonate inside my mind. The different fragrances of her perfume and body lotion mixed in with her lip gloss and the smell of her hair, all those sweet feminine smells caress my nose at one time while my fingers tingle to touch her clear glowing skin. With an Aaliyah disposition and features like Lisa Raye, her exotic beauty makes it impossible to look away.

This woman sitting across from me, seven months pregnant with my seed, has all kinds of feelings flowing through me at this moment, but I hold my composure and continue to listen as she talks.

"Every since you showed up at the club and I found out you were still alive; all I've been able to think about is you. For four months I had been mourning you, regretting that I would never get a chance to talk to you and explain why I did what I did. Then there you were. Alive and as beautiful as the first day that I ever laid eyes on you at the bus station. My Dabo...." She pauses and seems to get lost in thought for a few seconds. Then she says, "Guess that's how I allowed you to play me so easily at the hotel. I was so determined to talk to you and make things right that I underestimated your level of hate for me."

I swallow all the angry responses that surface on the tip of my tongue and hold on to my silence.

Dena stands up and removes her leather jacket giving me a clear view of her baby bump before moving around the table to my side. Gently she grabs my hand in both of hers and places it over her belly. Then she moves it around until she has it where she wants it.

"You feel that?"

The sudden movement underneath my palm

catches me off guard causing me to jump, but Dena holds my hand in place.

With a laugh she says, "It's a baby Click. Our baby. See..." She pulls the front of her dress up revealing pink paternity panties stretched up over her round stomach. I'm more than amazed when she pulls the top of them down and I see the outline of a small hand emerge and move across the interior of her skin before disappearing. The complexion of her stomach lighter than the rest of her already light skin tone except for the dark line running vertical down the middle of her stomach, giving it the appearance of a well-developed peach.

Excited and amazed at the sight of the little me growing inside of her, I can't hold back a smile as I place both hands around the flesh of her large globe

and say, "I can't wait to meet him."

"You mean her. It's going to be a girl."

"No, I meant him."

"Her."

"Him."

"Whatever." She shakes her head with a smile knowing that it's pointless trying to change my mind. "The bottom line is, I need you to understand what I was up against. I had to make some hard choices to protect our child. Lafu knows how close me and Finesse are. Once he found out we were trying to kill him, he used that against me and threatened to pull the plug on her while she was in a coma if I didn't go thru with setting you up. One thing I know about Lafu, he doesn't make idle threats. I didn't know you at the time and all I cared about was Finesse. So, yes you were expendable. But somewhere along the line of us being together every day, I fell in love with you." With her hands covering mine on her belly, she looks deep into my eyes. "You got in my system without my permission Click and I don't know how to turn that off. I need you to know that everything that happened between us was real. None of it was fake. You're the first man besides my father that I ever let get close to me. You're the first man that I've ever been with or fell in love with. Tell me that you believe me."

  Slowly I remove my hands from her belly and lean back in my chair without answering. There's no doubt in my mind about this being my child because we were together during the time of conception and I know she couldn't have faked her virginity. I even believe that she may have genuinely caught feelings for me. But at the end of the day, she had committed the ultimate betrayal, and to me there's no coming back from that.

CHAPTER 12

Click

    With a defeated sigh at my rejection, Dena props her rear end up on the edge of the table in front of me and says, "I found out that I was pregnant the day after we threw Lil-Eighty's birthday party at the hotel. We had so much fun that night. Remember? We snuck off and locked ourselves in one of the rooms and made love for hours?"
    I nod my head at the vivid memories that flash through my mind. How I felt like I was on top of the world with Dena and thought that we would be together forever.
    "The next morning after I left you, I took a pregnancy test. Actually, I took three of em. And they all came back positive."
    "Why didn't you tell me?"
    "I was so scared and confused that I didn't know what to do. Then I got the call that Finesse woke up right afterwards, so it really didn't have time to sink in. All I could think about was how perfect the timing was. Finesse waking up out of her coma meant that Lafu didn't have anything to hold over my head so I figured that me, you, Finesse, and the baby could all leave and go somewhere and start over. By the time you made it to the hospital that evening, I had made up my mind to sit you down and tell you everything, but then you're cousin got killed before I got a chance to talk to you."
    Her bringing up my cousin instantly ignites the inferno of anger that I feel whenever I think about my last living family member and best friend both murdered because of Dena and her lies. Uncomfortably, I shift in my seat trying to sit on my anger as I continue to listen.
    "Nurse Shelly was a good person and didn't deserve what happened to her. You have to believe me when I say I didn't know anything about that. But now that I look back on it, I know that Lafu did it to throw everybody off since he had lost his leverage."
    It does makes sense. First Mechi's hand got cut off and delivered to Reece's apartment in a box and the next day my cousin got murdered at her house. All immediately following Finesse waking up out of her coma. Lafu being the strategist he is, had already planned for that day when it came.

"I was waiting until you came back from burying your cousin in Milwaukee before I told you about the baby because I knew you needed time to mourn. But Lafu came to me while you were away. Somehow he knew that I was pregnant. I can't figure out for the life of me how because I hadn't told a soul at the time. Not even Uncle Fresh."

"Uncle who?"

"Uncle Fresh, that's my nickname for Johnny Ray. I gave it to him when I was just a little girl."

"Your father?"

" Yes..." She looks at me strangely. "But how did you know?"

"Because he told me. He told me when he told me you was carrying my seed."

"I didn't know myself until the night before my mother was murdered. That's the last conversation she and I had before she died."

"So before that you thought Lafu was your biological father?"

"Yes and no. Something inside of me always knew the truth. I knew I couldn't have come from someone as evil as Lafu. Plus, all my life Uncle Fresh has been like a father to me anyway. Lafu and I have never seen eye to eye or had that father daughter bond."

I sit trippin to myself off of their soap opera situation. How Johnny Ray must have been fucking his right hand man's wife behind his back all those years and had gotten her pregnant. I wonder if that's the reason why Lafu ended up killing Dena's mother, because he found out the truth.

"Does Lafu know?"

Slowly she nods her head up and down.

"He came to me while you were in Milwaukee. He told me that I was the seed of betrayal birthing the seed of deception. I didn't know what he was talking about at first because he's always talking in riddles. Then he said that Uncle Fresh and my mom had planted the first seed and you and I had planted the second one. Then he touched me..." Her eyes close and her body recoils as if shrinking away from a physical touch. "He told me that he had been molding me to be the princess of his empire, but now I was tainted. I was carrying the seed of the enemy. He kept on touching me..." Unconsciously, her arms come up and wrap around her body as a lone tear escapes down her left cheek. "He touched me in ways no father is ever supposed to touch his own daughter."

Ain't no way she saying what I think she is.

"Did he rape you?"

She doesn't answer, only hugs herself and rocks while tears stream down her face. When my hands touch her shoulders, she jumps, opens her eyes and looks up into mines. I see that same haunted glare that's always there whenever she speaks about Lafu.

I can't explain the instant anger that I feel at the thought of Lafu violating Dena or the sudden desire I have to wrap my arms around and comfort her right now.

Cautiously I ask again, "Dena, did Lafu rape you?"

Her "No" comes out on a broken cry as she collapses against my chest. "...he just kept feeling on me and told me if I didn't go through with what we started and finish the job on you, then he was gone make sure that my bastard child never got to breathe its first breath of air. Then he...he put his hand down my pants and told me he was gone show me what being with a real man felt like. All I could think about was all the horrible things Finesse told me he did to her.... I hate that muthafucka..."

Her sobs cause her body to convulse as I wrap my arms around her and kiss the top of her head.

"It's all good ma. That muthafucka gone get what's coming to him."

Holding on to me tightly she says, "You don't know how many times I wanted to break down and tell you what was going on but couldn't because I was afraid of what he might do."

For some reason, I believe every word she's saying. I know how ill this nigga Lafu is and the lengths he'll go to get what he wants. Dena had chosen to try and save our baby's life over mine which is the same decision I would have made had I have been the one who had to choose so I can't even be mad at her. All this time I thought she was a major player in the big scheme of things when she had just been another piece on the board that Lafu was playing along with the rest of us.

I kiss her forehead then her eyelids and say, "Shh, don't even trip Suabo, Lafu gone have to see me one day. That's my word ma. But I don't need you stressin over him right now. I need you focused on giving me a strong and healthy newborn baby boy."

Still sniveling and crying she says, "You mean a strong and healthy baby girl."

"Man shut up." I say before covering her lips with mine.

Dena's minty mouth meets mine with the same hunger that I feel for hers. Her tears wet my face as we kiss with lost abandonment trying to fill in that what's been missing since our lips met last. We kiss until we both have to come up for air or risk suffocating on each other. Her sexually aroused face laced with tears makes me want to take all of her pain away and leave her with nothing but pleasure.

My hands explore the ripened swell of her breast before moving down to caress her thick thighs as I try to overdose on the taste of her tongue. Her baby bump leaves just enough room for her hands to find their way inside my pants to grip my nature. Her small fingers hold enough heat to raise my body temperature ten degrees. She wraps her legs around my waist and the contour of our bodies fit snugly together, yet it still feels like we aren't quite close enough. I'm tortured by her thumb rubbing back and forth across my tip as she continually strokes me. Her moist mound moving against me speaking her desires.

Urgency takes over and we fight the battle to remove the material that separate us.

I lose my breath when she pulls her panties to the side and guides me inside her paradise. Everything seems to shift into slow mo.

"Dabo...I'm sorry baby. I never meant to hurt you..."

"Shhh...." I lift her chin and attach my lips to the tender flesh of her neck, as I slowly submerge myself in and out of her heat. I'm rewarded with her erotic moans as her body wraps tightly around me. Each stroke deliberate, I take my time loving on the mother of my child as all the feelings that had been lying dormant inside of me come to the surface and boil over. I don't think about us being in a jail or how the jailor could walk in on us at any minute. I don't think about me being on my way back to prison. All I know is how perfect right now feels. Nothing else matters. My whole existence is right here in this moment.

On the edge of the table with her legs up in the crook of my arms, I take my time making slow, sweet love to Dena. We make love like we never made love before. Her hands travel across my face, neck, and back like a blind person reading braille, like she's trying to memorize every detail of my physique with her hands. Somewhere along the line, I lost my shirt.

Never breaking my connection, I scoop her up with ease and sit in the chair with her straddling my lap. We exchange more kisses as she takes control with the roll in her hips making me submit to the motion of her body. For long minutes we get lost in the groove. Her hazel eyes lock into mine as she rides me nice and slow. The pleasure in her pussy indescribable. My upward strokes meet the thrust of her hips with perfect timing giving me the perfect angle to all of her secret spots. The temperature in her box is scorching hot. I'm loving the sexy faces she's making as her moans grow louder and louder. Her tight wetness convulses around me and her love comes down as I continue to rotate in and out of her with no intentions of stopping. Even when I bend her over the table and start hitting it from the back, my strokes are relentless. The sight of her juicy, round ass cheeks jiggling as they back up against me turns me on even more and I feel myself growing inside her.

"Yes Dabo, fuck me just like that...keep fucking me just like that...Oh shit you gone make me cum again..." This is no longer sweet love making. This is more urgent. More aggressive. More animalistic.

I grip her hips and pull her back into me over and over again. When she arches her back and looks back at me with that why-are-you-fucking-me-like-this-face, I back off afraid that I'm hurting her or the baby.

But Dena is insatiable.

She places one of her knees up on the table and throws it back at me demanding every inch.

I give her what she wants.

A knock at the door.

"Miss Givens, are you alright in there?"

"...yes...yes!" Her word mixed moans make it hard to tell if she's talking to him or me.

I can't hold it any longer, I chase that good feeling inside her until the table legs begin scraping across the floor. Until the rhythm of our bodies slapping together sound like the beat to house music.

Until the jailor opens the door again and asks, "Miss Givens, are you alright? "

CHAPTER 13

Finesse
FINESSE da GAME

Damn this nigga got some good ass dick!

Repeatedly he hits my spot taking me up to the edge of my peak, then pushing me over making me fall into the abyss of ecstasy. I lay on my side and cream all over his dick as he holds one of my legs in the air and continues to work me from behind.

"You like this dick don'tcha?"

"Yes daddy! I love this dick."

"You want daddy to keep on fucking you like this?"

"Yes daddy keep fucking me just like that!"

"You want daddy to beat this pussy up all night don'tcha?"

"Um hmm... " What I really want daddy to do is shut the fuck up. He killing my vibe with all that talking. Niggas be killing me thinking that just because they got a big dick and can blow a bitch back out, that they all the sudden become the boss. No nigga, that means that you're qualified to come fuck me when I want some dick then move yo ass around. I'm the only real boss around here. I can't front tho, this nigga Lil-Eighty is a king at eating pussy and his sex game is off the chain. Too bad it's time for me to expose his ass. The only reason I started fucking him in the first place is because I discovered how much he despises Click and Mechi.

It was right after I turned Mechi on to the first one of Lafu's clubs that they ended up robbing. Mechi and I had a presidential suite at the Peabody Hotel in downtown Memphis, which is where I was chilling and waiting while him and his crew went and handled the business. I'd made it clear to Mechi that no one involved could know my name or anything about me because Lafu's name held weight and if it ever came out that I was involved, it would be an instant death sentence for me. That's why I was so heated when he popped back up at the room with Lil-Eighty, Click, and the rest of his crew on some rowdy shit after they successfully pulled off the robbery. I had just enough time to dash off into one of the rooms of the suite, and out of sight before they all came in talking loud.

I hear Mechi's voice first. "Man, yo scary ass act like you was scared to shoot the bitch."

"I wasn't scared nigga. That bitch was just fine than a muthafucka. I hate wasting good pussy."

"Well which would you rather have, some of that good pussy or all this paper we got right here? Look at this shit." I crack the door and peek out in time to see Mechi dumping a duffle bag full of money on the table. "Racks nigga!"

"Oh shit, Look at all that fetty!"

"We did that shit!"

"Hell yeah, it's time to get paid." They all chime in excitedly.

"Fuckin well right. It gotta be at least two, three hundred thou here."

"At least."

"And that ain't even including the dope. Y'all niggas hurry up and count this shit up. I'll be right back."

It was about eight of them in all with Mechi, but I thought my eyes were playing tricks on me when I spotted Click over by the bar fixing himself a drink. How was that even possible? Last time I saw him, Lafu had officially punched his clock and gave Johnny Ray the order to finish him. Not once had I seen a person who Lafu had marked for death continue breathing past their appointed expiration date. If Click had somehow got the drop on Johnny Ray and escaped, then Johnny Ray would be dead right now. Since he ain't, that meant that him and Click were in cahoots together, which wasn't surprising being that Johnny Ray was down with me and Dena's original plan to double cross Lafu. Guess it's true what they say, nothing beats the double cross but the triple cross.

I watched through the crack in the door as Click and the other guys got busy counting the money while Mechi began poking his head in and out of rooms, no doubt looking for me. He found me on the third door he tried when I grabbed his arm and pulled him inside with me.

"Why you bring them here?"

"Huh?"

"Huh hell. Why you bring them here? You know I ain't tryna let them niggas see me."

"Look shawty," he said grabbing my waist and pulling me close to him. "Why you trippin? Everything went just like we planned it. Now we finna split this money up real quick then they outta here. After that we can do us."

"But what if they would have saw me? Then what?"

"They would have just seen that I got a fine ass bitch waiting for me. That don't automatically mean they would have known you were involved. Besides, those niggas so geeked up from the lick that they ain't thinking about nothing but the money they finna count."

"You still shouldn't have brought them here." I said crossing my arms across my chest with a pout.

"Be cool shawty." he said pulling a brick of powder out the front of his pants where he had it tucked and handing it to me. "Take you a couple of bumps and lay back till me and the fellas finish handling business." Then he smacked me on the ass and walked back out closing the door behind him. I almost threw the brick of cocaine behind him but thought better of it. I could use a lil wake up.

Mechi is my boo and everything, but sometimes I be wanting to choke his ass. He has no idea what we're up against. I found out that he was out to get Lafu not long after I woke up out of my coma when he and I reconnected, and I asked him how he ended up with a prosthetic. He told me the story of the crazy Jamaican who drugged him and cut his hand off trying to get at his homeboy Click. I didn't let on that I knew who Click was, but I did tell him that I knew Lafu personally and had a way that he could get back at him. Once I made him promise to keep it between me and him, I told him what I knew about Lafu's clubs.

Since me and Dena's plan to have Click kill

Lafu had backfired, I had all but given up on killing Lafu. Especially when I woke out of my coma to find that not only had Dena fallen in love with Click, but she had also gotten pregnant by this clown. I mean come on now, he was a mark. How could she be so damn gullible? That's why I was more than happy when Lafu finally got tired of playing games with Click and gave Johnny Ray the order to take him out. I thought everything would go back to the way they were before, but I couldn't have been more wrong. Dena was so devastated over Click's death that she fell into a state of depression. She stayed in bed crying for a week straight. She wouldn't eat, I couldn't get her to talk to me, and worst of all, she cut me off sexually. She was just starting to come around, around the time that I discovered that Click was still alive so there's no way in hell I was telling her about it. Instead, I needed to find a way to get Click out of the way for good so that I could have Dena all to myself. My answer came that night after Mechi left out of the room and I went into the bathroom to powder my nose.

I heard a voice say, "I gotta make a call real quick. I'll be right back." before someone came into the room. Luckily, I had the bathroom door already closed.

Quickly, I cut the lights off then cracked the door

and peeked out into the room. He was dark-skinned and kinda on the heavy side with gold in his mouth. Definitely not my type. He had a deep baritone voice, so it wasn't hard to make out what he was saying.

"What up big man...yea everything went smooth. We bout to count up now...should be close to half a mil...I know but we at the Peabody now and we can't do shit up here with all these cameras...yea that makes sense. Plus that fuck nigga Click been watching like a hawk anyway...Right right. It's only a matter of time before him and that nigga Mechi slip up. And when they do, Ima be on they ass like white on rice...No doubt...Aight big man, keep ya head up and just know, I'm out here handling shit....no doubt...aight. One." He hung up just as Mechi opened the door and stuck his head into the room.

"Eighty, fuck you doin, in here caking?"

"Nah man, just checking a couple traps."

"Well come on mane for one of these lil niggas get sticky fingers out here, and I have to smoke one of em."

"You ain't gotta worry bout that. My team loyal bra." Lil-Eighty said before walking past Mechi and back out into the suite.

Mechi took one more look around the room,

probably wondering where I had disappeared to, before pulling the door closed behind him as he left.

The wheels in my head instantly began turning.

Mechi and Click had no idea that they had a snake in their grass, and I could definitely use that to my advantage.

It wasn't hard to work my magic on Lil-Eighty once I spotted him and a couple of his guys come into the 'Hot Spot 'about a week later. I waited until I saw him headed towards the restroom alone before I made my move. He was coming out and caught up talking on his phone when I accidentally on purpose ran into him spilling my drink all over the front of my new Roberto Cavalli blouse.

"Damn nigga watch where the hell you going!"

"Oh shit, my bad beautiful."

"Damn right it's yo bad. You know how much this
blouse cost?"

"Actually I don't but tell me the price and I'll reimburse you. "he said pulling a bankroll out of his pocket.

"This is a one of a kind Roberto Cavalli that my father had specially made and shipped to me straight from Italy before he died you idiot. It's irreplaceable. "I said freestyling and lying through my teeth.

"Aw man, I'm really sorry. I uh...guess I wasn't paying attention to where I was going. Is there anything I can do to make it up to you?"

"No thank you. You've done enough." I said before attempting to walk off.

Just as I expected, he grabbed my hand stopping me. "Wait a minute. I can't let you leave like that. I know I can't replace the shirt your father bought for
you, but at least let me take you shopping and out to eat." I stood there giving him my blankest stare. "And..." He put his bankroll in my hand and closed my fist around it. "You can still keep this. What do you say?"

I looked down at the money in my hand then up into his waiting face before blowing out a breath and relaxing my body.

"Look you don't have to do all that. I know you didn't mean to."

"No, I insist. It's the least I can do." he says pushing my hand back like the thought of taking it back was insulting.

"Well..." I said with a smile relenting. "I do loves to get my shop on."

"Then it's settled." he said flashing his gold teeth smile and sticking out his hand. "My name is Lil-Eighty."

"Finesse." I said taking it.

We exchanged numbers and ended up hooking up the next day. Lil-Eighty kept his word and let me tear the mall down at his expense. I didn't spare his pockets either. I bought all kinds of expensive shit that I know I would never wear just getting a kick out of watching him try to keep a straight face and play it cool while I put a dent in his pockets. I had already made up my mind to give him the pussy, but I needed him to know that he wasn't dealing with one of those cheap ass sack chasers that he was probably used to dealing with. He was gone have to step his game up if he wanted to dance with this diva. I had fun tho. We smoked blunt after blunt after blunt and he kept me laughing throughout the whole day.

My second surprise came when we finally made it to the bedroom and got busy. I had never been with a heavy guy before and had always heard that they all had small dicks. That myth got broken the moment that Lil-Eighty took off his clothes. The boy was packing! That didn't stop me from working my pussy power on him though. By the time I finished squirting my black girl juice all over him, he was curled up in the fetal position, sucking his thumb, and sleeping like a baby. I could tell from the beginning that he was a tender-dick because I hadn't been fucking him but two weeks before he was telling me that he loved me on top of tricking off all of his money on me. It would have crushed his heart to find out that I was messing around with Mechi too. Especially after he and Mechi got into it after they came off of the third robbery. Each new club that I turned them on to produced more money than the one before, and each time the friction between Mechi and Eighty grew a little more just as I was hoping. I knew things had come to a head when I met up with Lil-Eighty at one of his spots and saw how distracted he was.

"What's wrong daddy?"

"Nothing man, just tired of mafuckas thinking they can play me any type of way."

"Who you talkin about?"

Shaking his head, he said, "Nobody. It ain't nothing you need to be worried about."

"Aw daddy, I don't like seeing you all uptight like that. Let mama make you feel better." I rolled a fat blunt, put on Juvenile and Soulja Slim's new club banger 'Slow Motion', and gave him some slow sloppy top while he smoked the blunt to the face. By the time I finished working my head game on him, he was relaxed and pouring his heart out to me.

"It's just these niggas still tryna treat me like Lil-Eighty from back in the days, like I'm a shorty or something. I ain't that lil nigga that they use to trade game cartridges with. Shit done changed."

"Who you talkin about daddy?"

"Just some older niggas from my hood that I been getting money with. They think they can break me and my team off crumbs while they keep the whole cake for themselves. Niggas got me fucked up. Without us they wouldn't be shit."

"If it's like that, why you still fucking with em then?"

"Cuz I still got some unfinished business with this nigga Click and Mechi pussy ass got the hook-up on the moves we been making. If I had a way to come up with the information he got, I would have been exed his junkie ass out of the picture."

"Damn, it sound like you really dislike this guy Mechi or whatever his name is."

"Yea that fuck nigga use to serve my mama before she died. He don't know that I know he was there getting high with her the night she overdosed. He didn't call the ambulance or nothing. Just left her there to die like a dog. Plus I'll never forget when I was little watching him let his brother Travis and Click run a train on my mom's when they thought I was in the back room sleep."

I was stunned. I knew Eighty disliked Mechi, but I had no idea it ran that deep.

"So let me get this straight." I said playing dumb. "This guy Mechi has the plug, I'm guessing on where you get your drugs from and the other guy, what's his name, Clock?"

"Click."

"Yea Click. You and him got some business going on to where you feel that you need him too. So you have to continue letting them treat you as less than the boss that you are?"

"Yea something like that. Well....not really. It's complicated. Like I said, it ain't nothing you need to worry about."

"Well what if I told you that I could hook you up with a guy who deals in major weight and could get you a price that's probably much better than what you're paying now? I could hook you up with a deal that's so sweet that you could feed your whole team by yourself and you wouldn't need them niggas no mo. Matter of fact, they would probably end up copping from you."

"Shiid, if I had that kind of plug, I wouldn't hesitate to cross both of they asses out for good."

So I went to Lafu and convinced him that I had

a guy who could move some major units at a quick pace and he agreed just like I knew he would. The only thing Lafu cares about is making money. Long as the numbers added up, he was down. Of course, I had to play the middleman because Lafu doesn't deal with anyone face to face, so Lil-Eighty had no idea that he was doing business with the same person who's clubs he was helping rob. See the way I figured it, If I put Lil-Eighty in position to make some real money then it would only be a matter of time before he got Click out of my way for me. Too bad that meant that Mechi would also get caught in the crossfire, but hey, all is fair in love and war. Fortunately, things worked out better than I expected.

Behind every real boss is a real boss bitch. A woman who's crafty enough to stand behind her man and play the background while really she's the one making all the decisions and calling all the real shots; at the same time letting him feel like he's the boss.

I had put Lil-Eighty on his feet and taken him to the next level by plugging him with Lafu. I had taught him how to think and move differently. Even convinced him to rent us a stash house out in Marianna away from all his partnas that no one else knew about but me and him. I told him it was necessary because now that he was the man and seeing real money, all his friends would soon become his enemies and try to plot on taking what he had. I raised his awareness and made him conscious of the jack boys and how they think. Now he's so on point that he won't even drive his own car out to our stash house in Marianna, afraid that someone would try to follow and rob him. Instead, he either took a cab or waited for me to drive him out there.

The night before the robbery of 'The Hot Spot ', I called Lil-Eighty and told him to meet me at the stash house but ended up never making it out there myself because I went to the hood with Dena looking for Click and ended up at the Ramada with her and Mechi. The next day, I waited until the last minute before I called him again. I had left Dena at the hotel room thinking that I was headed to get us some weed to smoke and to the Chinese store to get the stuff to do our toes and nails when really, I just used that as an excuse to get away from her ears and make the call.

The phone rung so long that for a moment, I thought he wasn't going to pick up but to my relief, he finally answered.

"Hello?"

"Hey daddy."

"Don't hey daddy me. What the hell happened to you last night?"

"Whoa, slow down. First of all, who you think you talkin to like that? Secondly, I had an emergency situation that I had to tend to."

"So you couldn't answer your phone? I called you a thousand times."

"I didn't even have my phone with me last night. But why are you iggin me about this dumb shit when we got more important issues to discuss?"

"Because I sat up all night waiting on you. And on top of everything else, I had to get that fuck nigga Click to pick me up this morning because you still wouldn't answer yo damn phone."

"What? You showed Click where the stash house at?!?"

"Calm down, it's not like I let him come inside. I told him that it was some new chick's house that I met."

"That still wasn't smart. Anyway, I was talking to the plug not long ago tryna set up our next play and he asked me did you have a strong team who was willing to make some extra money putting in some work. I told him that I knew for a fact that you had some hittas on yo squad and he told me to tell you that someone had been robbing all of his clubs and he would be willing to double your next load if you could find out who they were and take care of them for him."

The other end of the line went silent and I could just imagine what he was thinking. He was already copping fifteen bricks at a time so not only could he double that, but this was also his opportunity to cross Click and Mechi out. Now all I had to do was put the final icing on the cake.

"Hello, you still there?"

"Yeah, I'm here."

"He also told me that he wanted to meet you personally, which is something he never does, so whatever you're doing right now, stop and come pick me up."

"I can't right now. I'm kinda in the middle of something."

"Are you serious? This is the opportunity of a lifetime. What can be more important than this? Lafu never meets anyone face to face so if he calls for you, you would be an idiot not to come. And he definitely ain't the type of person you leave waiting." I had intentionally said Lafu's name leaving Lil-Eighty no room to wonder: yes he had been copping bricks and doing business with the same Jamaican drug lord who had set up Click, cut off Mechi's hand, and who's club he had been helping rob.

"Fuck it." Lil-Eighty said "Where you at? I'm on the way."

I told him that Lafu wanted us to meet at the same club that he and I met at, which also happened to be the same club that he was sitting behind with a car full of niggas and guns when I called him. My plan was to get Lil-Eighty to leave Click and Mechi hanging on the robbery so that the already existing beef between them would escalate into a full blown war. I knew that Lil-Eighty and his crew of goons were the real muscle in their hood, so Click and Mechi wouldn't stand a chance going up against them. I later found out that someone had tipped the police off to the robbery, resulting in Click being locked up and heading back to prison. And there is no doubt in my mind that Lafu was behind the massacre that happened inside the club leaving everyone including most of Lil-Eighty's goons dead.

    By the time Lil-Eighty picked me up and we made it back to 'The Hot Spot', the whole block was taped off with reporters and spectators everywhere. And to my surprise, Johnny Ray followed by Mechi were being escorted out alive. Somehow my baby Mechi had managed to survive what is now being called 'The Mysterious Strip Club Massacre '. Now all I have to do is expose Lil-Eighty's ass and let nature take its course.

CHAPTER 14

Dena

No one has seen hide nor hair of Lafu since the strip club massacre.

Uncle Fresh told me that he was pretty sure that he was somewhere in Jamaica hiding out, but he wasn't taking any chances. There are so many armed guards posted up around the perimeter of the mansion that it looks like some type of military fortress. A few are even stationed inside at every possible entrance and exit. It's been like this for weeks now. And to make matters worse, Uncle Fresh won't let me go anywhere without being escorted. He said that Lafu knows that I'm his weakness and he isn't taking any chances when it comes to me. He and Lafu are officially at war. The whole situation has me feeling uncomfortable and like a prisoner in the home that I've grown to love over the past six years. But what Uncle Fresh just discovered has me wanting to leave this place all together and never look back. The whole state of Arkansas for that matter.

"How did you find this?"

"I hired an electrical technician to sweep the place for bugs and he found a whole slew of em. In every room, office, kitchen, hallway, you name it. He told me that with this many being found in such close proximity, there had to be a central receiving source somewhere close by. And he was right."

I can't believe my eyes. Over a hundred tv monitors stare back at us from almost every wall surrounding Lafu's private quarters. Walls that were covered with uniquely designed paneling and expensive artwork before Uncle Fresh's electrical technician stumbled upon the soccer trophy disguised handle that opened the secret compartment revealing tv monitors behind them.

"I don't understand. How can he have cameras in all those obvious places and we not see em?"

"They're called lipstick cameras, Babygirl. Small cameras about the size of the tip of a ballpoint pen, mostly used by international spy groups such as Mossad and MI6. You would have to have a trained eye to spot them. They're mostly hidden in common household utensils like clocks, lamps, light fixtures, and even in ordinary pictures hanging on the wall."

My eyes scan from screen to screen. I see a bunch of different locations in the mansion, including several different angles of the Rainforest Room where I spend most of my time. I'm more than appalled when I see the inside of my bedroom and personal bathroom knowing that he has intruded on some of my most personal moments. And especially when I realize that more than likely, he's witnessed Finesse and I being together sexually. That also explains how he knew that I was pregnant.

"Sick bastard." I hear myself say out loud.

"Sicker than you know, watch this." Uncle Fresh says directing my attention to a main screen that's bigger than the rest located behind Lafu's desk. He uses some kind of remote control to change from one camera to the next. When he stops, I recognize the familiar interior of the dancers dressing room at 'The Hot Spot'.

"You mean he has access to more than just the hidden cameras in the mansion from here?"

"Yes, but from what I can tell, the mansion's cameras are the only ones giving live feed. The rest are recordings." Which makes sense because 'The Hot Spot ' has been closed down since the day of the killings and the dressing room on the screen is filled with several dancers in different stages of dress or undress.

The audio is clear as we watch the video close in on different parts of the dancers anatomy before scanning over to capture two dancers assaulting another one in the corner. No one tries to break it up or help the overpowered girl. Not even when one dancer pulls out and sprays pepper spray in the girls face, while the other one pulls out a box cutter and starts slicing her up. Instead, they all scatter and exit the dressing room leaving the three women alone fighting. It turns into a very bloody and gory site that's hard to watch. The girls ear-shattering screams send chills through my body.

"I remember this incident, they beat her unconscious and cut her over seventy times. She almost died."

"Yea me too. Her family tried to sue us. But there's more." Uncle Fresh changes the monitor to a different screen that shows the inside of one of our V.I.P. rooms that are reserved for our elite clientele.

I watch as a young attractive dancer lays on her back across a sofa with her head resting in the lap of an Italian man in a business suit. I recognize him as Jimmy Damoochie, an Italian mob boss who is one of Lafu's number one and only clients out of the mid-west. The two indulge in casual conversation as Damoochie drinks from a champagne bottle and runs his hand all over the young woman's body. Eventually, his hand travels down her stomach and inside her thong where it stays for a while. She doesn't seem to mind as she lays there with closed eyes while he continues to entertain her with charming conversation. Their banter goes on for a bit with her giggling periodically and seeming to enjoy his company.

Damoochie says, "How about you use that pretty mouth of yours to help ole Damoochie relax?"

"Now Mr. Damoochie, you wouldn't be asking me what I think you are would you?" she coos while already rolling over and beginning to undo his belt buckle.

"Well you know, seeing how I's being a good guy and all, spending all this money..." His words trail off as she reaches inside of his pants.

"I guess I could do a little something to show my appreciation." She says before taking him into her mouth.

Damoochie's eyes roll into the back of his head as he turns up and gulps loudly from the champagne bottle. For a moment he relaxes and enjoys the pleasure he's being given. Then he places his hand on the back of her head forcing her to move faster as he raises his hips off the sofa to meet the motions of her mouth. This causes her to begin choking.

"Mr. Damoo...Mr. Damoochie wait...." she attempts to stop and talk but he only forces her head back down and continues pumping roughly into her mouth causing her to gag more. It's obvious by the sinister grin on his face that he's getting enjoyment out of watching her struggle and choke.

Suddenly he screams, "Aaah shit, you fucking cunt! You bit me!" Violently, he swings the bottle down hitting her in the back of the head. The girl rolls off his lap onto the floor where she lays groaning and holding her head.

Enraged, Damoochie stands up over her with the bottle in his hand. "You fucking bite me?!?" He swings the bottle down and with a loud smack, it lands on her back. "I'll fucking kill ya, you stupid bitch!" Again and again he hits her in the back with the bottle making her scream out in pain. Grabbing a hand full of her hair, he pulls her up from the floor and unto her knees. "I'll teach ya to bite me." Using her hair, he forces the top half of her body face down onto the sofa. Then he yanks her thong down and brutally shoves the top half of the champagne bottle up inside of her. Despite her pleas for him to stop, Damoochie continues to mercilessly violate her with the bottle.

"Oh my God, I can't watch this anymore." I finally turn my head away from the gruesome molestation on the screen. "Who keeps stuff like this?"

"Lafu. He has a bunch more to go with these, all listed under 'favorites'. The next one is the one I brought you up here to see. It was labeled under 'Betrayal'." Uncle Fresh switches screens again and I find myself looking at him and my mother sitting in the plush interior of our company's private jet engaged in conversation. I instantly recognize the ensemble that my mother is wearing as the outfit that she had on when her and Uncle Fresh returned from Chicago bearing gifts the day before my twenty-third birthday. The day before she was murdered.

On the screen my mother says, "Oh Johnny Ray, this can't be true. Please tell me I'm reading this wrong." In her hand is a small, worn booklet that slightly favors my poem book except smaller.

"I wish I could baby. Someone sent it to my P.O. Box about three days ago. I didn't show it to you because I didn't want to ruin your trip. Lord knows I wish I never had to show it to you at all."

"Oh Nessa, my poor baby. It's all my fault. If I would have at least been there maybe..."

"Now Theresa, don't you go blaming yourself." Uncle Fresh wraps his arm around my mother's shoulder pulling her firmly against his side. "It ain't nobody's fault but his. He's the bad guy here. Not you."

"I know, but I should have at least been there." My mother is devastated. "I can't believe this. What if he's done something to my Dena too?"

"I seriously doubt that. My Babygirl would have come to me." Uncle Fresh pauses the video and I look up to see him watching me intently.

"You knew didn't you?" he asks me.

My heart drops down into the pit of my stomach as pangs of guilt coarse through my body.

"Not at first. Not for a long time. Nessa told me one night after I woke her up from a nightmare. Even then, I had to twist her arm before she finally came out with the truth."

"How long has it been going on?"

"Since she was five."

Uncle Fresh closes his eyes and cringes. After a few seconds he opens them, looks at me closely and asks, "I'm right aren't I?"

"About what?" I ask although I know perfectly well what he's asking me.

"You would come to me. If that bastard even so much as looked at you funny, you would tell me right?"

Ever since Lafu put his hands on me I've been wanting to tell my father. I wanted him to know because I knew he would go and beat Lafu to a pulp with his bare hands. I wanted him to break every bone in his body and make him pay for touching me the way that he did, but I could never find a way to broach the subject. If ever there was a perfect time to tell him, now would be it. Instead, I find myself saying, "Yes daddy, I would tell you." I watch as relief floods his face and his body relaxes.

Uncle Fresh puts his arm around my shoulders and pulls me close just like he did my mother in the video and says, "I know you would Babygirl. I know you would." He kisses my forehead then continues the video again.

My mother says, "You would think Finesse would come to one of us too."

"Nessa is different. She doesn't react to things like normal people. Her and Babygirl are like night and day. Babygirl knows how to express herself. Nessa holds everything inside."

"Well she can't stay here any longer, she has to go."

"Now hold on Theresa, let's think about this."

"What else is there to think about Johnny Ray. Nessa has to leave!" My mother screams before breaking down crying. "I have to get her away from here. I can't leave her alone with that monster ever again.... he raped my baby.... he raped my baby..."

"I know baby. I know..." On the screen Uncle Fresh holds and comforts my mother while I revel in the fact that at least she found out how much of a monster Lafu really is before she died.

By the end of the video, Uncle Fresh was able to get my mother to calm down and they discussed and decided that she would quit the family business for good so that she could stay home and be with her "babies".

****

Three o'clock in the morning and I still can't seem to fall asleep. Too many troubled thoughts invade my mind. Namely, the video with my mother from earlier. Uncle Fresh showed it to me for two reasons: One it proves that Lafu knew about his and my mother's secret affair. And two, Lafu also knew that my mother had found out what he had been doing to Finesse all those years and was quitting the family business because of it. Both the perfect motives for murder.

Still one unanswered question keeps plaguing my thoughts; who mailed Finesse's diary to Uncle Fresh? Was it Finesse? Was this her desperate cry out for help? And since when did Finesse start keeping a diary? I'd never seen her write in one.

The overactive child growing inside of me coupled with the need to empty my full bladder has me climbing out of bed. Seems like the closer I get to my due date, the more often I have to use it. I slip on my night gown and go inside my bathroom to relieve myself. Sitting on the toilet, I can't help scanning the ceiling with my eyes knowing that there's a camera up there somewhere. At the exact spot of the camera angle I watched on the monitor in Lafu's quarters earlier is a smoke detector. Even as I'm walking through the eastern wing of the mansion where most of the bedrooms are located, the knowledge that there are invisible eyes on me is giving me the creeps.

I stop at Finesse's bedroom door and poke my head inside. I'm not the least bit surprised to find her bed still made without her in it. I was so stressed at one point when I thought that Click was dead, that the doctor ordered me on complete bedrest for two weeks because my child's health was in jeopardy. After that I just stopped Finesse from sleeping in my bed altogether and cut her off sexually. Now she rarely ever sleeps at the mansion at all. I still worry about her a lot, but I worry about my child's health even more.

I find myself climbing up the stairs that lead to Lafu's private quarters for the second time within a few hours. Out of the six years that we've lived here, I can count on one hand how many times I've made this journey. My desire to stay as far away from Lafu as possible has always caused me to make big circles around this part of the mansion. Now here I am again.

The double doors open without so much as a squeak. Somehow I know that isn't by chance. I'm willing to bet that Lafu intentionally oils the hinges regularly so that he can slither out of his hole undetected whenever he wants to.

Inside it's dark with the exception of the small lamp sitting on the desk. Cautiously, I step inside and move through the darkness towards the light with the intention of figuring out how to turn on and watch the tv monitors again. Curiosity has me wanting to find and see what a lipstick camera actually looks like up close. The ones in my bedroom and bathroom are too high for me to be trying to reach in my pregnant state, but I remember seeing several more that are angled from lower positions.

I'm no more than ten steps away from the desk when I feel the hairs on the back of my neck stand up.

Suddenly, I feel a presence behind me.

Before I have a chance to turn around or react, I'm

rushed from behind as strong arms wrap around me. A hand covers my mouth enabling me from screaming.

"Now Dee-nah, me show ya whata real mon can do." His harsh breath heats the side of my face as he walks me forward towards the desk. I'm horrified to feel his erection pressing against me as he forces my body to crash roughly into the side of the desk with no regards for my baby.

Without warning, he slams my face down onto the surface of the desk so hard that I almost pass out. Then he does it again leaving me on the brink of unconsciousness. With one arm wrapped around me just beneath the swell of my belly holding me up, I feel Lafu raising my nightgown up over my hips. Next my underwear get yanked down.

Mustering up every ounce of strength that I have left, I throw my head backwards into his face as hard as I can. Bingo! The back of my head connects with the bridge of his nose causing him to yell out in pain. Then I shoot a sharp elbow into his ribcage for good measures before I reach forward and get my hands on the desk lamp. I swing it like it's a baseball bat and I'm trying to hit a homerun. It shatters against Lafu's head sending him falling backwards into the shadows. Discombobulated with blood running down my face, I pull my underwear up and stumble towards the double doors in complete shock. I run down the stairs as fast as my swollen feet will carry me.

"Uncle Fresh! Uncle Fresh! He's here! Lafu is here!" Tears and blood blur my vision as I frantically race through the mansion slipping and falling along the way. Soon as I bend the corner into the west wing where the small kitchen is located, I run directly into Uncle Fresh and several armed guards. I collapse into my father's arms on the verge of hysteria.

"Babygirl!" The look on his face is pure horror.

Uncle Fresh kneels to the ground with me in his arms. "Nooo...Babygirl, who did this to you?"

"He's...he's...in... he's, I..." I can't seem to form a straight sentence.

"Slow down baby. Talk to me. Who did this to you?"

I try to calm down and take a deep breath. "La.. La... Lafu is here."

Uncle Fresh immediately starts barking orders to the guards. "Go now! Secure all the perimeters and make sure that bastard doesn't get away! Only kill him if you have to, I want him alive!"

The vision of Uncle Fresh standing above me begins to get blurry. Black spots appear before my eyes and I feel myself about to pass out.

"Stay with me Babygirl. Whatever you do, don't close your eyes." Effortlessly he scoops me up into his arms and begins moving quickly through the mansion. "Can you hear me?"

I nod my head against his chest. Although his voice is clear in my ears, the desire to close my eyes is too powerful. If I could just rest them for a few seconds.

"No Babygirl, stay with me." I feel him patting my cheek. I look up into his face as a gush of liquid comes from between my legs.

"Uncle Fresh."

"Yes baby, Uncle Fresh is right here."

The last thing I remember is saying, "I think my water just broke." before passing out.

****

Voices all around me. Blinding light sting my eyes as I try to open them and see. I can tell by the frenzied movement surrounding me that something is wrong. I try to sit up, but someone puts a hand on my shoulder holding me down.

"Whoa Miss Givens, relax. We're going to take good care of you."

"What's going on? Where's Uncle Fresh?"

"Just relax. Everything is going to be fine." So many unidentified voices around me saying things that I don't understand. I feel a prick in my arm as a plastic mask comes down over my face covering my nose and mouth. Faces that I don't recognize amidst a bright light come in and out of focus above me then I fade back out.

Next thing I know, I'm alone. A sense of emptiness fills me as I begin coming around. It's not hard to tell that I'm in a hospital. My hands instinctively move to my stomach.

"My baby!" Frantically, I look around as I try to sit up. "Where's my baby?"

A nurse walks into the room and comes over beside me.

"Well hello Miss Givens, glad to have you back with us. You gave us quite a scare."

"What happened?"

"You suffered a severe concussion caused by a blunt force trauma to your head. Do you remember anything?"

Instant memories of Lafu attacking me flood my mind. Then I remember feeling safe in Uncle Fresh's arms right before my water broke.

"My baby. What happened to my baby?"

"Well there were some complications and..."

"What kind of complications? Is my baby alright?"

"Yes your seven pound, four ounce, beautiful baby boy is fine. Almost as fine as his granddad." Uncle Fresh says walking in beaming with pride carrying a small bundle wrapped in a turquoise and white Burberry print baby blanket.

No words can describe the feelings I feel when he places him in my arms, and I look down into my son's eyes for the first time. Eyes like mine surrounded by a face like his father's look back up at me filled with curiosity. His smooth, creamy complexion somewhere between Click's mocha brown and my sun kiss yellow. Head full of curly hair and dimples deeper than mine, he's adorable.

"Hello baby. I'm your mommy. Oh my God, you are so handsome." He just looks up at me sucking on his little fat fist and slobbering. "It's like my first crush all over again. I haven't been this smitten since the first day I laid eyes on his father." I laugh while fawning all over my son.

"Yes, he is very handsome and very active." the nurse says. "Somehow he got himself tangled in the umbilical cord and flipped upside down. We had to perform an emergency Cesarean Section."

This surprises me and I begin inspecting my bandaged lower stomach.

Uncle Fresh says, "I don't know who scared me the worse, you with your concussion or him with his acrobatics." We all share a laugh.

The nurse says, "You're going to experience a bit of discomfort over the next couple of days and you're still going to be on bedrest, but you and your baby should be cleared to go home no later than tomorrow."

"That's great news."

"The doctor is going to want to have a few words with you, so I'm going to inform him that you're woke and give you some time with your baby."

"Okay." I say still not able to take my eyes off my child.

"Oh, and he's also going to want you to sign his birth certificate. I assume you already have a name picked out?"

"Of course. He's going to be named after his father, DeShawn Jr."

I wait until the doctor is gone and the baby is fast asleep before I ask Uncle Fresh, "Did they catch him?"

"Nah Babygirl, they didn't catch him. I believe that Lafu already had an exit route before he came back into the mansion. There's no way that he could have gotten past all those guards undetected unless he has more than just video monitors hidden behind those walls."

"You mean like a secret passageways or something?"

"Yea, I think so. I know for a fact that he had the mansion specially designed and built from the ground up. Same thing with the club. He always creates an emergency escape route in case the day comes when the government finds out of his existence."

"Just like with the Safe Room."

"Exactly. Lafu is very crafty. That's part of the reason why I haven't removed all of the lipstick cameras yet. We have them wired to our central database with someone watching them around the clock. Of course we've already removed the ones out of the inappropriate areas like bedrooms and personal bathrooms, but we were hoping that he did exactly what he did, and we could catch him on camera. You must have walked in and caught him in the middle of something when he attacked you. The only problem is, he has cameras everywhere but in his private quarters. That's how we know that the entrance has to be somewhere in there, but so far we haven't been able to find anything."

I digest everything Uncle Fresh is saying to me and instantly conclude, "I don't ever want to go back there again." And just like that the door to my previous life, where I'm the boss lady and club owner closes and I transition into a whole new life where I'm a mother living in a whole new city and state beginning a whole new career.

CHAPTER 15

Click

"Aiight bra, you all set." I say cutting off the clippers and using a towel to knock the excess hair off of Playboi's shirt after I finish trimming his goatee up for him.

"Fa sho. Preciate it. It should be about that time." he says looking up at the clock on the wall.

"Yea, they should be coming to getchu any minute now. You ready?"

"Shit how much more ready can I be. These crackers done railroaded me into taking this time so I'm just ready to get it over with."

Today is Playboi's court date where he either accepts or denies the deal that the state is offering him. His lawyer told him that the state wasn't budging on the probationary deal that they were asking for and going to trial isn't even an option. Someone had paid a lot of money to make it look like he had a strong motive; even had a guy willing to take the stand and testify under oath that Playboi paid him to burn down his club. Basically, he's in a lose lose situation and the state isn't accepting anything less than him doing some time. Although he's only going to end up serving three years on a lesser charge, someone had successfully shut him down and gotten him out the way.

"I feel you bra. One thing about it though, I wish I was in your shoes right now. By the time you get out, I'll probably be just getting started on my bid good."

"Yea you right. I ain't sweatin it. It's just a minor
setback for a major comeback."

"No doubt." I say repeating the phrase that we've been using to uplift each other. "A minor setback for a major comeback." We shake it up and give each other a shoulder bump before Playboi heads back inside our cell to finish getting ready for court.

Me reminding him about the amount of time I'm facing is my way of telling him that things could be worse. There are a lot of brothas who are locked up right now, myself included, who would love to trade places with him. Lately, life has been showing me that there is a positive to be found somewhere in every negative. Like my situation with Dena. Although I didn't get back at Lafu, Lil-Eighty is out there trippin, and I'm headed back to prison, at least now I know that the woman I gave my heart to isn't a snake after all. She didn't have anything to do with my cousin being killed and her decision to protect our child is one that I would have made myself.

Speaking of which, I go into the cell to check the BlackBerry that Dena gave me on the night of her surprise middle of the night visit to see if I have any missed calls or messages. She told me that she brought it for me so that her and I could talk without our conversations being monitored on the jail phones. Her and I have been talking every day since that night except for the past two days, which is why I keep checking my phone. It's unusual for me to go this long without hearing from her.

Playboi is under the bunk when I walk into the cell, no doubt securing all of his contraband in the secret stash spot that he had built under there. Come to find out, not only did he have weed, liquor, and two free world butcher knives, but he also had a cellphone himself. He ended up showing it to me when I came back with mine and offered to let him use it.

"Nah, I'm cool. I got my own." he said reaching under his pillow and pulling it out to show me with that sneaky laugh of his. I couldn't do nothing but shake my head and smile.

"I should've known."

He really threw me for a loop when a bunch of jailors burst into our pod a couple of days later screaming "Shake down! Shakedown! Everybody out of your cell!"

Playboi, who sleeps on the top bunk, jumped down and said, "Give me yo phone and watch the door real quick!" I give him a questioning look. "Hurry up nigga, give me yo phone!"

Knowing that we don't have much time, I hand it to him then go peek out of the narrow window that's built into the cell door. I see four jailors in our pod, two of them going from door to door rushing inmates out of their cells. Seeing that they're only two doors away from ours, I look at Playboi, whose feet are sticking out from under the bunk.

"Hurry up bra."

"Almost got it."

By the time they made it to our cell door, we were
already coming out. Seemed like they searched our cell longer and harder than all the rest. At one point, all four of the jailors were in there searching at one time, which is something I hadn't seen them do to no other cell. After they strip searched us, ransacked our pod, and left, Playboi and I returned to our cell to find it in complete disarray.

"Snitchin ass niggas."

"Man bra, I'm standing here thinking the same damn thing." The good news was they didn't find the stash spot. I got a chance to really see what it looked like a little later that day after we finished getting our cell back in order and it was time to get our phones back out.

"Squat down bra, I want to show you how the spot works just in case there's an emergency and I can't get to it in time." Playboi said from under the bunk.

I kneeled down and watched as he inserted what looked like a straightened paper clip that's bent at the end into a barely-there hole in the wall right between the crease where two bricks meet.

"This is the key." he said explaining. "All you have to do is insert it, turn, and pull." He did just that and I watched in amazement as the entire center piece of the brick slid out. "The beauty of it..." he continued while removing our phones and a bunch of other stuff "is that although the entrance is basically invisible, there's enough room in here to fit ten phones."

"Man that's some double 0 seven shit. How the hell did you get that made?"

He just looked up at me, shrugged, and said "I got a couple of connections."

Now I stand back and wait for him to get done before I go check my phone. I'm more than happy to discover that I have a picture message from Dena waiting for me.

"Bout time." I say sitting on the bed waiting for it to download.

I hear the jailor call out "Eric Frierson, Barry Dean, court!"

"That's me." Playboi says "Time to get this shit over with. Hold the fort down till I come back."

"No doubt."

He walks out of the room just as the picture of a little curly haired, hazel eyed baby with features like mine pops up on the screen of my BlackBerry along with a text that says, 'Guess I'm going to have to be your genie in a bottle for twenty- four hours '.

I'm beside myself with happiness. I got a son! I'm a father! I finally got a little me! I want to tell someone. I want to scream it out loud for the whole world to hear. Instead, I sit there and stare at the picture of my son in amazement. I don't know how long I sit there; long enough for my happiness to fade into sadness at the reality that I'm about to miss out on the beginning and most important years of my lil man's life. His first words, watching him take his first steps, teaching him how to ride a bike and catch a football. That train of thought possesses enough pain to break me down, but the sheer joy of knowing that Deshawn Jr., the newest and only other living member of the Fever legacy, is finally here keeps me smiling despite of.

I call Dena and she answers on the third ring sounding like I woke her up.

"Hello?"

"You in there sleep?"

"Hey Dabo. Yea me and the baby were just taking a nap."

"How you feeling?"

"Tired." she answers with a laugh.

"Congratulations Suabo, you did it. You gave me a healthy baby boy."

Again she giggles "Thank you, but I couldn't have done it without you."

"Not technically, but you did all the real work. You're the Super Woman."

"Aw baby, thank you."

"Did you have a hard labor?" Ten seconds of silence from the other end. "Hello?"

"Oh I'm sorry, it's just that...I didn't have a normal delivery. I actually had a C-Section."

"C-Section?"

"Yea, somehow he got himself tangled up in the umbilical cord and they had to go in and get him."

"Oh okay. Is that why he's here so early, cause if I'm not mistaken he's not due for another month right?"

"Um yea." Something about the way she answered, the sound of her voice doesn't sound right.

"Dena?"

"Huh?"

"What's wrong? What aren't you telling me?" More silence. "Dena?" I hear precious baby noises in the background.

"He's waking up. He's so adorable. Hey mommies creamy baby. Guess who's on the phone. It's daddy. Say hi to daddy." she coos into the phone before I hear more baby sounds in my ear. I picture his little body in her arms stretching and moving around. Then a couple of little whines before he really starts crying. "Oh alright, alright, he's hungry baby. Let me feed him real quick and I'll call you right back."

"Aiight that's cool." We hang up and I lay back on the bunk with the feeling that I just missed something.

So caught up in my thoughts about Dena and the baby, I'm startled when the phone starts vibrating beside me. It's Reece. Her and I have also been communicating on the regular since I got my phone.

"What's up big head?" she clowns when I answer.

"Not shit, just coolin. Sup witchu?"

"Wondering why you ain't tell me yo lil skank had the baby."

"Because I just found out myself, but how you know already?"

"Because it's all over the news. They still trying to figure out how her attacker got in and out of the mansion."

"Her attacker? What the hell you talkin bout?"

"Oh, you really don't know do you. Sooo..." she says sounding more than happy to be the bearer of bad news. "Apparently, someone broke into their mansion and tried to rape yo lil skank. Guess they beat her up because she ended up with a severe concussion and went into labor. They say she alright, but the baby had to be delivered prematurely through emergency C-Section."

"Damn Reece, you don't have to sound so happy about it."

"Oh, I'm glad the baby okay. I just wish that whoever whooped her ass would of at least broke a few bones, knocked out some teeth, or something."

"Listen at you."

"What? If I'm not mistaken you use to feel the same way too?"

"I'm saying tho, she's the mother of my child so I was gone have to get over it eventually anyway. Besides, I'm on my way back to prison. Don't none of that matter to me anymore."

"Uhm hmm, whatever. She came up there and put that pregnant pussy on yo ass and gave you a little phone now you in love all over again."

"You just a hater."

"Call me whatever you want to, I'm still kickin that bitch's ass whenever I see her." I had given Reece the whole rundown, explained Dena's whys and reasons and told her that I had forgiven her. Reece told me how much of a sucker I was and now she clowns me about it every chance she gets.

"So you said that someone beat her up and tried to rape her?" I ask nonchalantly although I'm going crazy inside.

"Yup. And they're still trying to figure out how he got in and out of that big ole mansion without being seen." It doesn't take but a few seconds for me to conclude that this situation has Lafu written all over it.

"Was she able to give the police a description?"

"Nope. The news is saying that she didn't get a good look at the perpetrator and is asking anyone with any information to come forward. You can go see for yourself. It just came on channel seven news."

"Aiight, I'm bout to go check it out now and call you back."

"Okay later."

I hang up and put my phone in the stash spot before going out into the dayroom where three of the guys in the pod with me are sitting in front of the tv watching Jerry Springer.

"Hey, y'all mind if I turn to the news real quick? I'll turn it right back."

One of them answers, "Nah mane, you gone have to wait. We watchin this."

"I feel you bra. I ain't tryna take nothing. I just got word that someone broke into my baby's mother house and tried to rape her. Shit all over the news right now. I'm tryna see what's going on." I didn't realize my mistake until later.

"Oh, you talkin bout ole girl who own 'The Hot Spot' right? Yea, I saw them talking about that earlier." Another one says as he stands up and begins changing the channels.

"Fuck you doing mane? I don't care nothin bout ole girl. I'm watching Jerry."

"Chill out bra. Let this man check on his folks. We gone turn it back."

"Whatever mane." the hostile one says before walking off mumbling under his breath. "Catering to this sucka ass nigga..."

I don't have time to entertain his bullshit. I'm too busy trying to hear what the news reporter is saying.

"Turn it up a little for me bra."

"I gotchu."

I hear the news reporter say,"....as we reported to you earlier, there are still no leads on the suspect who broke in, assaulted, and attempted to rape twenty-four year old club owner, Dena Givens at her residence out on Bear Hill Road Thursday night. Police reports reveal that Miss Givens woke up to use the restroom at approximately three a.m. and was assaulted while returning to her bedroom. The big question that have investigators scratching their heads is, how did the intruder get inside the highly secured twenty- two point five million dollar mansion undetected. Investigators report that no alarms or motion sensors were triggered, nor were there any signs of forced entry. If you have any information that may lead to the arrest of the perpetrator please contact Crime Stoppers at 1-800-..."

The rush of adrenaline coursing through my blood causes a vein to pulse at my temple. I feel my palms begin to sweat as I flex my fingers. Internal anger has me clenching my jaws and gritting my teeth. I can't believe this Jamaican pussy is still busting shots at me after all he's already done. Trying to rape Dena while she's carrying my seed is the ultimate violation.

The news flashes several different pictures of Dena across the screen from advertisements of her franchise. The highlighted glamour shots of her face enhancing her already alluring skin tone and exotic beauty.

"That's your baby mama right there?" the guy next to me asks.

"Yea." I answer without taking my eyes off the screen.

"No disrespect, but she bad den a muthafucka. Whoever did that shit is foul."

The lock turning in the main door to the pod draws everyone's attention. In walks Playboi and an older guy in our pod who went to court with him. I make eye contact and hit him with the head nod. He nods back then heads straight to our cell. I let him be because I know he probably ain't trying to do nothing more than lay back and get his mind right after having to go in there and face those white folks.

I turn back around to finish watching the news. A few seconds later I hear Playboi's voice.

"Fuck you doing coming outta my cell nigga?"

"I wasn't in yo cell. I just looked in there to see if I could find my dictionary." I turn around in time to see Playboi exchanging words with the same cat who was talking shit about me watching the news a little while ago.

"Yo dictionary? Fuck would yo dictionary be doing in my cell? That don't even make sense. And even if you did think that something of yours was in there, you could have asked that man over there sitting in front of that tv." he says pointing at me. "You ain't have no business in my cell partna."

I get up and go over to where they are.

"Damn nigga, you all in my cell when my back turned?"

"Like I said, I was looking for my dictionary, but what you getting all up like yo gone do something for? Y'all niggas ain't talkin bout shit."

I just found out that Lafu had beat up and tried to rape Dena. Playboi just came from court accepting time for something he didn't do. We're both frustrated and on edge. The dark-skinned, stocky dude standing in front of us had picked the right time to say the wrong thing.

The older brother who had come back from court with Playboi steps in and says "Now young man you know you wrong for going into their cell without asking. They supposed to be on your ass right now."

"They ain't gone do shit. Fuck them and fuck you too old..."

Before he gets a chance to finish his sentence, I'm leaning into his jaw with a right hook. He bounces off the wall and Playboi catches him with a two piece that sends him down on one knee in front of us. I finish him off by grabbing his head and driving three consecutive knees into his face knocking him out cold.

"Punk ass nigga."

"Come on bra." Playboi taps my arm and we go inside our cell and close the door. "Fuck that nigga." We look around and instantly notice the signs of someone rambling.

"Looking for a dictionary my ass. What he thought it was under my mattress or something?" I say noticing that my blanket isn't tucked the way that I left it. "I ought to go back out there and stomp his ass up off that floor."

"Naw peep game tho, the only reason I saw him was because his partna stopped me on the way to the cell talking bout could I sell him a half ounce. I instantly knew something was up because I don't even talk to dude like that. That's when I saw his boy coming out of our cell."

"Which one stopped you?"

It's three of them that be together all the time; the one who just got his ass whooped, another buffed up dude who be working out all the time, and a tall, skinny, light-skinned cat.

"The tall one."

"Might as well go whoop his ass too." I say still pumped and already heading for the door.

"Hold on, let's grab these blades first." Playboi goes into the spot and comes back out with the two knives he had stashed. "Here." he says handing me one. We tuck them and step back out into the dayroom.

I notice that the big mouth one who was knocked out on the floor and both of his partnas are nowhere to be seen. The other three guys who live in the pod with us are all posted up in the TV area waiting to see what's going to happen next.

"They all down there in that last cell on the end." the older guy who spoke up earlier whispers to us. "And watch that tall fellow too. I saw him with a shank earlier."

"Preciate that old school, but we ain't worried about these fools." I say ready for whatever.

A few seconds later the door to the last cell opens and they all come out looking like they've just finished eating Super Mario mushrooms or some shit.

Big mouth says, "So y'all niggas want to jump huh?"

What's up now?!" And comes straight at me fist first.

I duck his first swing and catch him in the ribcage with a solid blow that leaves his mouth hanging open. Another body blow has him grabbing trying to wrap me up and stop my arms from swinging. He outweighs me by about twenty pounds and uses his weight to overpower and wrestle me backwards against the iron table near the tv where the other three guys are sitting. They all scramble out of the way. Then Big mouth lands a hard fist to my mouth that fills it with the coppery taste of blood.

I grab the knife out of my waistband and sink it into the back of his thigh as far as it will go. He instantly lets go and falls back screaming like a bitch.

"Aaaggh, he stabbed me! This nigga stabbed me!"

I see that Playboi has the buffed dude on the

ground giving him the business raining blows down on his face. That's when I spot the tall light-skinned cat coming up behind him with a shank in his hand.

"Playboi, behind you!"

He turns around and rolls out of the way just in time for the shank to miss his back and land in his arm.

By the time I make it over to them, Playboi is on his back on the ground wrestling with the tall dude over the shank while his partna is recovering and climbing to his feet.

Without hesitation I kick the tall one in the ass and stab him twice in the back of the head before I spin on the buffed one.

"What fool, run up!" He throws his hands up in front of him and starts back peddling. I turn back around to see Playboi getting back to his feet holding his arm.

"You good?" I ask him.

"Yea I'm straight. Pussy ass nigga stabbed me." He pulls his knife out and we stand side by side.

"Wassup, what y'all niggas wanna do?"

"Put the knives down." The big mouthed one who started all of this says while limping backwards. His whole right pant leg is covered in blood. Playboi has a stab wound in his arm and a small cut over his right eye. My mouth is busted. The buffed one's face looks like he forgot to bob and weave with one of his eyes already swole shut and his nose twisted and bleeding. Looks like he's missing a couple of teeth too. Tall light-skinned has blood leaking out of his head yet he's still frowned up, gripping his shank, and looking like he still wants some more. Everybody is battle wounded, but it looks like the war is far from over.

Again I ask, "Whatchall wanna do?" as Playboi and I close in on them.

"Come on." The tall one with the shank says.

Just then, we hear a bunch of footsteps outside of the pod followed by the key turning in the lock.

"Drop the knives! Everybody on the ground!" One of the jailors scream as five of them rush inside the pod carrying pepper spray guns. Nobody hesitates to follow instructions knowing that they won't hesitate to spray us all. The jailors cuff us and take us out one by one. I'm taken to a dark, nasty, one-man cell filled with spider webs and a bunch of foreign insects that have me continuously scratching and rubbing over the next couple of weeks. Outside of the flap opening and closing to deliver and pick up my daily meals, I've had no contact or communication with anyone outside of this cell.

****

Late into the wee hours of my twenty-third night in the hole, the flap to my cell opens jarring me from my sleep. Something drops inside, hits the floor and rolls, then the flap is abruptly shut back. I lay still listening until the retreating footsteps fade. Another couple of seconds of my brain processing and separating what just happened from my previous unconscious state of mind. It doesn't take long for my eyes to adjust and identify the white oval shaped object laying on the floor not far from me. I get up and go pick it up. Just like I suspected, it's a ball of socks except this one is three times bigger than the size two socks would be. One after another, I begin unfolding them. Seven socks later, I'm left holding a single sock with something heavy inside. I'm more than overjoyed to reach inside and pull out my BlackBerry, a small tightly wrapped and taped package, and a folded piece of paper with a strip of tape around it. I peel the tape and begin reading

What up my guy,

I just found out that I'm shipping out in the morning and wanted to drop you a couple lines and put you up on game. Your phone and an ounce of weed should be in here with this kite. (Just a lil sumsum to keep your mind elevated). I had some of my people's put the squeeze on one of the niggas that we got into it with and found out the whole scoop on what went down that day. One of them niggas (the one you left limping) go by the name Pipe G. He has a cousin on the streets named Lil-Eighty who has it out for you. Once he found out that you was in the pod with his family, he put a price on your head and had the nigga laying on you waiting to catch you slippin. The only reason Pipe G hadn't made his move yet is because he knew I was getting it in and wanted to find my stash spot first. Guess he figured he could get two for the price of one. Somehow you slipped and exposed the fact that you had a phone while I was at court, so dude figured it was the perfect time to make his move. Don't sweat it tho, I got some of my people laying on him right now. He violated me so now it's personal.

Anyway bra, keep ya head up and stay focused. This is just a minor setback for a major comeback. You'll be hearing from me real soon........

Playboi

I put the kite down and let what I just read settle in my mind. There's no doubt about it, Lil-Eighty has officially flipped the script. And the crazy part about it is, I don't even know why. I had mad love for him before all of this went down and as far as I knew the feeling was mutual. From the time we had linked back up, I had kept it more than a hundred with him and considered him to be my number one partna next to Mechi. Crazy how as soon as you think you've got it all figured out; life throws you a curve ball. Guess it is what it is though. I pick up the kite and read it again. Playboi said that I'd somehow exposed the fact that I had a phone while he was in court. But how though? From day one it was understood that we couldn't let anyone else in the pod know we had phones because it would start a chain reaction. For that reason, I'm always careful not to talk loud while using it. Especially at night when it's quiet. Playboi is so cautious with his phone, that I've never even heard him talk on it. All he ever does is text. It was early afternoon when he went to court. The tv's were on and everyone was up conversating so I know no one could have heard me talking. Then it hits me. I was so caught off guard with what Reece told me about Dena, that I reacted without thinking. I had left my room and went straight into the dayroom and told them that I had just found out that someone had attacked my baby's mother and it was on the news right then. It didn't take a rocket scientist to figure out that I didn't have a television in my room so how could I possibly know what was on the news right then. No one had saw me use the jailhouse phone either so how else could I have found out such immediate information from my room? I was definitely slipping.

CHAPTER 16

Finesse
Finesse da Game

  The beat of the new Usher, Lil-John and Ludacris banger 'Lovers and Friends' pulsates through my body as I cruise through the Forrest City streets on the passenger side of Mechi's new burgundy 2004 Avalanche sitting on twenty-fours. His amped up system pumping the sound crisp and clear as the bass thumps and I sing along with the words.

  "Tell me agaaiin...."

  Smoke clouds from our second blunt hang in the air as we continue to smoke and ride through the mid-afternoon Spring day. Lately, I've been spending more and more time with Mechi. Especially since Dena had abandoned me by packing her and the baby up and moving to Atlanta, Georgia, claiming that she didn't feel comfortable here since the incident with Lafu. I can't lie, knowing that she would leave here and not take me with her hurts me to my core. I remember a time when even the thought of her going anywhere without me was laughable. But Dena didn't even try to protest or convince me when I tried to play a little hard to get the first time that she asked me to go with her. Instead she responded with a halfhearted, "Well it's your choice. I can't force you to come if you don't want to." And continued packing.

  I mean damn, have I really become that unimportant to her? We used to be so close. There was once a time I was at the center of her world, where you couldn't find one of us without the other but, ever since this nigga Click came into the picture things have been different. And even after using Lil-Eighty to get Click out the way, she still found a reason to leave me, so it was all for nothing.

  Mechi turns down the music and asks me, "What's on ya mind shawty?"

  "Nothing, I'm just over here vibing to the music and zoning."

  "I can tell because you been boss hoggin the blunt for like five minutes. Can I smoke with you?"

  "Oh, shit my bad." I say with a laugh as I pass it. "My mind is just zoned out."

  "What you over there thinking about?"

  "Everything and nothing at the same time."

"I know what you thinking about." he says with a raised eyebrow giving me the side eye.

"What Mr.-think-you-know-me?"

"You over there thinking about my dick."

"What?!" I bust out laughing. "Nigga please, ain't nobody thinking about yo dick."

"Yea you is. You over there thinking about how turned up my sex game was last night."

"What-ev-err, you was aiight. It wasn't all that." I say smiling from ear to ear knowing that I'm lying through my teeth. Last night me and this nigga literally put on an exhibition from a hotel balcony, having crazy sex while the people on the next balcony over sat there and boldly watched. I don't remember ever being that turned on or cumming so many times.

"You turned to the exorcist on the dick. I thought you were possessed or some shit."

I can't stop myself from blushing and smiling. "You had a bitch feeling some thangs."

"You got me feeling some thangs right now sitting over there lookin all good. Lips all glossed up."

"Oh yea." I say getting turned on all over again and going with the moment. I reach over into his lap and pull out his manhood.

Just then an old-school U.G.K. joint blares from Mechi's phone.

"Hello?" he answers just as I'm wrapping my lips around him. "Ah shit, whatup Click....not shit. Just out here riding around chasing this paper." Hearing Click's name makes my ears perk up as I continue doing what I do. "....in the hole for what? Who, Lil-Eighty?" He puffs the blunt and listens for a while before saying, ".... yea, I been peeped that nigga was sour when he left us hanging on that last move.... right right, but don't even trip. It's on sight whenever I see his ass....no doubt...That's what's up, consider it done.... aight. One." Mechi hangs up then decides to find a spot to park so I can finish handling my business. Although he seems to be enjoying my deep throating skills, I can still tell that his mood has changed.

"What's wrong baby?" I stop and ask. "Seems like your mind is a million miles away."

"I'm sorry shawty. I'm just really trippin off of this phone call that I got."

"What happened?"

"That was Click. He just told me some foul shit about one of the guys on the team."

"Let me guess. His name is Lil-Eighty, right?"

"Damn was you listening that hard?"

"Nah, but I saw something a few weeks ago that had me debating if I should tell you or not."

"Wassup, why wouldn't you tell me?"

"Cuz, I don't want you to do nothing stupid."

"Don't play with me shawty. Whatchu see?"

"Alright, but you didn't get this from me. I met one of your boys at the mansion about a month ago. The dark-skinned heavy set one with gold in his mouth. I recognized him from that night you brought them all up there witchu to the Peabody. He was there meeting with Lafu and introduced himself to me as Lil-Eighty."

"Lafu?" It takes a moment for it to sink in. "Fuck would he be doing meeting with La.....oh so that's where that nigga been getting all of that work from. He been playing both sides the whole time." He sits nodding to himself as he continues to smoke like things were finally starting to make sense. Mechi sits there quiet for so long that I eventually just turn the music back up and finish sucking his dick. Afterwards we swing by the barbecue joint on Franklin St. to pick up some red links with cold slaw and fries to get our munchies off before going to pick up some more weed. Mechi parks in his favorite little duck off spot on the side street right across from the main parking lot of the barbecue joint. I stay in the car while he goes inside to pick up our orders.

Soon as I'm alone, I pull out and check my phone which has been at the bottom of my Chanel purse on silent since yesterday afternoon when Mechi first picked me up. Just as I expected, there are several missed calls and messages from Lil-Eighty. He's been blowing me up like crazy for the past couple of weeks. Since Click is already locked up facing football numbers, Lil-Eighty is no longer any use to me, so I've been giving him the cold shoulder. Now, I dial his number knowing that it's the perfect time to execute the final part of my plan and tie up all loose ends.

"Finesse, wassup mane. I've been trying to contact you all week. Why you ain't been answering my calls?"

"Cuz I've been out of town. I just got back today." I lie easily.

"Well I'm glad you finally back cuz I need the hook-up like yesterday. I've been outta work for over a week missing all kinds of money."

"No problem daddy you know I gotchu." I say although Lafu has been missing in action since the day of the massacre at 'The Hot Spot ' and there's no way for me to possibly get him anymore drugs. "Let me make a couple of calls real quick."

"Okay, but make sure you hit me back and let me know something."

"I gotchu." I hang up just as Mechi is crossing the street towards the truck carrying a white bag.

"I'm bout to demolish these polishes." he says while climbing in the truck and handing me our food. "These bitches smelling good!"

"They sho is." I say pulling out and separating our food. We don't hesitate to get our grub on. Something about chowing down on some good hood food after getting your smoke on just makes it all taste better.

The U.G.K. ringtone on Mechi's phone sounds out again as we sit watching all of the traffic coming and going across the street in the barbecue joints parking lot and stuffing our faces.

After slurping the excess condiments off of his fingers, Mechi answers his phone still chewing a mouth full of food.

"Hello...Tayo my man what's happenin...yea I'm headed yo way now...Okay that'll work too. I'm at the barbecue spot on Franklin right now, so you can just meet me up here...aight see you in a minute." He hangs up.

"Hey boo, you got some wet wipes in here?" I ask while frowning and holding my stomach. "I got the B.G.z."

"Nah, but you bet not be pooting in my new truck I know that."

"Boy ain't nobody poot in yo truck, but you bes believe if I had to, I would let it go right here on yo new leather seats." I say before sticking my tongue out and climbing out of his truck.

"Stankin ass." is the last thing I hear him say before I push the door shut. I flip him the bird and put a little extra twist in my hips as I walk in front of his truck. I cross the street over to the barbecue parking lot where it seems like more and more people are coming to get their eat on.

Inside the warm food flavored aroma greets me along with a long line of black people waiting to get them some soul food. I maneuver around them and into the women's restroom where surprisingly, I find myself alone. Just to make sure, I check both of the stalls before calling Lil-Eighty back.

"Hello?" he answers eagerly on the first ring.

"Hey daddy."

"Wassup, tell me something good."

"Everything good. I'm with Lafu right now. He wants you to meet us at that Italian restaurant out by the interstate, but could you please do me a big favor first?"

"Wassup beautiful, whatchu need?"

"Can you stop at the barbecue place on Franklin and pick me up a Catfish plate? I am not Italian. I need some soul food in my life."

"Yo ass. How you bougie and ghetto at the same time?"

"Nigga, I ain't bougie. I'm from the streets."

He laughs. "Yo family live in a big ass mansion and own a multi-million-dollar franchise but you from the streets? Yea, aight."

"Whatever nigga, just hurry yo ass up because we already on our way up there and make sure you grab some extra hot sauce with my food too."

Still laughing he says, "Aight, I'm on my way." and hangs up.

Lil-Eighty has been bugging me to set him up another meeting with Lafu ever since the first one had gotten canceled. At first, I kept giving him the run around telling him how busy a man Lafu is and how rare it is for him to agree to meet with anyone face to face. Then I just stopped answering my phone for him altogether. I know Lil-Eighty is so desperate to meet Lafu that he's probably breaking every traffic law there is right now trying to get there. I hurry out of the diner and back out to Mechi's truck.

"That was quick." He says when I climb back in.

"It's so nasty in there that I couldn't even use it. Stuff all on the walls. Yuck!"

He gives me a look. "Witcho bougie ass."

Just then a huge white milk truck with tinted windows pulls up on the side of Mechi's Avalanche, sounding like it has something under the hood that's more suited for a racing car. When the window rolls down, I have to take a second look to make sure I'm really looking at what I'm seeing.

"Mechi my nigga, what the fuck goin on!" he explodes displaying a big Kool-Aid smile. Light-skinned with blonde dreads dancing around his shoulders, he's full of energy. The single white contact lens in his right eye along with the pyramid tattooed boldly on his forehead is what's giving me a moment of pause. I've never seen anyone who looks quite as eccentric.

"Tayo, just the man I'm lookin fo!" Mechi greets back just as animated as him. "What's good?"

"From the looks of it that polish sausage over there you eating. You got that outta there?" he asks indicating the barbecue joint across the street.

"Hell yea. I got another one over here if you want it."

"Hell yea." Tayo climbs out of the milk truck leaving me once again struck by his appearance. He has to be at least six-eight with a lanky build that contradicts his massive size. Dressed down in all black from head to toe, he puts me in the mind of the Undertaker as he steps up to Mechi's window grabbing the polish sausage. "Thanks, my nigga."

"No problem but let me ask you a question. What made you choose to drive a milk truck outta all vehicles?" I don't know how Mechi knew but I was wondering the same thing.

"Aw man this is just my means for nurturing my neighborhoods. You know weed is nutritious like milk so I'm like the milk man in this bitch riding around making sure all of my people stay with a healthy supply of what they need to ensure another good day in the hood."

"Nigga you wild." Mechi says as we both laugh. "I hope you got some fresh milk for me right now cuz I think I'm gone need about ten gallons. Ya feel me?"

"Most definitely, I got something for you. Come check me out."

"Get out and come look at this shit." Mechi says to me as he begin climbing out of the truck. "This nigga is like the mad scientist of weed or some shit." I get out and we both stand waiting while Tayo parks his truck on the opposite side of the street.

We end up with both doors of the milk truck open, Tayo on the driver's side, Mechi and I on the passenger side.

Tayo says, "Aight check it out, I know you told me that you wanted some of that Arizona popcorn, but I got something here that's a little better than that."

"Aw shit, don't tell me you finally got that Northern Light that I been asking you about?" Mechi asks rubbing his hands together with a kid-in-the-candy store kind of excitement.

"Nah, I got something that's a little better than that too." Tayo says reaching under the seat with his right hand. He uses his left hand to pull up and the top half of his seat comes up like the hood of a car. Underneath it looks like the display case of a jewelry store except the nuggets that I'm looking at ain't diamonds and gold. All I see is buds. A bunch of different colored, exotic looking bud nuggets covered by a glass case. At least twenty different kinds, all sitting in little jars looking to be about three to four grams a piece each with a label.

"Let me introduce you to the next best thing on the weed scene. This my nigga is Kush or what me and my partnas like to call that 'Loud Pack '.

"Kush? What the hell is that? I ask with a laugh.

"Sounds like the name of some cologne."

"Trust me baby, you smoke some of this and you definitely gone be able to smell it on yo clothes. Kush is a new strand of weed that's taking over the game. It comes from the Northern region of Afghanistan in a place that's actually called Kush. What me and my team have been doing is taking the Kush strands and cross breeding it with other strands of Indica weed and creating some of the most potent weed ever manufactured. Now we got Blueberry Kush, Cotton Candy Kush, Lemon Lime, Coconut, you name it we got it." he says proudly pointing out the different brands of weed.

"That shit sound fly." Mechi says getting even more excited. "What's the street value?"

"Depending on what you getting, anywhere from seventy-five hundred to ten thousand a pound. Wholesale value of about four or five thousand."

I let out a whistle.

Mechi says, "This shit gotta be fie to be selling for that much."

"Don't take my word for it. Try it out for yourself." Tayo produces a cool looking woodgrain and brass weed pipe with a built in lighter and a black bud of reefa with red and gold hairs in it that resembles those on a deadly spider sealed in a little vacuumed package. "I call this that 'Black Widow Kush'." He cuts the package open and the smell of weed grows so strong that it seems like you can catch a contact by simply breathing.

"Damn that shit loud."

"Why you think we call it that 'Loud Pack'?"

He slides the brass lid on the top of the one-hitter back, stuffs the exotic buds inside and passes it to Mechi. "Here try it."

"Black Widow? I'm damn near scared to smoke it with a name like that."

"Well I'm not." I say taking it out of his hand and firing it up. The smoke is thick and its effect instant. "Damn! Now this the shit we need to be buying right here. How much for some of this?"

"Sorry sweetheart," he says easing the pipe out of my hand "but this ain't for sale. All I got is a personal stash of this." He tries to hand it to Mechi so he can get a toke, but Mechi's attention is elsewhere.

"What's wrong baby?" I ask following his eyes with mine.

Across the street, Lil-Eighty's Lexus GS400 is just now pulling into the parking lot of the barbecue place. Without any words, Mechi races over to his Avalanche and reaches under the driver's seat pulling out a big ass chrome Desert Eagle.

"Wassup bra?" Tayo asks going over to Mechi with me following two steps behind. He sees the gun in Mechi's hand, and the killer look in his eyes and says, "If you finna pop it off, I got something over there that's gone handle it a lot better than that little shit right there."

"Oh, I'm definitely bout to pop it off."

"Step into my office then." Tayo says once again

showcasing his joker smile and seeming more than happy to be contributing to a deadly cause.

Playing my role, I say, "Come on baby let's just go before you do something stupid." My words fall on deaf ears as Mechi and Tayo are already headed back over to the milk truck. By the time I make it over there, the tall dude with the blonde dreads and white contact lens in his eye is pulling something from under his front seat that looks like it came from the same place that he got his weed from.

"This my nigga, is a modified AR-15 with the fitted

scope and enough accuracy to hit a mosquito from a mountaintop. Only way you'll miss with this bitch is if you do it on purpose. Wait a minute tho...I forgot you got a prosthetic. You definitely ain't gone be able to shoot it with that."

"I don't see why not." Mechi says laying his Desert Eagle down on the inside of the milk truck.

"Because ain't no way you gone be able to control the recoil from an AR and maintain a steady aim with only one hand."

"Wanna make a bet?" Mechi asks grabbing the high powered assault rifle out of Tayo's hand and rounding the truck to the passenger side. We watch as he struggles to brace the gun on the open door and find a comfortable position to shoot without being able to grip with his right hand.

"Hell, yeah I wanna bet. You drop ole boy with that, and I'll give you a pound of that Black Widow. But if you miss, you owe me ten G's nigga."

"You ain't said nothing but a word." Mechi says aiming at the parking lot across the street while looking through the scope.

I look to see Lil-Eighty just getting out of his car and heading inside the barbecue place.

"Mechi, you're not really going to shoot him out here in front of all these people, are you?"

He ignores me and asks Tayo, "Why is it all blurry? I can't see shit."

"That's because you gotta use that little knob on the side to adjust the sights and bring the picture in clear." That simple act alone proves to be a challenge for Mechi and his prosthetic. Tayo stands there getting a kick out of watching him try to balance the gun, look through the scope and turn the knob all at the same time.

Finally, Mechi says, "Got it! I can see the stretch marks on lil mama ass cheeks over there."

"Mechi, would you please put that thing down let's go before somebody sees you."

"Be cool shawty. Let me handle this lil business real quick and get this weed for us to smoke." I can't do nothing but shake my head. This fool is dead serious about committing murder and winning this bet. Although I'm the one who orchestrated this whole thing, my nerves are shot sitting here knowing what's about to happen. Especially when Lil-Eighty finally walks back out carrying my Catfish plate and a soda in his hands.

My heartbeat can't help but to speed up as I watch Mechi squat down behind the passenger door of the milk truck and take aim.

It all happens so quickly.

Lil-Eighty amongst a group of others walking towards his Lexus looking good and probably feeling like money before the sound of a single gunshot shatters the air. Blood explodes out of his shoulder and his body does a backwards zombie dance, slinging catfish and hot sauce everywhere. There's a moment of disbelief followed by panic as the people around him begin screaming and running for cover.

Tayo's words prove to be true. The AR jumps out of Mechi's hand and clatters to the ground as soon as he fires it. I don't hesitate to take cover behind the Avalanche. Tayo jumps behind the wheel of his milk truck and starts it up. To my horror, I look up to find that not only is Lil-Eighty back up and climbing into his car, but most of the people outside are already pointing and looking in our direction. Although we're parked on the side street, the burgundy Avalanche and huge milk truck are sticking out like sore thumbs and this nigga had just set it off in broad daylight.

"Mechi bring yo crazy ass on!" I yell. Instead of listening, he reaches into the cab of the milk truck and comes back out firing the Desert Eagle. I watch as bullets knock gaping holes in the windshield of Lil-Eighty's Lexus as it starts up and comes screeching out of the parking lot. Mechi has enough time to come from behind the milk truck and dump two more slugs through Lil-Eighty's back windshield before his Lexus careens up the block and out of sight.

CHAPTER 17

Dena
June 2005 1 year later

    The heat from the afternoon sun greets me as soon as I step out of the air-conditioned lobby of the Peachtree Towers where I've been living in downtown Atlanta for the past year. The news forecast predicted a high of ninety-two degrees which is the perfect temperature for what I have in mind today.

    "Come on Creamy Baby, you ready to go see the fish?" I ask my overactive one year old son who's holding onto my hand and teetering along beside me.

    "Fish." he answers in his usual one word baby monotone.

    "Yes baby we're going to the Aquarium to see the fish."

    "Fish, fish, fish!" he chants while jumping up and down and pointing at the tall abstract building that he's so fascinated with. Being that the Aquarium is located right across from the Peachtree Towers, he has a clear view of it from our twelve story condominium window. He loves to stand marveling at it for sometimes an hour at a time. Since today is Saturday and the first official day of summer, I decide that it's the perfect day to surprise him with his first real up close view of underwater life.

    "Ma ma!" he squawks excitedly while yanking on my hand and pointing as we cross the street. "Dook."

    "Yes baby, I see it. Come on you wanna go see the fish?" I scoop him up into my arms and kiss his chubby cheek as I head towards the entrance. For the next three hours my son and I tour the amazing sights of the underwater world and mysterious creatures. Nothing gives me greater joy than seeing the wonder and awe on his face as we stand in the underwater tunnel watching the Beluga Whales swimming gracefully through the water.

    "Ma ma, fish."

    "No baby, that's a whale."

    "Waal." he utters in wide eyed amazement. He's just as taken with the sharks and dolphins who streak back and forth making sharp turns and maneuvers through the water, but his reaction to the penguins is what takes the cake.

    I can't control my laughter watching my creamy

baby jumping up and down and clapping at seeing the penguins playing around the pool pushing each other in and belly-flopping into the water.

By the time we leave the Aquarium, we've both worked up quite an appetite. I take him with me to this five star restaurant that I discovered called Canoe, that overlooks the Chattahoochee River. I normally come here alone in between trips to the Gateway Center or Peachtree and Pine. Those are the places I spend most of my weekdays doing charity work and feeding the homeless. Today is the weekend, which I reserved especially for me and my son to spend quality time together.

My transition from the life I was living to the one I'm living now wasn't an easy one. I spent my first eight months in Atlanta bonding with my creamy baby and adjusting to motherhood. Going from being the "Boss Lady" dealing with strippers, a bunch of drunk ass niggas, and drug dealers, to a single mother living alone in a new city was quite a big step for me. Especially without Finesse. This is the first time since her and I were kids that we've been apart, but something inside of me keeps telling me that it's time for me to let her go. Besides talking to her, Uncle Fresh, and Click over the phone, I mostly stay to myself.

I knew that I would have to eventually get out and do something with myself, so I hired a nanny to watch my son while I started venturing out on my own exploring the city. As I walked down Peachtree Street, I couldn't believe the amount of homeless people I encountered. People panhandling and inhabiting the downtown area like they had traveled down every road in life and had come to the conclusion that the dead end spot that they were in now was their final destination. It broke my heart to see so many people who had given up on life and lost all ambition to succeed. Right then, I truly understood what compelled my mother to do what she did. Knowing that I had a nice cozy condo with all the luxuries of wealth while these people out here don't even have a roof over their head or enough money to afford a ninety-nine cent cheeseburger bothered me. Even more so, all the coldhearted people who walked passed them with no empathy at all. One of the main reasons why my mother had begun to despise her own wealth. After her death, I began adopting her same outlook. I started spending the majority of my days and even some of my nights donating money and helping out at organizations such as The Salvation Army, Goodwill, and Homeless Shelters around the city. The more I dealt with Atlanta's overwhelming population of homeless people, the more passionate I became about them. And the less time I spent with my son. Eventually, I had to set some limits on the time I spent away from him. Now the evenings and weekends are reserved especially for him.

"You want some ketchup baby?" I ask my son who sits next to me in a highchair overly excited that our food has finally arrived. I squirt a generous amount on the side of his plate knowing that he prefers to dip his fries rather than have it applied directly on top.

"Fies." he says grabbing a handful, dipping them, and trying to stuff them in his mouth but dropping the majority on the front of his shirt.

"No." I admonish. "One at a time. Remember how I showed you?" I pick one up and demonstrate.

"Fies!" he shouts again slapping the tabletop flipping his plate and slinging food everywhere.

"No baby! Look what you did." I get up and begin cleaning up the mess.

"Fies?" he points at the wasted food on the floor.

"You wasted them now they ain't no good." As soon as he sees me throwing them into the trash can, he begins falling out and having a fit.

"Fiies!" His cries echo through the restaurant causing people to look in our direction.

"Shhh. Okay okay look, you can have some of mommy's." I try to put one into his mouth, but he rejects it and cries even harder already too caught up in the throes of his tantrum.

My first time alone with him and experiencing one of his tantrums, I almost came undone. No matter what I tried, he wouldn't stop crying. After making sure he had a full belly, dry diaper, no fever or any signs of physical harm, I didn't know what else to do. Desperate and at my wits end, I picked him up and began singing the first song that came to mind. Surprisingly, his cries stopped immediately. From that day forward, that song has never failed to do the trick.

"Okay Creamy Baby." I say removing the tabletop to the highchair and picking him up. "Come're mommy sorry. Shhh." I hold him close to my bosom and begin singing what has now become his favorite song. "If I could write a silly love sooong yea...I would write it all about yoooouuu.." And as always his cries instantly begin to dissipate.

I close my eyes and rock him gently while harmonizing the words to the old school song that my mother use to play for me; 'Silly Love Song' by the group Enchantment. By the time I make it to the bridge of the song, I'm pretty sure he's already fallen asleep, but I still continue rocking and singing until the last note. I'm more than shocked to hear applauding when I'm done.

I open my eyes and look around to find every set of eyes in the restaurant focused on me. Had I let myself get that loud? So engrossed in my moment of comforting my son that I had no idea that I had drawn attention to myself. All the patrons and even some of the waiters are smiling and clapping their hands. I'm so embarrassed that I don't know what to do. It feels like my cheeks are on fire.

"Oh um...thank you." I manage lamely before quickly sitting down wishing I could find a hole to climb into. "See what you did?" I say to my son who's sleeping soundly in my arms without a care in the world.

"Excuse me Miss."

I look up to find a tall, slim guy with a milk-chocolate-skin tone standing beside my table looking down at me. His pleasant smile and youthful face are disarming.

"Yes?"

"I hope you don't mind me saying but, you got it."

"Got what?"

"It."

"Huh?" I give him a confused look.

"Look, I don't mean no harm, but you just single

handedly hypnotized me and everyone in this restaurant without even trying. Your voice is amazing. You got that "It" factor that everyone in my line of work is looking for."

"Thank you, "I say" but what exactly is it that you do?"

"Marko Humphrey." he says retrieving a business card from his wallet and handing it to me. "But everybody call me Chicago Slim. I'm a talent scout." I look at his business card and see that it names him as a Talent Scout, Promoter, Artist, Author, and Relationship Specialist.

"Wow. This is impressive. You really do all of these things?"

"I sure do. And then some. Have you ever thought about going into the studio and recording?"

"Sure. I've thought about it, but that's about as far as I've gone with it." I say with a laugh. "Now actually doing it, I doubt if that will ever happen."

"Only if you don't want it to. I just so happen to have over five hundred hours of paid studio time. You ever heard of Blue Room Studio?"

"Actually, I haven't. I'm kinda new to Atlanta."

"Oh, well it's on Bishop Street in Northwest. If you're interested, I would love to get you in there and let you listen to a couple of tracks to see if any of them are appealing to you. Do you write?"

"What, you mean songs?"

"Um huh."

"No. I write a little poetry from time to time, but I've never actually composed a song."

"Well songs are just words of poetry put to a beat and turned to music, so actually you have."

"I've never heard it put quite like that before."

"Music is simply rhythm and melody, but the words are the heartbeat to the melody that makes the song. It's what gives the song meaning."

"You have a way with words. You're definitely a writer."

"Thank you Miss..."

"Oh I'm sorry, how rude of me. Givens, Dena Givens." I say extending my hand for him to shake. "Please have a seat."

"Thank you." He shakes my hand and takes the seat across from me. "So are you gone let me hear one of your pieces?"

"What, right now?"

"Yea, why not?"

"No. I think I've made enough of a spectacle of myself for one day."

"Nonsense. You've made these people's day in here. Look around." I do and notice several people still stealing curious glances in our direction. The ones that I actually make eye contact with give me shy smiles and nods.

"See, I told you. You got it." His inspiration and positive energy feels good and I can't stop myself from smiling.

Chicago Slim and I end up sharing a meal together while we continue discussing music, poetry, politics, people, relationships and a number of other topics that naturally come up. I find his conversation to be intriguing and him to be a genuine person. And definitely a gentleman insisting on paying for our meal and not letting me take the city bus, which I've become accustomed to doing. I gently refuse his offer to give me a ride.

"Are you sure?" he asks as we exit the restaurant together.

"I appreciate it, but I'm fine. Really. Plus, I love using city transportation."

He laughs. "I don't think I've ever heard anyone say that before."

"I think it's exciting, plus it gives me a chance to sightsee without having to wrestle with traffic. You have to understand that this is all very new to me. Prior to coming to Atlanta, I've never experienced riding a bus or a train before."

"Really? Why not?"

I don't want to tell him that it's because I've always had my own driver and a multiple of luxury cars to choose from, so I simply say, "I just moved from a small town in Arkansas that didn't have buses or trains."

"So that's where you're originally from, Arkansas?"

"It's where I've been living for the past six years, but I've been moving around basically my whole life."

"Let me guess, you're a military baby right?"

"Something like that." I answer evasively. "Come on Creamy Baby." I call to my son who is walking in between us but struggling to keep up.

"If you don't mind me asking, why do you call him Creamy Baby?"

"Because his skin complexion is so creamy and smooth like warm peanut butter spread evenly across a slice of bread."

"Spoken like a true writer." We share another laugh.

He ends up escorting me to my stop and waiting with me until my bus comes.

"So where you headed to now?"

"Thinking about stopping at Fifth Plaza to do a little shopping before I head home."

"You sure you won't change your mind about letting me drive you?"

"I'm sure, but you will be hearing from me soon Mr. Marko Humphrey." I say holding up his business card before scooping up my son and boarding the bus. He stands waving goodbye as we pull off.

****

It's close to eleven by the time I make it back to my condo. Wrestling with the dead weight of a sleeping baby along with several shopping bags has me exhausted by the time I make it up to the concierge's desk in the lobby of my building.

"Good evening Mrs. Gracie." I greet the cool, older black lady who's been working shifts here since I first moved in.

"Hey Dena honey, how you doing? You out kinda late tonight aint'cha?"

"Yea. I missed the last bus and it took forever for the taxi to come."

"I so wish you would hurry up and buy yourself a car. It ain't safe for you to be out with that baby at night traveling alone like that."

"I know Mrs. Gracie. I'm gone get one soon."

"You've been saying that for a whole year now."

"I'm for real this time. He's getting way too heavy to be carrying around."

"Here, let me take him for you." she says easing

him out of my arms and resting him across her heavy breast. "He's so adorable. You're going to have to fight the women off with a stick by the time he's a teenager."

"Don't I know it. Do I have any mail today?"

"No, but you have had a couple of visitors. A young lady showed up here earlier looking for you. She said she was your sister and asked me to let her wait in your apartment for you, but I don't remember you ever mentioning having a sister. She hung around waiting for you for a while, but I guess she gave up because she disappeared a couple of hours ago." Mrs. Gracie leans in and whispers, "And he just showed up about a half hour ago." before cutting her eyes past me and to the right. I can't believe my eyes when I turn around.

CHAPTER 18

Click
June 2005

    I look at the time and see that it's ten minutes after ten. I've already shaved, showered, and gotten fully dressed in preparation for my visit this morning.
    Niesha normally arrives somewhere between ten and ten thirty so I know they should be calling my name at any moment. So far she has kept her word about holding me down, not missing a single visit or letting a day go by without letting me into her world in some way. Even if it's something as trivial as a five minute phone call or text message. Niesha always finds a way to let me know that I'm somewhere in her thoughts.
    Dena does the same thing just in her own way. She expresses her love for me through pictures of my son and sharing her everyday life with him with me. Our actual conversations are limited to once maybe twice a week and for some reason that's enough for both of us. I think that things are like that because it's easier for Dena to except the thought of me going away better than Niesha can. Although Niesha tries not to show it, I can tell that this whole situation is starting to get the best of her. She met me and was able to enjoy four months of her life with me. Four months of developing feelings that were able to grow more and more with each passing day. Then to have that taken away so abruptly is something that she's still struggling to cope with. Dena on the other hand spent four months of her life believing that she'd lost me forever. And to have a reminder of our love growing inside of her each day was probably pure torture for her. So just the thought of knowing that I'm still alive and able to come home to her one day and be a part of our child's life is enough within itself to keep her content. What she doesn't know is that one day is coming sooner than either of us could have expected.
    A quarter till eleven and still no Niesha.
    I go into my cell and take my BlackBerry out of its hiding place, which happens to be in between two honeybuns off of the commissary that I smash together to make it appear to be just one. The secret is to use a razor blade to cut down the natural seal line and remove the honeybun without damaging the wrapper. After that it's just a matter of using a thin strip of clear tape to seal it back up. Not as sophisticated as Playboi's hiding spot but it's been working for me for over a year now. Thankfully, I don't have a

roommate at the moment. After my slip-up in the last pod, I'm extra careful not to let anyone in this pod know that I have a phone.

I power on the BlackBerry and dial Niesha's number. No answer. Taking that as a sign to mean that she's already up front, I make quick work of stashing my phone again before going back out into the dayroom. Another thirty minutes of me watching the clock and telling myself that it will be any minute now passes by before I go back into my cell. Once again, I go through the tedious process of removing and powering on my phone. Still no answer from Niesha. I send a text:

Where are you?

Still playing it safe, I go through the process of hiding my phone again, but this time I don't cut it off just in case she tries to call or text back.

By twelve o'clock, I'm blowed that she hasn't shown up yet. Niesha and I stayed on the phone well past one o'clock last night which is something normal for us. With Queen Bee being the alarm clock that she is, Niesha never has to worry about oversleeping. The last thing Niesha said to me before we hung up last night was "I love you baby. I'll see you in the morning." She'd even hinted about having a surprise for me today. If something had changed between then and now, I know she would have at least called or texted me. She hasn't missed a visit in over a year so I definitely wouldn't complain if she did. It's the not knowing that's pissing me off and making me start to worry.

At exactly two forty-three, the jailor finally opens the door to the pod and calls my name. But it's not for a visit.

"Fevers. Deshawn Fevers, pack it up, you've been bonded out."

"Bonded out?"

"Yes bonded out. Now let's go unless you like it in here and wanna stay. In that case, I'm pretty sure any one of these other gentlemen would love to leave in your place." A couple of them make remarks in agreement.

In shock, I hesitate briefly before going into motion. I experience a moment of deja vu as I begin packing my stuff. This has to be some type of mistake. I've had a no bond parole hold on me since the day I came here fifteen months ago. So how is it possible that I'm being released? The only reason I'm still here and not in prison already is because Niesha's aunt, who she hired to be my lawyer, has been arguing the fact that my fingerprints weren't found on any of the weapons nor were they actually found in my possession. The arresting officer reported that he recovered three guns from a duffle bag that he witnessed me drop on the ground after I emerged out of the back entrance of the Hot Spot Gentleman's Club. Dena's bodyguard Pitbull made a formal statement saying that he emerged out of the same entrance at the same time that I did and had confiscated that same duffle bag from one of the killers who infiltrated the club while he was on duty there. With that being the case, they can't violate my parole unless I'm found guilty or convicted. Now the state has resorted to constantly rescheduling my court dates hoping that I'll get tired of sitting in the county jail and settle for taking a plea agreement.

I make it to the booking and release area still wondering what the hell is going on. The jailor takes me to a holding cell and hands me a box containing the clothes I had on the day that I got arrested.

"Here. Throw your sheets, blankets, towels, and jail uniform in those piles over there and get dressed." I have a million questions, but I know better than to ask any of them. This could be my blessing in disguise.

I'd left all my personal property, hygiene, and commissary with the guys in my pod who needed it the most before I left. Everything except the honeybun containing my phone, which I slide in my pocket after I'm finished getting dressed. The release process takes thirty minutes. The whole time I'm waiting for someone to come and tell me that they had made a mistake and I was the wrong person, but it never happened. By the time I finally make it to the last step of signing my release papers, I see the lawyer who Johnny Ray sent up here to talk to me. He'd been up here a total of three times, twice since Niesha's aunt had become my lawyer. He told me that Johnny Ray wanted me to know that his services were still available to me if I ever needed them.

"How you doing Mr. Fevers?" he greets me with a firm handshake.

"I'm fine. How bout yourself?"

"I can't complain. I know you have a lot of questions, but I think it would be best if you wait until we get out of here before you ask them." He gives me a meaningful look.

"I think you're a smart man Mr. Bonman."

Light-brown with a bald head, wearing glasses, and a business suit, he gives off the image of importance.

The jailor says, "Ok Mr. Bonman, he's released into your custody. It says here that it's a conditional release of..." he consults his paper. "Seventy-two hours. That means you should be returning him here on Tuesday at four o'clock."

"Retuning?"

"That's correct." The lawyer quickly responds while grabbing the paper and scribbling his John Hancock. "We'll be here." Then without further ado, he escorts me out of the jailhouse.

Stepping out into freedom for the first time in over a year is a bittersweet moment for me. Bitter because of the word 'returning ' that's still echoing in my brain. How do you make reservations to return to lock-up before you're even released?

"What's he talking about I'm being released into your custody?" I ask the lawyer as we walk through the parking lot. He doesn't respond immediately. It's not until we make it into the back of a black stretch limo where Johnny Ray is waiting that he's ready to talk.

"How you doing young brotha?" Johnny Ray greets me with an extended hand as I climb in.

I shake it as I take the seat across from him. "Sup old man."

Johnny Ray is dressed down in a dark blue Brooks Brothers suit with the blue Dob hat to match. The last time I saw him, he'd just taken a hot one to the chest at close range from a 44 magnum. Not many people experience that and still live to tell about it. Yet here he sits across from me as smooth and dapper than ever. The lawyer takes the seat beside him still holding the paperwork from inside.

"Ok Mr. Fevers, here's the situation."

"Click. Call me Click."

"Ok Click, to answer your question, yes you've

been released into my custody. Thanks to Johnny Ray having connections in high places, we were able to get you a conditional seventy-two hour release. Conditional because..." he pauses and shuffles the papers in his hand before looking up into my eyes and saying, "You have a court date scheduled for Wednesday June fifteenth where you'll be sentenced to serve ten years fed time."

"Excuse me? Fuck you mean ten years? I just got done serving ten years for some shit that I didn't even do!"

"Well unfortunately, you are guilty of these charges. No matter how we look at this situation, we can't get around the fact that the officer is saying that he witnessed you with the guns in your possession."

"But my fingerprints weren't even found on any of the guns. Plus..."

"Plus Pitbull claimed possession of the guns himself and your lawyer has filed a thousand motions on your behalf." Johnny Ray cuts in. "We know all that already. And trust me young brotha when I say, I've been doing everything in my power to get you off or at least the best possible deal. But the racist cracker who arrested you isn't bending. He's adamant about testifying and making your charges stick. The sad part about it is, his credibility outweighs yours, Pitbull's, or anyone else involved."

"Can't we just pay him off or something?" I ask hearing the desperation in my own voice.

"Jabbar already tried that."

"Jabbar?"

"Mr. Bonman here."

The lawyer takes over the conversation. "I made

him a generous proposition, which he promptly refused and told me that if I so much as looked in his direction again, he would file bribery charges against me, and have me disbarred and arrested." He takes off his glasses before saying, "Look, what you have to understand Click, is that the law enforcement of this town are embarrassed. They have seventy-two unsolved murders without so much as a lead. And no one is giving them any details about what went on inside the club. Including you."

"I ain't no damn snitch."

"I understand that, but what you fail to understand is that you were the only arrest that they made that day."

"Meaning," Johnny Ray says, "you're the only person they have to take all of their frustration out on." I hadn't thought about it like that. Convicting me, no matter that it's on gun charges rather than murder charges, is the difference in them getting "somebody" as opposed to "nobody".

"So I'm going to prison no matter what?"

"Put it like this," the lawyer jumps in again "even if we found a way to somehow silence him and make it to where he couldn't testify at all, his arrest report alone is enough to still guarantee them a conviction."

I sit in silence as my last hope of freedom fades away. Up until this point, Niesha's aunt had given me hope, making me believe that there was a chance to escape the crunch and be there to help raise my son. She truly believed that by law, my case was beatable. Now I realize that this isn't about law at all. It's about politics.

"Click, I know that this is a hard pill for you to swallow, but no one put you in this situation but you."

I look up in shock. This is the first time since I've known him that Johnny Ray has actually called me by my name instead of "Young Brotha". The look he's giving me is one that a father would give his son in a moment of manhood. Although I know he's speaking the truth, I still can't help but to feel some type of way.

"Your right. I did put myself here, but what's the point of coming to get me if I still have to come back to this hellhole?"

"Funny you should ask. Ten years is a long time to be away. Especially for a man who had a newborn child that he never got a chance to hold. Now technically, you're not supposed to leave the state, but seeing as how you've been released into Mr. Bonman's custody and he just so happens to suddenly have an emergency situation that he needs to tend to in Atlanta Georgia..." He pauses to let the full meaning of his words sink in.

I look from Johnny Ray to the lawyer. They both have knowing smiles on their faces. All of this happened so unexpectedly that I haven't had a chance to entertain the possibility of me being able to actually hold my son for the first time or being able to spend time with the mother of my child. Now the thought of it, knowing what my future holds, is enough to almost bring me to tears.

"Aw man, you serious?" I ask in disbelief.

"Yeah." Johnny Ray nods his head up and down looking directly into my eyes. "We're actually about to head to the mansion right now where our private jet is waiting to fly us to Atlanta."

Mr. Bonman the lawyer says, "Just so we're clear Click, I'm putting my neck on the line for you. If you so much as think about running, not only will I do everything in my power to help apprehend you, but the state will revoke your ten year agreement and you'll have to serve the maximum sentence for your charges. Meaning, your son will be old enough to legally buy liquor by the time you come up for parole.

Do we understand each other?"

"I understand." I say more than grateful for the opportunity.

Just then, Johnny Ray's cell phone rings. "Excuse me." he says before answering it.

Hearing his phone ring reminds me of my

BlackBerry. I take the honeybun out of my pocket and remove my phone from inside. The lawyer watches me with curiosity but remains silent. There's a text from Niesha waiting for me. It says:

Sorry I missed your visit but something bad happened to Nadia

The last text that I sent was at 11:33. Her text came in at 12:06. Why didn't she try to call me? And what happened to my Queen Bee? My confusion grows even more when I try to call her phone twice back to back and get no answer.

I tell the lawyer, "Look, I got something that I need to go take care of before we catch this flight."

"Um..." He looks at Johnny Ray who is still engrossed in his phone call. "I don't think that will be a problem. Where is it that you need to go?"

Not wanting to disrespect Johnny Ray by taking him with me to check on another woman, I say "I have a personal matter that I need to go check on. Can you drop me at my car and give me a couple of hours?"

He looks at me skeptically. "I'm not sure if that's such a good idea."

"Look, I give you my word. I'm not trying to run. This has something to do with a loved one and it's very important."

Johnny Ray hangs up his phone and looks rather pale.

Mr. Bonman tells him, "Click wants to know can we postpone the flight and allow him to go take care of some personal matters."

Johnny Ray looks at me and says, "Lafu is on the move."

"Lafu?"

"Yea. I was planning to fill you in on the flight to Atlanta, but things just took an interesting turn." I give him a questioning look. "As you already know, Lafu attacked my Babygirl about a year back." I nod my head at the bitter memory. "Ever since then he's been underground hiding out knowing that I won't rest until I find him and snatch the last breath from his body." Johnny Ray speaks with so much conviction that there is no question that he means every word he says. "I created the monster known as Lafu and I know exactly what it takes to destroy him. His main weakness is his love of money, so I destroyed his financial stability. I sold our entire club franchise and closed every bank account that he had access to. Then I cut off all the connections that I gave him with the Colombians disabling him from getting anymore drugs and trying to set up shop somewhere else. Lafu is a very smart man so there was no doubt in my mind that he had money stashed away for a rainy day, but with his excessive lifestyle and expensive taste, I figured that it would only be a matter of time before his stash began to run low. And I was right."

I watch as Johnny Ray retrieves a CD from its case and inserts it in the bottom of a T.V. that's located on the side console next to a mini bar. A few seconds later, the screen comes to life with an infrared view of what appears to be an office. I see a large marble desk that sits directly in the middle of the office and seems to dominate the room. On each side of it is a very large golden statue of a lion. A glass case filled with trophies cover the majority of the walls to the right. The rest of the walls are covered with expensive paintings and some kind of intricate paneling. Around the office are a couple of leather chairs, potted plants and trees, and a bunch of paraphernalia representing Lafu's native country.

Johnny Ray continues, "When Lafu broke into the mansion and attacked Babygirl, I figured that she must have walked in and interrupted him in the middle of looking for something. I later found a safe inside his quarters hidden inside one of those lion statues you see right there. Inside it was a couple mil in cash, so I figured that's what he was after. What I couldn't figure out, was how he got in and out the mansion without being detected. We knew that the entrance had to be somewhere in his quarters because none of the other cameras in the mansion captured him coming or going. So I left the money where it was, and had it bugged with a tracking device. Then I had a hidden camera installed in his quarters hoping he would get desperate enough to come back looking for it again. I had just about given up hope until two days ago."

On the screen everything remains normal for several moments. Then suddenly the marble desk begins to move. The entire right side comes forward turning the desk in a circular motion clockwise beginning at three forty-five and doing a complete three sixty. When it stops, I notice that the desk is now sitting on a three foot raised platform. I watch in disbelief as Lafu emerges from what appears to be a hole in the floor beneath the desk. He pauses momentarily to look around before climbing completely out. The angle on the T.V. places the hidden camera somewhere high up on the wall above the entrance to the office. When Lafu's eyes swing around and face the direction of the camera, they light up and glow like those of a nocturnal animal roaming the jungle at night. His once clean-cut pretty boy look is long gone. The neat, low cut, fade that he once wore is now replaced by long, wild curls, and his smooth baby face is now covered by a thick, scraggly beard.

Johnny Ray, Mr. Bonman, and I watch as Lafu removes the head of one of the golden lion statues, pulls out a net sack, fills it with bundles of cash from the statue, then disappears back down through the same way he came in. Moments later, the desk begins turning again, this time counterclockwise, returning it to its original position sitting level with the rest of the floor.

"That was two days ago. We've been tracking him closely ever since and for some reason he's been staying in the area. I told my guys not to move in on him so I can see what he's up to." Johnny Ray explains. "One thing you can't do is make the mistake of underestimating Lafu. He's a very crafty individual who thinks outside the box. His level of intelligence is rather surprising. And as you learned firsthand young brotha, so is his ability to hold a grudge."

Johnny Ray's words bring to mind how Lafu plotted and waited ten long years to execute his plan of revenge on me because he believes that I killed his brother. And thinking outside the box is an understatement. He had Dena and Finesse meet me at the bus station, set me up to rob him, faked his own death, and let me go months of living it up and spending his money, only to pop back up and kill me. If it wasn't for the smooth old man sitting across from me now, I would have been dead a long time ago.

"It's been over a year without so much as a peep from him. Now that he's surfaced, you bes believe he has something up his sleeve." he says "And now he knows that you're not dead and I'm the reason you're still breathing, so he won't rest until both of us are dead."

"Man Fuck Lafu! That muthafucka bleed just like me!" I explode thinking about how he brutally murdered my cousin Shelly.

"I feel the same way young brotha, but emotions have no place here. Remember, this is chess not checkers. Now whatever personal business you need to take care of, I suggest you get it done then hop on the next thing smoking to Atlanta, but I'm leaving right now. I just got a call that Lafu has left the area. And from the sounds of it he's headed straight towards my Babygirl."

CHAPTER 19

Click

"Up there, third house on the right." I direct the limo driver as we approach Niesha's house. It was decided after we dropped Johnny Ray at the mansion, that the lawyer would be coming with me to Niesha's and from there he and I would be boarding the flight to Atlanta together. Guess he still found me to be untrustworthy despite my promise not to run. My mind was way too distracted to really care. Not only had Johnny Ray's revelation about Lafu left me rattled, but I tried several more times to get in touch with Niesha with no luck.

Once we park, I tell Mr. Bonman, "I'll be right back."

As I open the car door to get out he says, "Before you go in, give me your phone number." I stop to give it to him, and he calls my phone. I answer then hang it up. He says, " Hopefully you'll come back out within a reasonable amount of time and I won't have to use this."

"Yea whatever." I say before getting out of the car. This guy is really starting to make me not like him.

The summer sun greets me with a bright scorching blaze. I don't stop to admire what a beautiful day it is as I make my way up to Niesha's front door. The more I think about this situation with Niesha and my little Queen Bee, the more I'm convinced that something is wrong. Although I don't see Niesha's car anywhere in sight, I still knock on her door anyway. No answer. I knock again and wait a few more seconds before I try the doorknob. Her front door comes open with an eerie squeak.

Niesha's house is a cozy little, one story, two
bedroom domain where she lives with just her and her daughter. A private nest that she always keeps tidy and welcoming whenever I come over. I look around in shock.

The house is in complete disarray.

Pictures and chairs overturned. Pillows from the couch thrown about. The large screen of the television smashed. A lamp broken on the living room floor. Obvious signs that some kind of struggle took place.

My heart drops to the bottom of my stomach as I take cautious steps inside. I'm careful not to touch anything as I move through the trashed living room into the kitchen. Thankfully, it appears to be in normal condition with everything neatly in place just the way Niesha insists her kitchen being before she goes to bed at night. The only thing that does concern me is the fact that her coffee pot is completely full. It appears to have been turned off and left to cool without so much as a cup taken out of it. Niesha's morning ritual consists of at least a cup or two to start her day, yet her favorite coffee mug hangs untouched from the cup rack sitting on the counter. Maybe whatever went down with her daughter happened in the early morning hours when she woke to begin her day. Maybe she turned on her coffee pot right before she went to wake Nadia, where she found her running a high fever and had only enough time to turn off the pot before she rushed out the door to take her to the hospital. Or maybe the coffee pot was an afterthought that caused her to rush back home after she had already left. Or maybe I'm just kidding myself.

Nadia is the most vibrant child that I've ever met. Even sick, she would make her way into her mother's room to wake her. And Niesha is so picky and meticulous about how she does things that it would take an extreme situation to make her break her routine. And there is no getting around the living room, evidence that something dramatic happened between the time I talked to Niesha last night and now.

But nothing can prepare me for what I find inside of Niesha's bedroom.

She's on the bed. Completely naked. Hands and feet tied to the bedpost. Gag in her mouth. Face swollen and bloody. Her skin dark and bruised. No signs of movement or life. Without touching her I know that she's long gone.

The most gruesome detail of the whole scene is the broom.

It's blood covered straws protruding grotesquely from between Niesha's legs. The handle lost somewhere up in the orifice of her body.

I stand frozen in shock at the horror before me.

Images that will haunt my mind when I close my eyes for a long time. I wonder how long she suffered. How long before she mercifully took her last breath and escaped the horrors of what became her last moments on earth.

The vibrating cellphone in my pocket snaps me out of my zone. I pull it out to see that I have another text. My face frowns in confusion when I see that it came from Niesha's number. It says:

Sorry about your girl Click. What can I say she SWEPT me off my feet. LOL

I can't stop myself from screaming at the top of my lungs and slinging the BlackBerry against the wall as hard as I can as a stream of tears rush down my face.

"Sick muthafucka!"

Lafu has done it again. Every time I try to forget

about the past and move on, he does something to let me know that it's not over with. I thought nothing could top the pain of knowing how he tortured and raped my cousin Shelly before setting her battered body on fire, but this one takes the cake. Niesha didn't deserve to die like this. Then to take her phone and wait for me to find her and..... wait a minute. How could Lafu have possibly known to send that text now? How could he know that I'm the one who's here finding her at this very moment? Unless....

My eyes begin searching the room looking for anything out of place or that doesn't belong. He has to be somehow watching me now.

Suddenly, I hear a noise come from the direction of

the closed bathroom door. It never dawned on me that Lafu could possibly still be here. But no, Johnny Ray said that he had already left the area and was headed towards Atlanta.

Not taking any chances, I pick up the closest thing that I can find to a weapon, which happens to be a black, African sculpture that got knocked off one of the shelves during whatever took place in the living room earlier. If he is on the other side of that bathroom door, I'm going to do my best to use Shaka Zulu here to cave his skull in.

First I place my ear close to the door to see if I can hear any more noise. Then I twist the knob and quickly push it open with my arm cocked back and ready to strike. Empty. Even the shower curtain is already pulled back, so I don't have to go through one of those scary movie moments of having to creep up and snatch it open.

Just as I'm lowering my arm and relaxing, I hear another noise. It came from the cabinet under the bathroom sink. Squatting down, I open the doors to find Nadia curled up in a ball squeezing her eyes shut in fear. Clothed in nothing but underwear, her body is shaking like she's laying outside in ten below weather.

She's terrified.

"Queen Bee?" The sound of my voice causes her eyes to come open and big crocodile tears to begin forming in them.

"It's okay baby. It's me, Deshawn."

"Deshawn..." She scrambles out from under the sink and wraps her arms and legs around me so tightly that I'm having a hard time breathing as I stand up cradling her in my arms. She holds on and cries quietly against my neck. Not wasting anytime, I head straight towards the front door trying to get her out of here before she sees anything more tragic than she already has. When I make it back outside with Nadia in my arms, Mr. Bonman looks up at me with curiosity.

"What's this?"

Numbly I say, "Call the police and tell them that there's been a homicide."

He looks at me searchingly while processing my words, then past me towards the house before getting out of the limo and heading inside to investigate for himself.

Taking the seat that he just abandoned, I pull the door closed and sit there still somewhat in shock clinging to Nadia as tightly as she's clinging to me. Long minutes of silence pass by. I can't believe that I just found my girlfriend dead, tied naked to a bed, with a broom stuffed inside of her.

A while later, the lawyer emerges onto the front porch with his phone up to his ear. I see him reading the address off of the mailbox and talking into the phone. It's so quiet inside the limo that I can hear my own thoughts.

The monster known as Lafu has to be stopped.

"Deshawn?" Nadia's little voice comes out of nowhere.

"Yes Queen Bee."

She uncoils from around my body and pulls back enough to look into my eyes. With a face full of tears and trembling lips she says, "The Boogeyman hurt my mommy......and he hurt me too."

My heart breaks in two when I look down and see the front of her underwear covered in blood.

CHAPTER 20

Click

    I'm exhausted by the time I walk into the lobby of the Peachtree Towers in downtown Atlanta. After having to practically tear myself away from a traumatized Nadia, who I had to leave at the hospital to be examined, then being interrogated by the Forrest City Police, who tried to treat me as if I was guilty of something, then having to be rushed across the bridge to Memphis and just barely making it there in time to catch my flight to Atlanta, and finally having to hail a cab from the Hartfield Airport to here, I'm exhausted. All I want is a fat blunt to smoke and a soft bed to lay in. But even if I had those things, I doubt if I'd be able to sleep. Every second that I'm not forced to interact with another human being, my thoughts are on Niesha and Nadia. It's eating me alive to know that everything they suffered today is because of me. Niesha is dead because of me.

    It's after ten p.m. by the time I make it up to the concierge's desk. An older, black, heavyset woman wearing the name tag Mrs. Gracie greets me with a motherly smile.

    "Hello sir, welcome to the Peachtree Towers. Is there anything that I can assist you with?"

    "Yea, I'm here to see Dena Givens. She stays in..." I consult the paper that Johnny Ray gave me with Dena's address on it.

    "I know exactly who you're talking about, but I'm pretty sure that she's not up there. I'd be more than happy to double check for you though."

    "Thank you ma'am. I'd appreciate it."

    "No problem honey." she says before picking up her desk phone.

    I wonder where Dena could be at this time of night. More importantly, where is my son? Maybe they're out somewhere with Johnny Ray. The lawyer was supposed to call and give him an update of my flight arrangements so maybe Johnny Ray had decided to take them out for a bite to eat and to spend a little time with them until I got here. I think about calling him, but then remember that I busted my phone earlier when I threw it against the wall at Niesha's house.

    Images of Niesha laying tied to the bed flash through my mind.

    Mrs. Gracie hangs up the phone and says, "No she's not up there. Sorry. I can take a message for you though."

"Um, could you just tell her that.... well to be honest with you, I just made it here from out of town and was trying to surprise her. I'm her son's father."

She looks at me in shock then gushes, "Indeed you are! I should've known. He looks just like you, as handsome as ever."

Her words give me a feeling of prideful joy that lifts the dark cloud that's been hanging over my head all day and causes me to smile.

"Thank you."

"I hope don't mind me saying, but Dena definitely needs something like this to happen to her."

"What makes you say that?"

"Well don't get me wrong, she seems happy enough, always pleasant and showing that beautiful smile of hers. But she's always alone. She never has any company over, and I never see her with any friends. Just her and that adorable baby boy of yours coming and going. And underneath that pretty smile, I detect a quiet sadness about her like she's hurting somewhere deep. You know what I mean?"

"Yea, I know exactly what you mean." I answer thinking about how subdued Dena sometimes sounds over the phone; like she wants to say something but feels that her words would be pointless. "Well, I hope we're able to put a smile on each other's face."

"I'm sure you will." Mrs. Gracie says with a smile. "Really you can sit here and wait for her if you want to. She'll probably be walking through those doors any minute."

"I think I will, but is there a bathroom around here somewhere that I can use?"

"Sure. Right up that hallway and to your left."

"Thank you." As I follow her directions, I can't help but to admire how nice it is inside this place. Everything's so upscale and plush. Just the kind of place to fit my Suabo's taste.

After I relieve myself, I glance at my reflection in the mirror while washing my hands. So use to looking at the blurry piece of metal that supplements as a mirror in the county jail, it feels like I'm seeing myself for the first time in a long time. Although my gear is the same grungy all black get up that I wore the day that I had robbery on my mind, my skin appears clearer and I can tell that my four times a week workout routine is paying off. Not to mention the fact that I've picked up a few pounds. It's been over a year since the last time I've seen Dena and I wonder how she'll react to seeing my new haircut.

Once I make it back out to the lobby, I find a spot on a sofa and lose myself in a Black Enterprise magazine that I find sitting on a table. Don't know how much time passes, but I see her as soon as she steps inside. With one hand gripping the handles of several shopping bags and my little man sound asleep against the opposite shoulder, she doesn't notice me as she heads towards Mrs. Gracie's desk. I watch as she talks, then hands my son over to Mrs. Gracie, before setting her bags down on the floor beside her. Gone are the beloved thigh-high stiletto boots that she's so fond of wearing. In their place is a pair of frilly blue and white tennis shoes. A snug white shirt sits on top of a pair of fitted jeans that display a thickness in her hips that wasn't there before. I can't take my eyes off her.

It's not long before she turns around and our eyes lock into each other's. Dena's hands cover her mouth in shock.

Everything that happened today from the time I woke up has been leading up to this moment. Suddenly I'm not so tired anymore. Time seems to fade away as we stand staring across the lobby at each other.

Steady at first, Dena begins walking towards me. Then with an overwhelming urgency, she races into my embrace and wraps her arms around my neck with a strength that I didn't know she possessed. Words can't begin to express how good it feels to have her back in my arms again, to feel her voluptuous body pressed against mine and be able to inhale her intoxicating scent. The thought of never letting go crosses my mind as emotions take over. All the pain from what happened to Niesha and Nadia today, all the pain from being locked away, all the pain of not knowing when I would see her or my son, all of it melts away with her embrace.

After a while, Dena brings her face around and rests her forehead against mine. Her hands make their way to my cheeks as she places slow lingering kisses on my lips.

"Hi." she says.

"Hi."

"I didn't expect to see you here."

Without a laugh I say, "I didn't expect to be here."

Face wet with tears, her hazel eyes seem to be trying to capture every detail of my face. She runs a hand across my waves.

"You cut off all of your hair."

"Yea."

She smiles and says, "I like it. Makes you look even more handsome."

"Thanks." My hands travel down to get two hands full of her healthy cheeks. "Where'd you get all this?"

She blushes and laughs. "Your son gave it to me. Come on, you want to meet him?"

"Yea sure." We turn to find Mrs. Gracie watching us with misty eyes and a wide smile. Dena takes my hand and leads me over to where she's standing with Deshawn Jr. sleep across her chest. Dena reaches for him and Mrs. Gracie eases him up.

"There you go." Deshawn Jr. makes no secret that he doesn't appreciate being disturbed as he begins whining.

Dena takes him and says, "Oh hush now. I got someone here that I want you to meet. This is your daddy. Say hi to daddy."

Obviously still half asleep with one chubby little fist rubbing his eyes, my son peeks at me through eyes the same color as his mother's. He let's go of a long yawn then drops his head down onto her shoulder and stares at me.

"That's your daddy. You want to say hi to daddy?" Dena tries to pass him to me and for some reason I get nervous. "Here take him, he's yours."

I hesitate, but then my son reaches for me and a feeling that I can't explain goes through me. I take him into my arms and hold him against my chest the way I saw his mother do. He smells like a mixture of baby lotion and fruity candy. A head full of short silky curls drop down onto my shoulders and within seconds I hear his light snores.

Mrs. Gracie says, " Well, it looks like someone's tired."

"Yea, he's had a long day out trying to hang with his mommy. Mrs. Gracie, I'd like you to meet Click."

"Yes we've met already." She shoots me a wink. "Now I see why you're so secretive about your personal life. If I had a man this fine hidden off somewhere, I wouldn't want to share him with anyone either."

"I wasn't being secretive. I just.... you never asked." Dena says face turning a shade of red.

"Oh chile, I'm just messing with you. It just warms my heart to see two young people in love like this."

"Who said I was in love with him?" Dena asks while frowning her face up and cutting her eyes at me.

" Honey child please, a blind person can see that y'all two are in love with each other." Dena and I share a look. "Now y'all go ahead on up so you can get that baby to bed. And remember what I said about getting you a car."

"Yes Mrs. Gracie."

I squat down to grab Dena's bags off the floor with my free hand before saying, " It was nice meeting you Mrs. Gracie."

"You too baby."

As we head towards the embankment of elevators, I ask Dena "You don't have a car?"

"No. I use the city transportation."

"But why? It's not like you can't afford one."

"I know, but I wanted to do something different. Plus Atlanta's rush hour traffic is horrific."

"I don't know if I like you lugging my son around on city transportation in a place like this. It's pretty rough out there. What if you get mugged or something?"

In the blink of an eye, she has a .380 in her hand pointed at my gut.

"Don't worry, I still never leave home without it."

After we make it into the elevator and begin ascending, Dena gets into my space again. "I still can't believe that you're here." She leans in for another kiss and I take my time savoring the taste of her tongue. By the time the elevator stops on her floor, I'm all worked up.

"See what you did? Now you got me all on front street and I can't even adjust myself cuz both of my hands are full."

She follows my eyes with hers down to the tented erection in the front of my pants and says, "Oh my. I see." Then she uses both of her hands to grab what she see and says, " Now both of our hands are full." before she recaptures my mouth with hers and kisses me with so much passion that I'm dizzy with lust by the time she pulls away.

"Don't worry, Ima take care of that for you once we get inside." She walks away leaving me leaking at the tip and hypnotized by how juicy her ass looks switching off in her jeans. I stand there taking a couple of deep breaths trying to calm down before I'm able to move.

I follow behind Dena with only one thing on my mind now, but when I finally reach her, I can tell that something is wrong by the stiffness in her body. That's when I look past her to see that the door to her condo is slightly ajar.

"Finesse?" she calls out while pushing the door open as she slowly walks inside. I walk in behind her to find all of the lights off except for what's coming from a large tv screen. When Dena clicks a switch to turn them on, the sight before us isn't pretty.

Johnny Ray is sitting at the dining room table, taped to a chair with dried blood covering one side of his face, knocked unconscious with a large chess board set up in front of him.

Sitting on a couch in the sunken living room sipping from a small glass with brown liquid in it, is Finesse. In front of her is a long glass table with a crystallized tumbler sitting on top of it that's half full of brown liquid that's obviously some kind of liquor. There's also what appears to be about a half ounce of powdered cocaine in a pile beside a straw and five lines already made out and ready to be consumed.

And to make matters worse, Lafu is sitting next to her in a chair that matches the rest of the furniture in the living room. He's smoking a gold tipped cigarillo blunt with a laptop sitting on his lap. There's also a gold-plated .44 magnum laying on the arm of the chair.

Sitting the laptop down and grabbing the gun, Lafu stands up and says, "Dee-nah, Click, me been waitin fer ya. Welcome to da party."

My heart feels like it just stopped beating in my chest. This muthafucka just don't quit. Lafu has to have the biggest nuts in the world. First he brutally murdered my cousin Shelly and now Niesha. Then he had the nerve to text and taunt me about it. There's no telling what he did to Nadia. He tried to rape Dena while she was pregnant with my son. Now here he is, obviously ready to do some more damage. One things for sure, it's all about to end right here tonight.

CHAPTER 21

Dena

"Well isn't this special." Finesse says standing up. "Mother, father, and child all together as one. Y'all just one big happy family aint'cha?"

"Finesse, what are you doing here with him?"

"What, you not happy to see me big sis?" Barefoot and wearing a skimpy red negligee with her hair all over the place, I can instantly tell that Finesse is high out of her mind. Her eyes are bloodshot red with makeup smeared under them like she's been crying, and I can see that she's lost a considerable amount of weight. She reaches down between the cushions of the couch and comes back up with a gun identical to the one Lafu is holding. She begins walking towards us.

"Seeing as how you left me over a year ago and haven't even thought enough to come back and check on me, I figured I'd come check on you. And look at my nephew. He's so handsome. He doesn't even know his Tee-Tee. Ain't that right nephew?" She approaches Click and my son making silly baby noises.

Click drops the shopping bags and moves the baby out of her reach.

"Get away from my son."

She stops and looks at him incredulously then raises the gun angrily and points it at him.

"Let me see my damn nephew before I shoot you in yo fuckin face."

Lafu, who is still standing in the same place watching says, "Nessa."

She turns around and they make silent eye contact for a few seconds. Then she turns around and just like that, lowers the gun and heads back over to the couch where she was, mumbling under her breath " Bitch ass nigga." I can't help but to wonder what kind of stronghold Lafu has over Finesse to be able to control her like that.

"Dee-nah." Lafu calls out to me in his thick Jamaican accent "go and lay ya bwoy down in em play pen. And Lovabwoy, you come over 'ere and 'ave a seat beside Nessa."

I look at Click, and without words he and I both agree that the play pen is the safest place for our son to be out of the way of whatever's about to go down. Easing him out of Click's arms, I cradle my son against my chest careful not to wake him as I take two steps down into the living room and across over into the far corner where the play pen is located. Once I get him laid down, I wind the musical toy that hangs over his head praying that the lullabies that it plays will help to keep him asleep.

When I turn around, I notice the video that Uncle Fresh showed me in Lafu's private quarters of him and my mother sitting on the company's private jet playing on my television. Slowly, I walk over to where Click is now sitting beside Finesse and I take a seat next to him. Lafu sits back down, picks the laptop back up placing it on his lap and continues puffing his blunt.

On the screen, Uncle Fresh says: "Babygirl knows how to express herself. Nessa holds everything inside."

My mother: "Well she can't stay here any longer. She has to go."

Uncle Fresh: "Now wait a minute Theresa, let's think about this."

My mother: "What else is there to think about Johnny Ray. Nessa has to leave!" My mother breaks down crying then the screen switches. I see myself in my bedroom laying on my stomach across my bed crying a thousand tears. It's the day before my mother's funeral. I remember being so distraught and confused wondering how could something so bad happen to such a good person. My mother was the nicest most giving person I've ever known. I remember questioning God that day wanting to know why he took my mother away.

On the screen, there's a knock on my bedroom door. A few seconds later, Uncle Fresh sticks his head into the room.

"Babygirl?" Then he steps all the way inside, goes over and sits on the side of my bed and begins rubbing my back. "Aw Babygirl.....I know it hurts, but you gotta understand that God don't make no mistakes. Believe me, I'm in just as much pain as you are, but I know that everything happens for a reason. I can't imagine what reason God had for taking my Theresa away, but....." he raises his face towards the ceiling like he's looking towards the heavens for answers. I can see the grief on his face as he fights back tears of his own.

On the screen, I raise up from the bed and just the sight of Uncle Fresh brings on a whole new wave of tears. I fall against his chest crying.

"I'm going to miss her so much."

Uncle Fresh: "I know..." he holds me and rubs my back comforting me while I soak the front of his shirt with my tears. After a while, he says, "Babygirl I got something I need to talk to you about."

I turn my head and lay the side of my face on his chest: "What is it?"

Uncle Fresh: "Well seeing as how you're Theresa's only biological child, you inherited her whole estate."

Me: "What does that mean?"

Uncle Fresh: "It means that you're now the new owner of the entire Dean Dynasty."

Me: "You mean Lafu's operation."

Uncle Fresh: "Yea, but as you already know everything was in your mother's name. Now everything gets transferred from her name to yours."

Me: "So what do I have to do?"

Uncle Fresh: "Nothing. Every since Lafu has been legally dead, your mother and I have run the whole operation by ourselves. I've always managed the illegal activities going on and your mother handled the legal stuff. Now that she's gone, I'm going to have to run it all on my own."

Me: "So now you want me to start traveling with you and do what she did?" I asked hopefully, loving the idea.

Uncle Fresh: "No, not quite. I need you to do something else." I sit up and look at him questioningly waiting for him to explain. Then he asks me, "How do you feel about changing your last name to mines?" I remember thinking how ironic it was that just days earlier, my mother had revealed to me that Uncle Fresh was my biological father and not Lafu. All our lives, Finesse and I have carried the last name Dean, which was my mother's last name that she inherited from Lafu when they got married. Needless to say, I was ecstatic about the idea. Instead of Dena Simone Dean, I would now be Dena Simone Givens.

Me:" I think it's a great idea, but why now?" I asked thinking that maybe my mother had told him that she had let me know the truth and now that she was gone, he wanted to start openly claiming me as his daughter.

Instead he said, "Because that way, I can change the name of the family business from the Dean Dynasty to the Givens Dynasty. It will make it easier for me to take care of business if the company's name matches my own."

Me: "Oh." I say disappointedly. "I guess it will be alright then." Then a thought hits me. "What about
Finesse? Will we be changing her name too?"

Uncle Fresh: "No, there's no need to."

Me: "Why not? Didn't she inherit something too?"

Uncle Fresh: "No Babygirl you have to remember you're the heir to the throne, Nessa is just a foster child."

Lafu pushes a button on the laptop and the tv screen turns to white static. I look at Lafu, who's red eyes are trained on Finesse. I look at Finesse and see her staring bitterly at me. Click is watching everyone. For a moment, everyone sits in silence with only the sound of the static from the tv.

Finally, Finesse says, "Yup, Nessa is just a foster child." before she unceremoniously picks the straw up from the table and snorts one of the lines.

"Not true Nessa." Lafu says sitting the laptop on the floor before standing up and grabbing his gun. "Ya always gon be me baby gal. Lafu's Babygal." Then he walks over to the dining room area where Uncle Fresh is sitting taped to the chair. He stops behind him, puts that big ass mini cannon to his head and says, "Come now, we all play a game."

Once again, Click and I make eye contact before we both submissively do what we're told. Finesse remains seated on the couch with her legs crossed, sipping her drink and occasionally rubbing her nose with a loud sniff.

When we make it to the dining room, Lafu commands us, "Ave a seat."

Click takes the seat across from Uncle Fresh and I take the one beside him. Now up close, I can see a deep gash on the side of Uncle Fresh's head. Although it's stopped bleeding, a nasty puss is still oozing out of the wound. A red tinge makes a trail through his wavy salt and pepper hair ending in crusted blood down the left side of his face. It hits me that this is the first time that I've ever seen him without his hat on. With his chin resting down against his chest, Uncle Fresh's face looks peaceful except for the piece of grey duct tape placed crudely across his eyes. Beginning right below his shoulders, grey duct tape is wrapped tightly around his body all the way down to his waist, trapping his arms and bounding him to the chair.

"Johnny Ray, me know ya can 'ear me." Lafu says putting his mouth close to Uncle Fresh's ear. "Me got ya Babygirl 'ere. Me know ya taught er well. Now it's time to put er tinkin skillz to da test."

Uncle Fresh raises his head but remains silent.

The sound of Finesse snorting a line up through the straw draws my attention; first one nostril then the other. She sniffs a couple of times and wipes at her nose.

Lafu moves around to stand behind me and calls to her. "Nessa, come bound Lovabwoy ta em seat." Then he places the barrel of the gun against the side of my head, grabs me firmly by the neck and says to Click, " Try anyting Lovabwoy, and me gon rock 'er ta sleep."

Click looks at Lafu with murder in his eyes as Finesse grabs a large roll of duct tape off of the countertop and approaches him from behind.   Starting with a strip across his chest, Finesse wraps the tape around Click's body repeatedly until he's taped to the chair like Uncle Fresh.

"Ooh Click, you're even more buff than before." Finesse says rubbing her hands all over his upper body as she rounds the chair to stand in front of him. "Jail sure does a body good."

She kneels down in front of him and begins taping his leg to the chair. "I bet you wouldn't last three seconds in some warm wet pussy right now would you. It's been what, a year since you had some last?" Click doesn't answer, but I see his body tenses up when Finesse caresses his crotch area seductively before starting on his other leg.

"Is that what was about to happen when y'all came in here, Dena was about to scratch that one year itch for you?"

She finishes taping his leg and says, "I remember a time when she used to share. Ain't that right big sis?" Then she begins unfastening Click's pants.

"Finesse would you just stop. Why are you doing this?"

"What, you don't like it when I touch yo baby daddy?" She's like Dr. Jekyll and Mr. Hyde. A few minutes ago she was threatening to shoot him in the face. Now she can't keep her hands off of him. She reaches inside of Click's pants and pulls out his manhood.

Though gritted teeth he says, "Getcho hands offa me you crazy bitch!"

Finesse only gives him a devilish smile before

dropping her head down and taking him into her mouth. She bobs her head up and down slowly between his legs like he's her lover and she wants to bring him as much pleasure as possible. She uses her hand to help stroke him to life.

"Finesse stop! What's wrong with you? Would you stop!" It seems like the more I yell at her, the more determination she puts into her movements.

I make a move to get up, but Lafu yanks me back down into my seat, presses the gun against my head harder and puts more pressure on my neck. I sit helplessly watching Finesse rape Click with her mouth. Seems like she sucks him forever.

Finally Finesse stops and comes up for air. "Damn, I forgot how good this nigga's chocolate stick tastes. I see how you fell in love D. Can't say that I blame you, although you might not be so protective of him if you knew about his other hoe."

"Finesse, what are you talking bout?"

She stands up and straddles Click while pulling the crotch of her negligee to the side. "Click, you didn't tell her about Niesha?" She uses her hand to guide him inside and begins riding him. "Tell her Click. Tell her about the lil hoe you were playing house with on the north side.....she was a cute lil bitch.....had a daughter and everything.... tell her about your lil readymade family that you ain't think nobody knew about."

I look at Click waiting for him to deny it and tell me she's lying. I wait for him to tell me that she's just making up stuff to piss me off. Instead, he avoids my eye contact and yells at Finesse.

"Get the fuck offa my dick! You and this Jamaican muthafucka both crazy!" He wiggles and yanks in vain. The tape has him tightly secured to the chair.

Finesse grabs him roughly around the neck and begins choking as she works her hips faster.

"No muthafucka, you crazy if you think I'm gone let you play my sister for a fool." I see the veins popping out of Click's forehead as she bounces up and down on top of him choking.

Lafu's voice comes from behind me. "Nessa." She instantly stops and turns around to look at him. "Me ready ta play me game."

"But I'm not done yet." She answers in an almost childlike voice.

"Don't spoil de fun."

Like a trained dog, Finesse releases Click's neck and muffs him in the face. "You lucky Lovabwoy cuz if it was up to me, I would have choked yo ass to sleep and nutted all over yo dick at the same time." Then she raises up off of him, goes back over into the living room and pours herself another drink.

Click sits there gasping for air and trying to catch his breath.

I ask him, "Is it true?"

His eyes reluctantly come to mine. He takes a few more minutes to catch his breath before saying, "It was when we were on the outs....and I thought you betrayed me."

I can't hide the pain that surges through me at
hearing this. Knowing that he was laying up sharing himself with another woman while I was grieving over him hurts me to my core.

"Do you love her?" Again, his eyes drop down away from mine. I don't understand. How can he claim to love me and another woman at the same time? Besides my father, I've never felt for another man what I feel for him. My mind won't even entertain the thought.

"Don't worry about it D, I had yo back. I took care of that bitch for you." Finesse says coming back into the living room. I notice that she's now carrying the other gold-plated .44 magnum.

"What you mean you took care of her for me?"

"They killed her. Her and this twisted Jamaican muthafucka right here." Click spits. "And they did something to her daughter too."

"I didn't have anything to do with the little girl." Finesse says, "But I did get a chance to taste ole girl's sweet pussy...right before I fucked her to death with a broomstick." Finesse busses out laughing and Click explodes calling her and Lafu all kinds of names until Finesse finally sticks a piece of duct tape across his mouth.

I can't believe my ears. Click was messing around with some chick and Lafu and Finesse killed her and did something to her daughter.

I look at Lafu and ask, "what did you do to that little girl?" Instead of answering, Lafu moves around the table and takes the empty seat across from me. He just sits there penetrating me with those evil red eyes of his. I stare back thinking about the messed up things he did to Finesse when she was a little girl. I wonder how old this poor little girl was. I think about how Lafu killed my mother and all the pain he's caused in my life. I've never felt so much hatred towards another human being.

Finally he says, "Me ear ya quite the chess player Dee-nah. How about you and I play a game?"

"I don't want to play chess. I want you to get out of here and leave us alone."

"Me could do dat. Take what me came fer an leave, but me wan give ya a chance first. Do ya love deez two bumbaclots 'ere?"

I look at Uncle Fresh then Click. "Of course I do.

Lafu holds up the gun in his hand, pulls the pin on the front, flips the chamber wheel open, and dumps the large bullets into his hands. "We gone play a game ta see which one ya love da most. Me call dis, Chess Roulette." He grabs one of the bullets and holds it up to show me that it's already been fired and is only a shell casing. Then he places the rest of the them on the table in front of him. He sticks the empty shell casing into one of the empty chambers, gives the chamber wheel a spin, then quickly slams it shut.

"Yer white, ya go first. Ya' ave five seconds ta move."

"I told you, I don't want to play yo stupid game. What do you want?"

He says, "Deez bumbaclots violate Lafu. Me com fa dem life." Then he thumbs the hammer back. "Ya' ave five seconds ta move. One...two.." The full understanding of his intentions becomes clear when he gets to five, points the gun at Uncle Fresh's head and pulls the trigger. Lafu looks at the chamber wheel then holds it up to show me.

The firing pin is resting against the back of the empty shell casing.

"Ya would' ave lost one. Da rules are simple. Ya ave one in six chance erytine the trigga pull. Ya no move witin five seconds...the trigga pull. Erytine me call check...the trigga pull. Me call checkmate...the trigga pull two time. Dey live after da checkmate, me leave an never com bak. Ya choose who get da trigga pull." Lafu removes the empty shell casing from the gun and replaces it with a live round. Then he gives the chamber wheel a hard spin before slamming it shut. I'm thrown for a loop when I look up and see Finesse standing behind Click doing the exact same thing with her gun.

"Finesse why are you helping him?"

She looks at me and says, "Why not. He's the only one who seems to be paying me any attention or showing me any love around here. Besides, I hate both of these muthafuckas too." I'm confused. It's obvious that she's upset about Click having another girlfriend and hurting me, plus I know Finesse well enough to know that she's grown jealous of my relationship with him. What I don't understand is her beef with Uncle Fresh.

"That's not true. I've spent my whole life paying attention to you."

She softens up and gives me a look filled with affection. "I know D, that's why I will always and forever love you and have your back."

"Uncle Fresh has been there for you too."

Her facial expression instantly changes to a frown. "That muthafucka don't care about me no more than mama did."

For the first time, Uncle Fresh speaks up.

"Ness, Theresa and I both loved you dearly and have always treated you like a daughter."

She looks at him sarcastically. "Sure didn't sound like it on the video we just watched."

"There's a difference in me loving you and trying to take care of business. Don't let..."

"Enough." Lafu cuts in. "Dee-nah, it's yer move. Ya' ave five seconds." He begins counting.

I look at the chess board in front of me and realize that the odds are against me. Although I do have a fairly good game, Uncle Fresh taught me to take my time and think through every move. I've never been forced to play under pressure or against the clock.

"Focus Babygirl." I look at the tape across Uncle Fresh's eyes and the dried blood on the side of his face. His vulnerable state reminding me that his life depends on me.

I take a deep breath and make the first move. Lafu doesn't hesitate following up. The first four or five moves are typical defensive and strategical set up moves, but it's impossible for me to stop him from calling a simple check.

Lafu says, "Ya choose who get da trigga pull."

Then he cocks the hammer back and points his gun at Uncle Fresh's head. Finesse presses hers against Click's head. "Ya' ave five seconds or me choose fer ya. One...two.."

I look at Uncle Fresh then over at Click who's looking back at me with fear in his eyes. There is no way I would put more value on one of their life over the other one. Both of them are very special to me.

".... tree...four..."

Panicking, my eyes bounce back and forth. One of them can't see. The other can't speak. I wish someone would say or do something.

".... five. Times up. Nessa.

"Without hesitation Finesse pulls the trigger.

"Nooo!" The sound of the firing pin slamming into the empty bullet chamber is drowned out by my scream. Click is visibly shaking but still alive.

"You lucky Loverboy. You almost didn't make it." Finesse says next to Click's ear before licking the side of his face and letting out a deranged little laugh.

Now crying I ask, "Finesse why are you helping him do this after all this monster has done to you. Did you forget how long he's been raping you?"

"No but...if you really wanna know the truth, I actually started liking it after a while. What can I say,

Lafu got some good dick."

"If that were true Nessa, you wouldn't be still waking up every night screaming and having nightmares. And what about mama? Did you forget that he killed our mother?"

"It's yer move Dee-nah. Ya 'ave five seconds."

"No! I'm not playing this sick game with you. I ain't gone let you put they blood on my hands."

"Ya don move, da trigga pull. One...two…tree..."

Uncle Fresh says, "Finish the game Babygirl. You don't have a choice now. Focus."

I look at him then at Lafu. Those evil red eyes burning a hole through my soul. Without giving it much thought, I make a move. Lafu counters. I can't focus.

Two moves later, he steals my queen. I freeze up. He begins counting.

"One...two...tree...four..."   I move.

He puts me in check.

"Ya choose who get da trigga pull. Ya 'ave five seconds or me choose fer ya. One...two...tree...."

"Lafu please...please I'll do anything. What do you want?"

".....four...five." He opens the chamber wheel and gives it a hard spin before quickly slamming it shut. Then he points the gun at Uncle Fresh's head...and pulls the trigger.

The loud gunshot echoes inside my brain causing me to squeeze my eyes shut. When I open them, those evil red eyes are trained on me.

"Da luck is on her side Dee-nah. Two trigga pull wit no casualties. Let's see 'ow long it 'old up. It's yer

move."

Emotionally drained and at my wits end, I break down sobbing. "I can't do this." My tears are all I have left.

Finesse says, "Don't cry D, we all gone die one day." I look up at her and realize that although she's out of her mind, she's also my only hope.

"You know what Finesse, today I met a guy who wants to help me start a singing career. He says that I got what it takes to go all the way to the top and become a big time star one day."

"You do D, I've always told you that."

"When he told me that, the first thing I thought
   about was you. I remember you always telling me that you was gone be my manager. Remember that?"

"Yea I remember." she says with a reminiscent smile. Through my tears, I begin singing the lyrics to a Mary J Blige song. Finesse closes her eyes and snaps her fingers.

"Heeey now, sing it Dena. You know you be blowin girl." I sing to her from the depth of my soul. Like a cobra being hypnotized by the sound of a flute, Finesse gets caught up in my rhythm and grooves with me.

"Enough!" Lafu yells interrupting the moment and scaring me silent. "Time ta finish da game. Dee-nah, it's yer move." I ignore him and continue talking to Finesse.

Looking directly into the dilated pupils of her eyes I say, "We use to all be a family Nessa. Me, you, mama, Uncle Fresh....remember?"

"Y'all all forgot about me. Y'all let the monster get me." Her voice cracks and a lone tear escapes her eye and creeps down her cheek.

Hearing the pain in her voice, Uncle Fresh says, "We didn't forget about you Nessa. That's what Lafu wants you to think so he can control you. We were trying to figure out a way to come and save you."

"But I mailed you my diary Johnny Ray, knowing that if anyone could help me it was you. But all you did was show it to that bitch. And all she did was try and get rid of me."

"What bitch Finesse? You talkin about mama?" I ask not believing my ears.

Lafu spins the chamber wheel on his gun, slams it shut and says, "Ya 'ave five seconds ta move.

One...two..."

Finesse says, "You saw the video. She said I had to leave. She was getting ready to get rid of me."

".... four...five. " The sound of the firing pin slamming into the empty chamber wheel causes me to close my eyes and almost stops my heart.

A couple seconds tic by before I reopen them, silently thanking the Lord that I didn't hear a gunshot.

"He tricked you Finesse. That video was cut. Mama was upset when she found out what Lafu had been doing to you. She was saying that she had to get you away from him. She told Uncle Fresh that she would never leave you alone with him again and she was quitting the family business. Don't you see? That's why he killed her."

Uncle Fresh says, "Lafu didn't kill your mother Babygirl....Nessa did."

"You shut up!" Finesse screams at him.

I look at Finesse praying that what I just heard isn't true. "Finesse?"

"Playtime ova wit." Lafu says snapping the chamber wheel open again. One by one, he picks up the remaining four bullets on the table and inserts them into the bullet chambers leaving only one empty. He points the gun at Uncle Fresh's head and cocks the hammer back.

"Let me do it." Finesse says angrily while laying her gun on the table. She holds her hand out to Lafu. "Let me be the one to blow his lying ass head off."

Lafu looks at her long and hard before the corners of his mouth turn up into a sinister grin. He passes her the gun.

Finesse raises it and points it across the table at Uncle Fresh's face.

"No Nessa, don't do it."

"Sorry D.....he gotta die." The explosion from the .44 magnum rocks the confine of my twelve story condo, almost knocking Finesse off her feet.

CHAPTER 22

Dena

"I love to dream because, a dream denied defies the sky's true color blue,
And when I open my eyes wide and look towards the sky, I see the true color of you.
The true color of us is just the sight of distorted light with a midnight hue,
Midnight dreams seem like nightmares but are really our subconscious mind giving us a birds eye view.
Of things we just discovered, but really already knew.
I knew you in a different life so it's like despite how tight we grew,
We were never really far apart our hearts just wanted to beat brand new.
I believe if we stand through the test of time and deny the lies that we try to disguise as true,
Then we can see each other as reflections in the mirror and say I'm just like you.
I look through these eyes of mine and my mind misinterprets the things it think it sees,
Like the fluttering of the leaves in the wind that I pretend is just a breeze.
But really I know is God, so it's hard not to pray,
That that breeze could be your breath giving you life, if only for just one more day.
So rather we sleep light or sleep tight, we always dream.
Even if we don't remember when we open our eyes we still realize that life is just a dream."

The loud applause from the patrons at 'Enchanting Voices' warms my heart and causes my spirit to grow.

"Thank you." I say looking out at all the smiling faces, clapping hands, and snapping fingers.

Dejhoun, my emcee comes up and embraces me in a warm hug. "Glad to have you back." He whispers into my ear before receiving the mic from my hand and saying to the audience, "Once again ladies and gentlemen, Miss Dena Givens." The feeling that I missed so much courses through my body as I soak up the audience's praise before exiting the stage.

It's been over a year since the last time I made the journey back here to Arkansas and visited my poetry club. 'Enchanting Voices ' has always been my personal sanctuary. There was once a time when I wouldn't dare go a whole week without coming here at least once, sometimes three times a week, to enjoy the therapeutic atmosphere. Now that I'm back, I realize how much I've been missing it.

"Sista Givens, I swear you do it to me every time." Jersey girl Shaleitha says with her usual over excited enthusiasm. "You always seem to take me to a place that I've never been before when I hear one of your pieces."

"Aw thank you. It's been so long since I've performed one, that I forgot how exhilarating it is. God I've missed this place so much."

"We're glad to have you back. It hasn't been the same here without you."

"I'm glad to be back and definitely glad to have you on as my newest staff member."

"Deciding to work here full-time was one of the best decisions of my life. I was a little skeptical when Dejhoun first offered me a job here, but now I can't see my life without 'Enchanting Voices'. It's like getting paid to do something I love. Not to mention all the interesting people I get to meet. Like my new little man right here." she says bouncing my creamy baby up and down in her arms. "Ain't that right handsome." My son smiles and indulges her loving the attention.

"Uh-un, see y'all gone have him more spoiled than he already is. Give me my son you cougar." I joke while taking him out of her arms.

"But he's so adorable."

I place a juicy kiss on his chubby cheek thanking the Lord for my child. If it wasn't for him, his father probably wouldn't be alive right now. When I reflect on that night in Atlanta at my condo, I know that God was truly with us all. Three times the barrel got spent with a live round in it and the trigger got pulled without Click nor Uncle Fresh getting shot. Only two bullets actually got fired that night. The one that Finesse turned away from Uncle Fresh at the last second and put into the side of Lafu's head killing him instantly. And the one that I ended up putting between her eyes in a split second decision.

In the aftermath of the ear shattering gunshot that killed Lafu was an eerie silence. After regaining her balance, Finesse stood in apparent shock still holding the smoking gun. Lafu laid out with his brains and skull fragments decorating my dining room wall while his blood leaked out slowly all over my hardwood floor. It seemed unreal that all that evil, pain and suffering could be eradicated with just one simple flex of a finger. For the first time in my life, I was able to confirm that Lafu was nothing more than just a human being. Not a monster or the boogeyman or some type of machine, but simply just a man.

"Finesse?" My voice snapped her out of her trance and drew her eyes to me. "It's over Finesse. You killed him. You killed the monster."

She looked over at Lafu again as if to confirm that my words were true before looking back at me.

"I killed him. I killed him. I..." A new wave of tears flooded her eyes as she paused then broke down and said, "I killed mama. He tricked me D. He...he made me kill mama." Hearing her say those words broke something inside of me.

"Nooo Finesse, why? How could you do that?"

"I'm sorry. I didn't mean..." She broke down all the way letting out gut-wrenching sobs.

Now that I look back on everything and put all the pieces in place, I figured that Lafu must have gotten Finesse all doped up and drunk like that night in my condo. He must have used those videos to manipulate her into thinking that my mother was about to get rid of her. He made her feel abandoned and unwanted. He convinced her that he was the only one who loved her and the only way to stop her from being sent away was to kill my mother. All it took was a hysterical call from Finesse to get my mother from lying beside me in bed to driving out in the middle of the night to a hotel in the country. I can imagine the confused look on my mother's face when she walked into the hotel room and saw Lafu standing in his disguise of long salt and pepper dreads and beard.

Her asking him, "What's going on? What are you doing here dressed like that and where's Finesse?"

Then Finesse coming from behind the hotel room door where she was hiding in a rage and attacking my mother with a knife.

I guess realizing that she'd been tricked into murdering our mother in cold blood was too much for Finesse to bear.

Still standing behind Click's chair, she suddenly raised the gun and pointed the barrel at the bottom of her chin.

"I'm sorry D, I swear I didn't mean to...." she sobbed with her finger on the trigger.

In an instant, I was on my feet. "I know Nessa! I know it wasn't your fault. He tricked you. I know you didn't mean to kill her."

"You believe me?"

"Yes baby, I believe you." I held out my hand. "Now give me the gun." She looked at me skeptically while her mind tried to fight through the haze of liquor and cocaine. "It's all over Nessa. He can't hurtchu' anymore. Everything can go back to normal. Now we can go hang out in the Rainforest Room and get our smoke on like we use to."

The memory caused her to smile. "That use to be our favorite spot."

"Yea," I said matching her smile with my own. "We used to get so high....and yo ass was always imitating a scene from one of yo favorite movies or tryna get me to sing. " Finesse and I both laugh at that memory. "It used to be just me and you."

"Yea, me you and that damn poetry book." More laughter as we shared a nostalgic moment. A moment reflecting on moments that seemed to have happened eons ago.

Finesse smiled while lowering her gun." I miss those days."

"Yea me too. I wish things could just go back to how they use to be."

"They can." Without warning she put the gun to Click's head and cocked the hammer back. "All we gotta do is get rid of him."

In a panic, I said, "No Finesse you don't have to do that!"

"Yes I do D. He took you away from me and the only way I'll have you all to myself again is to get him out the picture for good." Then she pulled the trigger.

Like I said before, God was truly with us that night.

Only one chamber out of six was empty on that gun and what were the odds that the firing pin landed in that one.

I know Click damn near pissed his pants when he heard that gun click against his head. He stared at me with duct tape covering his mouth in wide eyed shock. I stood staring back just as shocked as he was. But neither one of us was more shocked than Finesse. She looked at the gun like it was a foreign object in her hand. That didn't stop her from cocking the hammer back and getting ready to pull the trigger again.

"Ma-ma." My son's voice caught us all off guard. So caught up in the twisted events taking place in my dining room that I hadn't stopped to think about that loud gunshot waking my son up out of his sleep. He stood holding on to the edge of his play pen watching us out of curious eyes.

That second of diversion saved Click's life.

I don't remember getting my .380 out. I don't remember pointing it and pulling the trigger. All I remember is seeing Finesse's finger applying pressure on the trigger and I just reacted.

Sometimes I sit for hours reflecting on my life with Finesse; wondering why some people are subjected to and suffer more evil than others. Why was she dealt such a bad hand? Only God knows the answer to those questions, but still I search my mind for the reasons why. From her first cry to her last breath, Finesse was a tortured soul. For reasons that were totally outside her control, she faced the most extreme vicissitudes of life. Sometimes I ask myself is my life better off or worse without her? She was a handful, always so reckless and needy. But Finesse was the salt of life. Her vivacious and sometimes downright outlandish personality brought flavor to the blandest moment. I miss her a lot. Does it bother me that she died by my hands? Yea, sometimes. I ask myself did I act too fast. Should I have kept talking to her? Could I have somehow still saved her? More questions that I'll never have the answers to. My comfort comes when I think about her terrible nightmares. How terrified she'd be and how much she hated to fall asleep. When she was woke, she could smile and pretend that everything was all good. But when she closed her eyes at night, her subconscious mind would conjure up the truth of her reality. The truth was that her reality was a nightmare. Knowing the details of Finesse's story made me realize that life is truly just a dream.

My son grabs my cheek and slobber on my jaw returning the kiss.

"What are you doing woke anyway? I thought you were supposed to be sleep."

"Girl he played me so many times that I gave up." Shaleitha says. "Every time I thought he was asleep and would cut off the light and try to ease out of the office, he'd go 'Ma-ma! When I'd turn around, he'd be standing there just a smiling with those dimples of his. After the third time, I finally caught on."

I can't help cracking up. "Girl he use to get me like that all the time. He loves playing possum."

Knowing that he's the center of attention, my creamy baby raises both of his arms in the air and says, "Yay! Fun fun!"

"No fun fun. Sleep sleep." I rub my nose against his making him giggle. "It's way past your bedtime. Now say goodnight to Shaleitha."

"Goodnight cutie pie." Shaleitha says pinching his cheek. Then to me, "I'm about to go help Dejhoun out. Let me know if you need my help with anything else."

"Okay, I will." I admire her Afrocentric garb and nice shape as she walks off. Just as I'm about to head down the hallway towards my office to put my son to sleep, a couple approaches me.

"What's happenin shawty. How you been?"

"Mechi, wow what a surprise. I didn't expect to see you here." I'm caught totally off guard.

"Yea I know. I just dropped by to check you out. Nice poem. I didn't know you was that deep."

"Thank you." I say still in shock as my eyes move to the person standing beside him. I definitely wasn't expecting to see her.

"You remember Reece dontchu?"

"Oh yea. How could I forget? The last time I saw her we were both living big-belly-style, waiting to give birth, and fighting like cats and dogs." She stands there eyeing me with stoic expression.

"How you doing Reece?" I ask attempting to be cordial and half expecting her to swing on me.

Surprisingly, she responds, "I'm fine. How about yourself?"

"I'm just living my life and tryna raise my son the best way I know how."

" I can definitely relate. I have one of my own about the same age who takes up most of my time."

Mechi say, "Damn, Click must have spit him

out. They damn near twins. Let me see my nephew." I don't protest when he takes him out of my arms. "Sup lil man. I'm Uncle Mechi."

"Tup." My son says giving him an upward head nod. It's so cute that we all end up sharing a laugh.

"I have no idea where he gets this stuff."

"Where else? He gets it from his cool ass daddy." Mechi offers.

"Um, if you don't mind me asking Mechi, how did you know I would be here?"

"Click told me." he says matter-of-factly. I should have known. Click is the only one beside Uncle Fresh who knew I would be here tonight. Actually, he's the one who convinced me to move back to Arkansas so that he could see his son regularly since he was now being housed at the federal prison here in Forrest City.

Mechi says, "If you don't mind, me and my nephew are about to do us a couple of rounds and listen to some poetry." Without waiting for an answer, he heads out into the audience carrying my son proudly in his arms.

Reece says, "You know he's about to use your son to pick up chicks right?"

"He better not. Mechi!" I call behind him, but he's already moving deeply into the throng of tables. I can't do nothing but shake my head.

"They'll be alright." she says. "I wanted to talk to you alone anyway. Let me buy you a drink."

"I don't drink, but if you want one, it's on the house."

"Hey, sounds good to me."

I lead the way to my reserved table that sits directly in front of the stage. I'm stopped along the way and given a couple of welcome backs and nice poem compliments that lets me know that I'm truly back home.

Once we get comfortable at the table, I signal the waiter. When he makes it over, I tell Reece,

"Order whatever you like."

"Um, I think I'll have a double shot of Patron."

"You can just bring the whole bottle over Clarence and bring me a large glass of orange juice too. Hold the ice."

"Okay ladies, I'll be right back with your drinks." he says before he walking off.

"Let me find out that you tryna get me drunk so we can pick up where we left off the last time we saw each other." Reece says giving me a skeptical look.

"Girl please, you're the one who had all the animosity. I was just asking for your help."

"Yea, I know. Click eventually broke everything down and made me understand what was really going on. At the time, all I knew was that you set him up, and I don't play when it comes to family. And Click is definitely family."

"It's all good. I go hard for those I love too." We sit for a second letting the silence confirm our peace. It gives me a chance to admire Reece's attractiveness. With her hair pulled back into a long, neat ponytail showcasing evenly cut bangs, her brown-skinned face looks young and smooth. Her tight, chinky eyes sit atop a cute button-nose and full lips. Heart-shaped diamond stud earrings sit in her ears drawing attention to her slender neck. A waist-length, black, leather coat and tight blue jeans cover her small but curvy frame. If I didn't know any better, it would be hard to believe that she'd ever birthed a child.

"I'm loving those boots. What are those Prada's?"

"Thanks and yes. I see you know fashion."

"Yea, I got a fetish for designer boots."

"Girl me too."

"Designer boots and some good weed." I say reaching down into my own boots and pulling a neatly rolled blunt from the stash pocket that I had sown inside of them. "Do you smoke?"

"Do I." Reece responds with a roll of her neck. "Whatchu need me to light it for you?" She digs into her jacket pocket, pulls out a lighter and sparks a flame.

"Thanks." I say leaning the tip of the blunt into it. After taking a couple of good tokes, I pass it to her and ask, "So what is it that you wanted to talk to me about?"

"Ooh, this shit strong." she says easing smoke out

of her nose and mouth. She looks at me and says, "Well just to get straight to the point, I love Click. From the day we met, he's been like a brother to me. As you already know, he and my husband Travis were best friends. Three days after Click got out of prison, my husband got murdered. That was a real ruff time for me." I nod my head remembering how distraught Reece was that night that I first saw her at the hospital after her husband got killed.

She says, "For a while, I even blamed Click for his death."

"Why did you blame Click?" I ask frowning in confusion.

"Because, as far as I was concerned, my husband wouldn't have even been in those projects that night if it wasn't for Click tryna sell some damn drugs."

"Oh." I say realizing that she's talking about the same drugs that Click had gotten from me. "So what made you have a change of heart?"

"Because I know something about Click that most people don't."

"Which is?"

She takes another puff of the blunt and passes it back to me. "That Click went to prison for a murder that he didn't commit." Now more confused than ever, I give her a look. She says, "Click took the charge and did ten years in prison for my husband."

My mouth drops open in shock. "Are you serious?"

"As a heart attack."

I'm blown away. From my understanding, the whole reason why Lafu made me set Click up in the first place was because he believed that Click had killed his brother Jamar. Now she's telling me that Click isn't even the one who killed Jamar.

"You mean to tell me that your husband is the one who killed the person that Click went to prison for killing?"

She nods her head up and down. "Yup. So while I was blaming Click, I should have been thanking him. Had it not been for him, Travis and I would have never even met. I realized that I owe him for every second of happiness that I ever shared with my husband. I owe him for my marriage, my memories, and most importantly, my son."

I sit puffing my blunt letting what she'd just told me sink in. I always knew that my Dabo was a real nigga but damn. Hearing this makes me love and respect him even more.

"I have to admit Reece, I've always been kinda jealous of your relationship with Click, but now it all makes sense."

"Click is the most loyal and genuine friend a person can have. Even after all that, he still looks out for me and my son on the strength of his relationship with Travis. That's why I will always have his back and be down for him."

"That makes two of us."

"Which leads me to my point."

The waiter comes back to the table with our drinks. "Here you go ladies, one bottle of Patron and a large glass of orange juice with no ice."

"Thanks Clarence." I say taking my glass and sipping from it. "Aah, just right."

He smiles. "Is there anything else I can get for you guys?"

Already busy pouring herself a drink, Reece shakes her head.

"Nah, we good."

"Alright then, you ladies enjoy the rest of your evening." He leaves and Reece picks up where she left off.

"Like I was saying, Click just got done serving ten years for a crime he didn't commit. He was only out for a year and now he's back serving another ten. That's a hard pill to swallow, but you know Click...he's taking it like a G." I nod my head thinking of how he's always in good spirits whenever I talk to him. "Me and him had a long talk the other night. And out of all the things I owe him for, he only asked me for one thing in return...." She looks at me pointedly. "That I make sure that his son and my son grow up knowing each other. That means that whatever disagreement or beef that you and I had in the past, it ends right here."

I look into her eyes now understanding the real reason for her coming here tonight.

"I don't think that's asking too much." I say picking up my glass of orange juice and holding it out to her. "I'm down if you down."

She bumps her glass with mine and we both take a sip.

"Speaking of sons, where is Mechi with mines?" I look around the room until I spot Mechi sitting at a table surrounded by women laughing and talking with my son sitting on his lap. "Look at this fool." Reece and I crack up laughing.

On the stage, Shaleitha grabs the microphone and says, "I don't know about y'all, but with each new poet that hits the stage, I fall more and more in love with poetry. There's definitely power in spoken words." The audience claps their agreement. "Okay y'all, coming to the stage next is a brotha who's a close friend of mine from the mid-west. In the famous words of R. Kelly, 'He was raaaised in Illinois.....right outside of Chicagooo'" she sings then laughs that infectious laugh of hers evoking laughter from the crowd. "He's not only a poet, but also a motivational speaker, writer, and published author. Y'all be on the lookout for him. My brotha-from-anotha-motha, Kuflo." The audience cheers as a short, stocky brotha with shoulder length dreads, and one of the coolest walks I've ever seen walks out onto the stage. Him and Shaleitha share a warm hug before she passes him the mic and exits the stage.

In a deep, raspy voice he says, "Hey how y'all doing? I got this piece I'm gone hit for y'all, but I'm going to need a little help from the band." He looks back at Dejhoun who's standing behind him. Dejhoun gives him the thumbs up then goes behind the piano and has a seat. He begins playing a smooth R and B melody that puts me in the mind of a Dave Hollister track. The rest of the band joins in and the vibrant sound takes over the room.

"Yea, I can vibe to that." Kuflo says moving his head slightly to the rhythm. "Aiight, I like to call this one, 'Garden of Thoughts'."

"OK now."

"Let's hear it then."

"Do yo thang brotha." Come a couple voices from the audience.

"Taking time to tend to my mental garden of thoughts, I find wild weeds of pessimism planted to perpetuate the continued growth of bad seeds....

In my moments of meditation, I mentally remove them to be replaced with pollinated plants of perspicuity....

A periodical thunderstorm of thorns poke from the rosebush of my beliefs to cause blood drops of reality to rain into the rawness of my emotions...

Beautiful colors all void of somber shine like summer in the winter months of my memories.....

Daily cultivation creates rows of optimism to develop in the soul of my mind...my thinking is sublime....

.....blinking at the sun when it shines its bright light into my eyesight and now I see.....

I see the good seeds cause even good weed can stimulate good thoughts....

Willing to pay for this day because it should cost...these are just the garden of my thoughts.... these and just the garden of my thoughts....."

"I like him. He has a nice delivery." I say to Reece.

"Yea, he's smooth and that deep, seductive voice of his is kinda soothing. Makes me wanna call my man right now and see if he wanna come over and water my garden of thoughts tonight."

"Man? I didn't know you had a man Reece."

"Yea, but please don't say anything to Click. I haven't found a way to tell him or Mechi about it yet."

"Why not?"

"Well you know, with them being Travis's brother and best friend, I don't know how they gone feel about it."

"I think you should just tell them. If they yo family and really love you then they should support you no matter what. Long as you happy that's all that should matter. Plus, I don't think Travis would want you to be alone for the rest of your life anyway."

"I don't know. Them two fools can be downright ignorant when they want to. Especially Mechi, he might try to jump on the man or something."

"Speak of the devil, here he comes now."

Mechi walks up still carrying my son. "Ay shawty, check it out. You think I could babysit my nephew tonight? I got this lil piece supposed to be coming over and she gone expect my son to be with me. Know whatamean?"he says with a gruff laugh giving me a wink.

Reece is beside me killing herself trying not to laugh.

"Boy if you don't give me my son." I say standing up and taking my baby out of his arms.

"What?" Mechi asks holding his hands out with a dumb look on his face.

CHAPTER 23

Dena
Ten years later 2015

Who would have thought?
Click's one request to Reece was that she make
amends with me so that our kids could grow up together and be close like he and Travis were. Who would have thought that her and I would grow to be such good friends? Who would have thought that she would help to fill that void that Finesse and my mother had left in my life? Who would have thought that she would eventually end up moving into the mansion with me and Uncle Fresh and stay for the next ten years? Who would have thought that my creamy baby and Travis Jr. would dislike each other so much?

Reece wasn't the only one that Click requested one thing from.

All I wanted to do was put the past behind me, raise my son and focus on my music career. What Click asked me to do was a constant reminder of a pain that would always live inside of me.

"Mama, they playing yo song on the radio again." My son says still excited at the success of my new hit single 'Gamechanja' that has been dominating the top of the billboard charts for the past six weeks.

"I know son, but they play it so much that even I'm tired of hearing it."

"Not me. I'll never get tired of listening to you sing."

"Aww, baby." I throw my arm around his shoulders and kiss the top of his head.

"That's cause you a mama's boy." Travis Jr. says taunting my son as usual.

"I ain't no mama's boy."

"Yes you is. Always under her like you still wanna be titty fed or something."

"T.J.!" Reece jumps in. "What I tell you about yo mouth? Don't make me come over there and whoop yo ass out here in front of these folks penitentiary. Now apologize."

T.J. drops his head and says, "Sorry Miss Dena."

"To both of them."

"Sorry Cream." Him and my son stare evilly across the interior of the stretch hummer at each other. I've long since given up on trying to figure out why these two can't get along.

"Nadia, you alright over there baby? Nadia?" I try waving my hand to get her attention, but she's in her own world with earbuds in her ears, eyes focused on her iPod.

Travis Jr. who's sitting beside her, nudges her with his elbow.

"What?" she says with attitude removing one of her earbuds.

"Miss Dena talking to you."

"Oh." she says straightening her face and looking up at me. "Yes Miss Dena?"

"I'm just checking on you making sure you alright over there."

"Yea, I'm fine."

"You sure?" She nods her head up and down then replaces her earbud and goes back to looking at her iPod.

Nadia reminds me so much of Finesse. Not the wild and crazy part of Finesse, but the introverted part where she closes up inside of herself and won't let nobody in. Nadia rarely talks. She's more of an observer who mostly likes to stay to herself. Even in a room full of people. The only exception is with her two "little brothers." That's what she calls T.J. and my creamy baby. She adores them both and their blind loyalty towards her is scary. She's the only one who can seem to mediate and keep the peace between those two. I worry about her a lot. It's bad enough that she was there and had to witness losing her mother in such a tragic way. But Lafu did a number on Nadia that left her scarred for life. After her examination revealed that she had in fact been severely molested and would probably never be able to have children, she was sent to a psychiatrist. But not even a shrink could get her to open up and talk about what Lafu did to her. To even bring up the subject is the quickest way to make her shut down and cut off all communication with you. On top of everything else, Nadia's grandmother had a heart attack and died two days after finding out that her daughter was found dead. Seeing as how no other family members were willing to step up and take Nadia in, they sent her to a foster home. That's when Click made his one request of me. At first, I was upset that he would even think asking me to adopt the daughter of his dead girlfriend knowing how bad it hurt me when I found out that he had been dealing with another woman. But then I saw Nadia for the first time and there was no way that I could turn my back on that little girl.

"Here he comes y'all!" Reece announces making

everyone look out the window towards the entrance of the federal prison that Click has been being held for the past decade.

"Ohmygod! My baby." My hands cover my mouth and begin shaking as I watch my Dabo walking down the sidewalk towards the parking lot where we've all been sitting in the stretch Hum-V waiting for the past two hours.

I don't wait for our driver to come open the door for me. Nor do I give anyone else a chance to move before I'm out of the truck running up the sidewalk towards him. Forget what you heard; I been waiting ten long years for this moment. All the weekend trips, waiting in long lines and being searched just to have guards standing over you and hovering around our visit limiting our conversation and interaction with each other. Then for it to all end after seeming to have just begun. All the sad goodbyes and long lonely nights in between waiting for his phone call or our next visit. Ten years of helping to keep his spirits up while trying to hide how low my own were. Ten years of taking care of, loving and raising the broken child of his dead girlfriend like she was my own. Ten years of raising and looking at his son being reminded every moment of the man I love and miss so much. Ten years of waiting for him to come home to me. I'm done waiting.

I don't hold back when I reach him and jump into his big strong arms wrapping my arms and legs around him. I kiss all over his face and neck giving him all the love that I've been saving up just for him.

"Damn Suabo, I've missed yo ass so much." he growls into my ear.

I respond by tonging him down while he grips both of my ass cheeks in his large hands. There ain't no shame in my game. I've gone ten long years with no form of sexual release besides the few times that I broke down and masturbated which only left me feeling hornier and longing for my Dabo's touch.

"Get a room!" I hear Reece yell.

"Ugh they nasty."

"Gross." I hear the boys saying which causes me to start laughing.

I wipe my lipstick from Click's lips as I look into his handsome face.

"Is this really happening right now or am I about to wake up in the next few seconds and realize it's just another dream?"

"It's definitely real ma. The nightmare is over. It's time for us to start living now."

"Oh baby..." My emotions take over spilling tears down my cheeks as I bury my face in the crook of his neck refusing to unwrap my arm or legs from around him.

"It's okay ma." He rubs my back letting me get my boo-hoo's out. After a few minutes he says, "Come on Suabo, you gotta share me with everybody else."

"No I don't."

He laughs. "Don't be like that. You got me for the rest of yo life. I ain't going nowhere. I'll never leave y'all again."

"You promise?"

"I promise." He kisses my lips again and begins wiping my tears away.

Reluctantly, I unwrap myself from around his body and try to pull myself together.

"It feels so good to be able to touch you without some guard standing there staring all in our face." I give his lips a few more pecks just to emphasize my statement.

"Like I said, that nightmare is over." He gives my butt a light smack and a tight squeeze. I'm all smiles as we walk the rest of the way down the sidewalk with his arm thrown around my shoulders and both of my arms around his waist.

Nadia is the first one to break away from the pack and rush Click when we make it to the parking lot. I stand in shock watching as she comes out of her shell. Nadia rarely ever gets excited about anything. The most you'll see is a faint smile when she's happy about something, which isn't often. Other than that, she mostly stays reserved and expressionless. Even on the occasions when she's come with me to visit Click, her disposition has always been quiet and sad. Now she's completely animated as she races into his embrace.

"Deshaaawn!"

"Hey Queen Bee."

"I thought they wasn't gone ever let you outta that place."

"Me either."

"Well I'm glad they finally did because the boys need you out here."

"Oh the boys need me huh?" Click asks amused.

"What about you?"

Instead of responding, she blushes and lays her head on his chest giving him a tight squeeze.

I notice the boys are still standing beside Reece looking half scared.

"T.J., Creamy, y'all ain't gone come say hi to Click?"

"Maaa, I keep telling you, it's Cream not Creamy. Creamy sounds gay."

"Ok my bad. I mean Cream."

"Creamy baaaby." T.J. teases.

"Shut up!"

Reece says, "Ok that's enough. Now go." She gives them both a light shove forward.

"Wassup my lil souljas." Click gives them each a one arm shoulder bump.

It's hilarious watching their body language change into their definition of cool in Click's presence. I can't believe how much they've grown up. Seems like yesterday they were both stumbling around, whining and about to start pre-school. Now they're both in sixth grade and on the verge of adolescence.

"Which one of y'all can run the fastest?" Click asks.

Cream looks up at Click with assured confidence and says, "I'll burn em daddy."

"You won't burn nothing over here boy!"

"Wassup then?" Cream lines up in a straightaway down the middle of the parking lot. "To that gray car and back."

"You ain't said nothin but a word." TJ goes over and lines up beside him. They both get in their starting position.

Click says, "Ready...set...go!" They take off in a furious battle towards the gray car.

Reece comes over and greets Click with a hug and kiss on the cheek.

"Hey bruh-in-law. Now why did you do that? We have enough trouble keeping them from arguing and competing over every little thing as it is."

"They boys, they supposed to compete. Competition is good for em." Click answers while watching the race closely.

"Well I'm glad you home now so you can deal with em cause I'm tired of it."

The boys sprint back towards us with pumping arms, legs, and determined faces, but TJ is no match. My Creamy baby beats him by at least five steps.

"I told you daddy! I told you I'd burn this fool!"

"Hey hey," Click checks him "that ain't what winners do. Win, lose, or draw you shake hands and tell each other good race."

"Sorry daddy." Cream approaches TJ with his hand extended for a shake.

TJ smacks it away and says, "You got lucky pretty boy." before storming off in a huff taking his loss hard.

"See what I mean?" Reece comments.

Click only smirks while following TJ with his eyes and says, "They gone be aiight. We just gotta teach em that they playing for the same team."

Suddenly anxious to put the prison in our review, Click rushes everybody to load up so we can head out. He tells the driver to take the scenic route through Forrest City so he can see the town. First through Sunrise then down Martin Luther King where we make a left on Highway 1. Next we swing past A through D street, down Rosser, and all through the South Side coming out at the end of Franklin and Broadway. Then we drive down Dawson Rd. past the Jackpot Projects and the Pickway Homes, past the high school and around to where all the stores and restaurants are located out by the main highway. The whole ride, Click asks questions and Reece fills him in on the happenings around the town. The boys talk nonstop about school, video games, and all the things that are important to eleven year old boys. I'm just happy to be up under Click and feel his hard body next to mine. Nadia seems just as content sitting quietly on his other side with his arms wrapped around both of our shoulders.

Finally, we drive deep back down Bearhill Road towards the mansion. Uncle Fresh is waiting for us in the driveway when we pull up.

CHAPTER 24

Click

The old man in the red Dob hat looks dapper than ever.

Crisp white button down, red slacks, and shiny red and white snakeskin Stacy Adams on his feet, Johnny Ray looks like he's ready to go out and cut a rug. Anyone who really knows him knows that this is just how he likes to get down. He's always fresh dressed and ready to impress. He greets me with a strong handshake and warm embrace when I climb out of the hummer.

"Welcome home young brotha. How does it feel to finally be back on this side of the fence?"

"Aw man, it feels good. Real good!" I answer with enthusiasm feeling my excitement begin to grow. Johnny Ray and I have long since put our differences to the side and gained a mutual respect for each other. Being that he doesn't believe in stepping inside of a prison unless it's by force, he never came to see me. Although we've spoke over the phone many times, this is the first time that I've actually laid eyes on him in ten years. He doesn't appear to have aged a day.

"What do you know that the rest of us don't?" I ask him.

"What do you mean?"

"You actually look younger now than you did before I went in."

Dena says, "I told you Uncle Fresh. He's been looking the same way since I was a little girl."

Johnny Ray releases a modest laugh before leaning in and saying in a conspiratorial tone, "Well I do have one secret..." Dena, Reece, and I are all ears. Even the kids are tuned in. "All I have to do is...keep my secret a secret and I'll remain young forever."

"Aw man."

"Uncle Fresh."

"He got us good." We all voice our disappointment at being played.

Then he says, "Now everybody get cleaned up. I have something special planned." He places a hand on my shoulder stopping me from going inside with everyone else. "Babygirl, if you don't mind, I'd like to borrow Click for a few minutes."

"I guess." She says turning and heading inside while shaking her head and mumbling to herself, "What is it with all this borrowing and sharing stuff? What if I don't feel like sharing? What if I feel like being selfish? I ain't even had a whole hour with my man and everybody wanna borrow him...."

Johnny Ray and I stand watching until her and the rest of the family disappears inside of the mansion.

He says, "We don't have long before she loses it. She's had everybody on pins and needles the way she's been running around trying to make sure everything is perfect just for you."

"Yea, I can imagine. That's why I feel so bad for what we're about to do."

"Well we don't have much time so if we're going to make our move it's now or never. You sure you ready to do this?"

I nod my head up and down. "I've never been more ready for anything in my life."

"Well let's go." I look back at the mansion one last time before Johnny Ray and I climb inside the Hummer and he tells the driver where to take us.

CHAPTER 25

Dena

"You seen Click and Uncle Fresh?" I ask Reece as we pass each other in the main corridor of the eastern wing.

"They still out front talking ain't they?"

"No. I just went back out there, but they gone." She shrugs her shoulders and continues on about her business.

Now where could they have disappeared to? I make my way into the surveillance room to check the monitors showing the camera angles covering every area of the property. They're nowhere in sight. I notice that the Hummer is gone as well. I wonder where they could have gone to that fast. Uncle Fresh said that he had something special planned so maybe they went to pick up some last minute detail while they talked. Wherever they went, I hope they hurry back so I can show Click all of the surprises that I have in store for him. For the past few weeks I've been planning how I'm going to make his first night home a night he won't forget.

First I check then double check to make sure that everything is set up exactly how I want it. Then I look in on the kids before heading into the main kitchen for a bottled water. After taking a couple of healthy swigs, I decide to call Uncle Fresh to find out where he took my man to. Before I have a chance to pull up his number, a call comes in from my manager.

Chicago Slim's excited voice comes from the other end of the line when I answer. "If you're not already sitting down, go find a seat because I got some news that's gone knock you off yo feet."

"What, you got me a collaboration with Beyoncé?"

"Close, but not quite. I just got a call from Evan Cliverson."

"From Tre R Records?" I ask in disbelief.

"Yes! They want to offer you a contract to sign with them."

"You lying."

"No I'm not. I just got the call a few minutes ago."

I drop the phone and scream at the top of my lungs at hearing that one of my biggest dreams has finally come true. After years in the studio, working with Slim, and building up my repertoire, we finally started releasing some of my music in a string of R&B mixtapes and YouTube videos that generated quite a buzz. My first single, 'Hurtchu Bad' dropped in the Spring of 2014 and was soon playing on several radio stations across the country. It was mildly successful, but when I dropped my second single 'Light Switch', the calls began rolling in. I've had offers from some of the largest named labels in the industry, but I've been holding out in hopes of signing with my favorite and by far the largest of them all. Realest Raw Records has been dominating the charts for the past five summers straight, dropping some of the hottest collaborations with some of the hottest artists the game has ever seen. Under the expert tutelage of powerhouse CEO Evan Cliverson, Realest Raw Records is the first label to ever have a number one hit in every genre of music from Country to Hip Hop and R&B to Neo Soul, Gospel, and Jazz to Rock and Roll, Pop, and even Reggae at the same time. Now after releasing 'Gamechanja', my junior and most successful single to drop, I've finally gotten the call I've been waiting for.

Chicago Slim's voice comes through the receiver.

"Dena? Dena, you still there?"

I pull myself together, pick up the phone, and put it back to my ear. "Yes I'm here."

"I knew you'd be ecstatic. He wants to meet with you today."

"Today?" I ask losing my smile as all of the excitement drains back out of me. "I can't do it today."

"What do you mean you can't do it today?"

"My man. He just...I...my son's father came home from prison today after being gone ten years. We've got plans. I can't do it today."

"Listen Dena, I understand that you've probably been waiting for this day for a long time, but this is Evan Cliverson. You've been waiting on his call your whole life. Now you have tomorrow...hell you have the rest of your life to make up this one day to your man. There might not be another opportunity like this with Evan Cliverson."

He's right. I know he's right, but I just can't see myself jumping on a plane and flying off to New York or somewhere knowing that Click just came home.

"Can't you call him back and reschedule a meeting. I understand that he's an important man, but clearly he had to consider that there was a chance that I would be tied up and not able to drop everything at the drop of a dime just because he called."

"Well that's the good news. He's over in Memphis right now meeting with Yo Gotti. He has another engagement to attend there after that at eight o'clock. He was hoping that you could join him there so y'all could discuss business. Shouldn't last more than a couple hours. You'd be back home by midnight at the latest."

I look to see that the time says four-sixteen. That leaves me three hours and forty-four minutes to jump in the shower, find something to wear, and make the forty-five minute journey across the bridge to Memphis. I can pull that off.

"Dena, I hear you thinking and I'm telling you, there's nothing to think about. This is the opportunity of a lifetime. Your man will understand."

"Okay, but I have to make a couple of calls first so just text me the address."

"That's what I'm talkin bout! "he shouts triumphantly. "I'm sending it now. Oh and Dena, it's an all-white formal event so clean up nice."

I hang up and call Uncle Fresh's phone.

"Hello. "he answers on the first ring.

"Uncle Fresh, where did you guys disappear to?"

"Oh Babygirl. I wanted to show Click the investment that he and I have been working on real quick."

"Oh." I say feeling some type of way about Uncle Fresh not being considerate enough for me to at least wait until I got to spend a little time with Click before he kidnapped him, but I decide not to say anything. "Well do you know how long it will be before you guys come back?"

"I just finished talking to the realtor and he said that he would be here in about forty-five minutes.

We should be back in about an hour or so."

An hour or so? Which really translated to two maybe three hours. Great. Now I know I won't be getting a chance to see my man before I leave.

Blowing out a breath of frustration, I say "Can I please speak to Click?" It's taking everything inside of me not to tell Uncle Fresh how I really feel.

A few seconds later my Dabo's voice comes over the line.

"Sup Suabo." Just hearing his sexy voice makes me wish he was here with me right now. Wishing he could at least go to Memphis with me to be my moral support. Damn Uncle Fresh.

"Hey baby. You know I'm upset right?"

"Yea, I kinda figured you would be."

"Not just at the fact that whatever it is that y'all got going on could have waited, but I just got some of the best news of my life."

"What is it?"

"Evan Cliverson called and he wants me to meet him in Memphis this evening to discuss me signing to Realest Raw Records."

"Aw man that's great news. Congratulations!"

"Yea I just wish you were here to share it with me."

"I'm sorry baby. What time do you have to be there?

"Eight o'clock."

"You still got a couple of hours. We should be back way before then."

"I hope so. Well, I have to start getting ready so hopefully I'll see you soon."

"Okay baby, love you."

"Love you too." I hang up then head to take a shower. Click coming home, the call from Evan Cliverson, it's all so much at one time.

I stand in my walk-in closet wrapped in nothing but a towel feeling excitement, nervousness, and anxiety as I choose and discard outfit after outfit. Finally, I settle on just hitting up a mall in Memphis and buying something new to wear. That decision also causes me to decide not to wait for Uncle Fresh and Click to come back. Knowing how indecisive I can be and how important this meeting is to me; I don't need anything distracting me while I shop. I'll make it up to my Dabo when I come home tonight. With that resolve in mind, I throw on a pair of black and white Air Max, some black leggings, and a white T-shirt, then head to the garage. It's ten minutes after five. Less than three hours to hit the mall and find something to wear that will blow Evan Cliverson's mind. I need a car with some serious horsepower to get me across that bridge as quickly as possible. My eyes survey the rows of expensive cars stretched out across the garage until they land on a bright red, brand new Maserati. Perfect.

Surprisingly, I don't get pulled over as I switched lane to lane driving ninety to a hundred miles per hour down I-40. Once I get there, finding the perfect attire proves to be a much bigger feat. Nothing seems good enough. I try on at least twenty different outfits before an all-white, mid-thigh, butterfly back dress with a plunging V-neck by Versace saves my life. It costs me thirty-five hundred bucks but it's money well spent. Every head in the store turns in my direction after I put on the white, six-inch stiletto heeled Christian Louis Vuitton's with the diamond crusted, spaghetti straps, and walk up to the counter to pay for my purchase.

"Whoever he is, the answer will be yes to anything you ask tonight." the attractive woman behind the register comments with a smile as I hand her my Platinum Visa Card.

"You don't think it's too much?"

"Too much? Girl you make that dress look so good that they ought to give you your money back and pay you for wearing it."

"Aw, thank you." I say feeling more confident and inspired by her words.

I keep that same energy going as I step out of the Maserati in front of the Alloriqui' Hotel and receive my ticket from the valet.

"Enjoy your night" he says damn near stumbling over himself trying to watch my physique as I walk towards the grand entrance of the hotel. The Alloriqui is one of Memphis's newest attractions that I often hear being advertised over the radio where star studded events are held. Whatever is going on here tonight must be big because the flow of luxury vehicles pulling into valet is nonstop.

I finger the princess cut diamond necklace that I haven't taken off of my neck since my mother gave it to me for good luck as I walk inside. It's a quarter till eight. I'd managed to do everything that I needed to do and still made it here on time. Now all I have to do is charm my way through this meeting and make it home before it gets too late. A tall white man wearing a black tuxedo is set up at a podium just inside the huge glass doors checking names on the guest list. I feel myself getting nervous as I stand in line waiting for my turn to arrive. Slim gave me the address and told me that this was an all-white event, but he didn't say anything about a guest list. Hopefully, my name is on there. It would be so embarrassing to get up there and be turned around. I start to call Slim, but it's too late. I'm already at the front of the line.

"Dena Givens," I say forcing a smile with a confidence that I no longer feel.

Surprisingly, he responds, "Ah Miss Givens, Mr. Cliverson has been waiting for you. Just one moment please." He begins speaking into a walkie talkie. I watch as he places a finger to his ear, obviously listening to a response through some kind of hidden device in his ear. Almost immediately another man wearing an identical black tuxedo emerges from a set of double doors labeled 'Ballroom'.

The man approaches me and says, "Right this way Miss Givens." before leading me to the Ballroom doors, which he holds open for me. I'm overwhelmed by the beautiful decor before me. The entire room is filled with red and white bouquets of roses giving the air a garden fresh scent. Large ice sculptures are strategically placed around the huge room in the shapes of music notes and microphones. The largest of them all being in the shape of the record labels trademarked Tre R symbol sitting beside the large stage that dominates the front of the room. Crystallized chandeliers hang from the ceiling with the lighting set low giving the atmosphere an intimate vibe. The Ballroom is already packed with several people sitting at the tables around the room and getting plates in the back where food is being catered. The entire place is beautifully decorated with a red and white theme. Now that I take a closer look, all the patrons in attendance are coordinated in some kind of red and white ensemble making me stick out like a sore thumb with my all white on.

The man in the black tuxedo leads me to a table in the center of the room that's in the shape of a horseshoe facing the stage. Evan Cliverson, a clean cut African American man in his mid-fifties, is sitting at the center of the horseshoe surrounded by an entourage of what I can now see is mostly artists who are signed to Tre R Records.

"Mr. Cliverson, your guest has arrived."

Evan Cliverson, who is dressed down in a red suit with a white tie, looks up from his conversation and says, "Ah, Miss Givens, you made it." before standing up and embracing me with an air kiss to the cheek.

"Yes, I managed to pull myself together and make it here in one piece."

"We've all been waiting for you." he says holding me at arm's length and looking me over from head to toe.

Now feeling self-conscious with all eyes on me, I say, "Sorry, but Mr. Humphrey told me this was an all-white event. Had I have known; I would have at least worn my Red Bottoms." My nervous laugh comes out sounding like a guffaw.

"Don't worry about it. Besides, you're absolutely breathtaking. Isn't she stunning?" he asks his entourage who all comment and nod their agreement. "I want you to meet your new label mates." he says as if I've already signed a contract and am a part of the team. One by one he introduces me to each person at the table. Although I'm a fan of more than a few, I try not to act star struck as we shake hands and exchange greetings. Most of them follow suit by embracing me with air kisses and saying, "Welcome to Tre R Records." The moment is surreal. Afterwards, I'm directed to sit in the seat next to Evan Cliverson.

"So Miss Givens." he begins.

"Dena. Please call me Dena."

"Ok Dena, I hear that you've had several offers from several different labels but have yet to sign with anyone. Any specific reason why?"

"To be honest with you Mr. Cliverson..."

"E.C. Everyone calls me E.C."

I smile. "Ok E.C. I've been a fan of your work since the late nineties when you first came out with 'New Vibe'."

"Ah New Vibe." he nods his head up and down with a reflective smile. "They were the first act on the label to go mainstream."

"The way you capitalized on their sound but enhanced their personal characteristics at the same time made the whole world feel like they knew them personally. Like who they were as people stood out more than the music itself. At first I thought that it was New Vibe themselves. How much of a relief they were from the usual trend following acts that were emerging at the time. They were like a breath of fresh air to R&B. But then the same thing happened with the Neo-Soul artist, Ink that you brought out. Then Givet blew up on the hip-hop scene as well as the other twenty-seven artists whose careers you've managed over the last twenty years. All in different genres. That's when I realized that it was you. Whatever formula you use, that thing you do to make the artist so relatable, is a personal gift that you possess. I told myself that if I ever made it to this point, that's how I wanted to be presented to the world."

"So what you're saying Dena, is that I didn't choose you, you chose me?"

"I guess you could say that."

"Well I'm honored. I hope I live up to your expectations."

"I'm sure you will. One thing about having a gift, you don't have to work at being good at it because it's something that comes natural."

"Touché." he says before grabbing a bottle of champagne out of the ice bucket sitting in front of us and filling up two champagne flutes. "Those are my exact sentiments when I heard your first two singles 'Hurtchu Bad' and 'Light Switch '. You're a natural. My instincts were to grab you then, but I was curious to hear what you would drop next. I was impressed to find out that you write your own music. Once I heard 'Gamechanja ', I knew I couldn't wait any longer because that song was exactly that; a game changer."

"Thank you Mr. Cliverson."

"E.C." he corrects me while trying to hand me one of the flutes.

"I mean E.C."

"I do believe a toast is in order."

"I'm sorry, but I don't drink."

"Surely you can make an exception for this occasion." he continues holding the champagne flute out to me.

I look around the table to see everyone looking at me expectantly. If there ever was an occasion to make an exception, this is definitely it. I take the glass.

"A toast in honor of our newest family member." He raises his glass in salute and everyone at the table including myself does the same. "Welcome aboard Dena. To success and longevity."

Our voices ring out in union. "To success and longevity!" The sound of glasses clinking can be heard all around.

I take a modest sip out of my glass. Having never tasted champagne before, the intense tingling sensation catches me off guard. I fight the urge to rub the back of my jaw like the comedian Martin Lawrence does in his over-the top comedy sitcom. Instead, I sit my glass down and ask E.C.,

"So is this the part where you present me with an enormous advancement check and a contract then we negotiate over the terms of agreement?"

"No. This the part where we kick back and enjoy the festivities."

"Speaking of which, what is this anyway?"

"It's Realest Raw Records seventeenth annual celebration." He leans in closer and whispers, "Between me and you, it's also a meet and greet for all of the singles in the building like myself to mingle and meet new people."

"For some reason, I always assumed that you were married."

"No not me. I enjoy the bachelor lifestyle way too much. The freedom to be able to travel to different cities and states at will without having to answer to anyone is something that I'm not quite ready to give up." I chuckle at his frankness. I like him already.

"So tell me, why is the celebration being held here in Memphis instead of New York where Tre R Records main office is located?"

"Because I'm originally from Memphis and this is where Tre R Records began."

"Oh I didn't know that."

"Excuse me everyone. Can I have your attention?" A heavyset black man who I recognize as one of the label exec's at Tre R Records say through the microphone on the stage. "I'd like to welcome you all to Realest Raw Records Seventeenth Year Anniversary Celebration." The entire room explodes in whistles and applauds. "In the famous words of founder Evan Cliverson, even when mankind fades away the music will still continue to play. And right now, I can definitely hear the music playing y'all. This year Realest Raw Records set the bar at a new height by becoming the first label in music history to ever have a number one hit in eight different genres of music at the same time!" Another eruption of applause take over the room. The energy is so intense that I can't help but to get caught up in the hype. It lasts a whole minute before it dies down enough for him to go on.

"Tonight we're going to celebrate by letting some of our artists get up on this stage and do what they do best. But first, a special tribute to love by our very own, New Vibe!"

All the lights in the room go off and the curtains on the stage open up revealing an enchanting background scenery of a nighttime forest filled with beautiful wildlife plants aglow under midnight stars and a cherry moon. New Vibe, which consists of a male and female duo, emerge one at a time from opposite sides of the stage singing their rendition of the Eric Benet and Tamia duet, 'Spend My Life With You '. It's a touching song reflecting on the power of love and the possibilities of spending forever with the one you love. When they reach the chorus asking that special someone can they see them every morning when they open their eyes, the nighttime forest scene brightens to daylight with the stars disappearing and the cherry moon being replaced by the sun. I find myself aching for my Dabo. So many days and nights I've lived with the emptiness of going to bed alone and waking up without him lying beside me.

The room goes dark again. New Vibe, at the bridge of the song, continue crooning beautifully in the darkness. Suddenly, a bright spotlight comes on from above the stage and shines on the Ballroom doors at the back of the room causing everyone to turn around.

My heart skips a beat when, dressed in an all-white tuxedo, Click walks through the doors. On his head is an iced out crown sparkling brightly in the spotlight. The diamonds in his ears and on his wrist flicker like a disco ball as he walks towards me. In his hand is a large, fancy, red pillow with another diamond encrusted crown sitting on top of it.

Another spotlight comes on shining directly on me.

I can't breathe.

I look over at Evan Cliverson to find him smiling happily at me.

"You set me up." I hear myself saying as my eyes turn into waterfalls. "All of you did."

He only shrugs his shoulders and continues smiling.

Click stops in front of us and hands the pillow to Evan Cliverson to hold. Then he picks the crown up and places it gently on my head. I'm an emotional wreck. My hands are shaking, and I feel lightheaded. Now that the crown has been removed from the pillow, I can see a humongous diamond ring sitting next to a microphone.

Click picks up the microphone and says, "Hey baby, you look beautiful. Congratulations on getting your deal with Tre R Records. I know you're about to take the world by storm. They're about to find out what those of us who are close to you already know. How amazing a woman you really are. I um...know how much you love poetry, so I put together a couple of words to help me express what I'm tryna say. Now I'm not half as good as you so don't laugh at me." My heart tries to beat its way out of my chest when Click grabs the ring off of the pillow and slowly drops down on one knee in front of me.

"Suabo, I didn't know that it could be so wonderful to have....that special someone to hold me down and turn all my smiles into laughs...since we crossed each other's path, the ride has been extreme...but it lead me to the seat of my throne which is why I crowned you my queen...and although sometimes it seems like this moment would never come...this ain't a happily ever after because our story has just begun...you, me, and our son together for me is like a dream come true...especially if I could see you every morning when I open my eyes...and spend the rest of my life with you....Dena Simone Givens, will you marry me?"

"Yessss...yes Dabo!" I'm out of my seat wrapped around him drowning him in a million kisses and tears.

The room explodes sharing in our joy as the lights come back on shining brightly and New Vibe picks up the chorus with a renewed vigor.

"Can I just see you every morning when I open my eyes..."

Everyone has their phones out snapping pictures and recording as Click slides the ring on my finger.

I look up to see Uncle Fresh at the forefront of the audience capturing everything on his iPad.

CHAPTER 26

Click

    I lay back in the comfortable bed in our luxury suite at the Alloriqui' hotel watching the video of my proposal to Dena playing on TMZ. This is probably the hundredth time I've seen it in the past three days that we've been here. It's been on Access Hollywood, Inside Edition, The View, Good Morning America, World News, you name it. Whoever leaked the video to the media had made Dena an instant celebrity and us one of the most talked about couples in Hollywood. The headlines read, "Evan Cliverson's newly signed songbird receives proposal from the man of her dreams." Truthfully, I could watch it a hundred more times and not get tired of seeing it. Dena and I dressed in all white, iced out from the crowns on our heads to the diamonds adorning our bodies is exactly how I pictured it in my mind when I planned it. It couldn't have turned out more perfectly.

    My cellphone vibrates on the nightstand beside the bed. All I can do is smile and shake my head when I pick it up and see who it is calling.

    "Playboi, wassup my nigga."

    "Man you still got that girl up there locked in the room witchu?"

    I laugh. "Yea we still up here chillin."

    "Man let that woman go before yo old ass have a stroke up there tryna make up for lost time."

    "You just talkin shit cause you was only gone three years. I just finished a whole dime. And who you calling old nigga? 38 ain't old."

    "It is when you up there tryna have sport sex like you a teenager."

    "Why you all in my business anyway? Whatchu want?"

    "I'm calling to see if y'all set a date yet. I wanna know how soon I need to reserve my club for yo bachelor party."

    Playboi had come home from prison and picked up right where he left off. He had his club rebuilt from the ground up and flooded the streets of Forrest City with some of the best Kush it had ever seen. He told me that he had saw my marriage proposal on the Wendy Williams Show and wanted to call and congratulate me. He and I have been staying in contact over the years, so he already knew that I was due to get out. What I couldn't figure out was how he got my new number. When I asked him, all he said was,

    "I got a couple of connections."

I tell him, "All I'm waiting for is her. You know how women are with details. She wants to have the perfect wedding so I'm letting her do her thing. As soon as she pulls it all together, we walking down the aisle so you can put the green light on the bachelor party."

"That's what I'm talkin bout. If you ever come up out of that hotel room we can link up so I can put you up on some of this other stuff I got going on out here."

"No doubt. We checking out in the morning, so I'm gone hitchu up some time tomorrow."

"Aight that's what's up."

"Holla." I hang up and lay my phone back on the nightstand. Then I use the remote control to click off the tv before calling out to my fiancé.

"Dena baby, you need some help in there. You been in there a long time."

"No, I'm coming out now. I still can't believe you making me do this."

A few seconds later the bathroom door comes open and what I see before me causes my breath to get caught in my throat. Dena steps out with her hair pulled up in a bun on the top of her head exposing the sleekness of her sexy neck. The crotchless red fishnet body suit with the red pumps that I bought for her hugs her hourglass frame, accentuating her beautiful, skin and causing me to get an instant erection.

With one hand on her hip she asks, "You happy now?"

I smile and nod my head up and down. "This is exactly how I pictured you the first day that I saw you at the bus stop."

"Yea, I saw you undressing me with your eyes. Nasty self."

"Who would have thought that one day I would have you as my own personal sex slave."

"After what we've been doing for the last past three days, you shouldn't want no mo sex." she says as she begins walking towards me.

"Oh this ain't just about sex. It's about you paying whatchu owe."

"But it was eleven years ago."

"Hey, a bet is a bet. Your twenty-four hours start now."

"Fine." she says crossing her arms in a mock
pout. "What you want me to do?"

I point to the tray of fruit that I had room service bring up. "Let's start with you feeding me some of those strawberries and pineapples over there. But there's one rule."

"Which is?"

"Being that you're my genie in a bottle for the next twenty-four hours, whatever I ask you to do, I expect you to reply with "Yes my king" and complete the task with a smile."

"Wait a minute now."

"Ah ah...and no back talk. Is that understood?"

She closes her mouth, takes a deep breath, then through a tight smile says "Yes my King" before coming over and doing what she's told.

I take great joy in chewing and savoring the taste of each piece of fruit that she feeds into my mouth. Even grabbing her wrist and slurping the excess juice off her fingers.

"You make me sick you know that." she says trying to hold in her laugh.

"And you make me horny."

She looks down at my firm erection standing proudly and says, "He needs to calm down because I'm a little sore right now. You ain't the only one who's been out of commission for the past decade."

"You were talking a lot of stuff over the phone saying what you was gone do to me when I got out. Don't try to cop a plea now."

"I've already backed that up all night the day you got out. Then all day the next day and yesterday. What more can I possibly back up?"

"All of that was before I saw you in this body suit. Now quit crying. You distracting me while I'm trying to taste yo fruit."

She shakes her head then picks up a strawberry and tries to feed it to me. Instead of taking it, I just stare at her.

"What?" she asks.

"I said I'm trying to taste *yo* fruit."

For a moment, she stands confused looking at the deviousness in my eyes. Then her cheeks blush bright red as the full understanding of what I'm asking sets in. Seeing how flustered she is turns me on even more.

To her credit, she recovers nicely by saying "Yes my King." before setting the fruit tray down on the nightstand beside the bed, then lifting her leg, and placing her high heel up on the side of the bed. "Shall I feed it to you too or are you gone come and get it."

It's my turn to be flustered as I admire the up-close view of her neatly trimmed peach with a strip of fine hair down the middle. Seeing my reaction seems to give her more confidence as she spreads her legs wider and slides a finger between the folds of her sex.

"Maybe I should taste it first and make sure it's sweet enough for you." Her middle finger disappears deep inside of her slit as she closes her eyes and begins stirring.

I couldn't be more turned on than I am at this moment watching my angel pleasuring herself. My hand involuntarily finds my nature.

Removing her finger, Dena stares boldly into my eyes as she places it in her mouth and makes an "Mmmm" sound while slowly pulling it out.

I raise up and begin kissing the inside of her thick thigh as she begins pleasuring herself some more. The sound of her moisture brings more eroticism to the moment. Her finger glistens with her juices when she pulls it out and slide it into my mouth. The taste of her essence is more than I can handle.

"Come're." I wrap my arms around her waist and pull her down on top of me. "Kiss me."

"Yes my king." Her soft lips press against mine three or four times before her sex laced tongue eases its way into my mouth and begins tangoing with mine. My hands travel the contours of her body as I roll her onto her back landing on top of her.

"I want you to do something for me."

"What is it my love?"

"Do you remember the first time that you sung to me?"

"Of course."

"We were on the highway in the new Range Rover you bought for me on the night you first took me to your poetry club."

A smile emerges on her face. "I remember that. That was the day that I finally admitted to myself that I had fallen for you."

"Do you remember the first song you sung for me?"

"Now that I don't remember."

"It was 'I like' by Kut Klose."

"Oh yea, that was my jam back in the day."

"Sing it for me."

"What, right now?"

"Right here right now."

She shrugs her shoulders. "Okay."

"Excuse me." I bite down lightly on the skin of her jaw.

"I mean.." she giggles like a giddy schoolgirl. "Yes my king!" Her first note comes out sounding like a harmony from heaven. The melody seducing my senses into removing my teeth and slurping her skin like it came wrapped in silky paper. My lips kiss her singing lips, her nose, her eyelids, her ears and neck before traveling down her body. By the time my tongue invades her secret garden, she hits a high note.

I'm the luckiest man on earth. About to marry a woman who's beautiful with a heart of gold. Sexy. Smart. Talented. Rich. Untouched by another man. Who's the mother of my child and hopelessly devoted to me. I'm one of the few men who can truly say that I've found my diamond in the rough.

I spend the next hour making her serenade me while I use my mouth to make her hit every note on the musical scale.

****

"Click, I want you to meet Jaye." Reece says when I walk into the living room.

He stands up and holds his hand out for me to shake. "How you doing Click. I've heard a lot about you."

I take it and say, "Wassup Jaye. Sorry, but I can't say the same." I look at Reece waiting for her to fill in the blanks.

"Click, Jaye is my boyfriend.

My eyebrows raise in surprise "Boyfriend?"

"Actually, I'm her fiancé. "he interjects.

"Oh, he's yo fiancé huh?" I ask incredulously.

"Yea Uncle Click, that means they getting married." TJ, who's sitting in front of the flat-screen playing the PS4 with my son offers.

I'm more than a little taken back by this revelation. Reece and I have been communicating on the regular for the entire time I've been locked up and not once did she mention anything about dating anyone; let alone marrying.

This is the last thing that I expected. It's been less than an hour since Dena and I made it back from Memphis and I'm running on fumes. We didn't get much sleep while we were over there, especially not in those last twenty-four hours. Only thing on my mind was crashing out for a few hours when we made it back to the mansion, was actually in the process of doing just that when Dena came into the room and told me that Reece needed to talk to me. Not wanted to but NEEDED to. Now as I stand here watching her nervous body language and evasive eye contact, I can't help but to feel blind-sided.

"So how long have you two known each other?"

"Jaye and I have been neighbors almost fifteen years."

"So that means you knew my homeboy Travis?" I ask directing my question to Jaye.

"Yea. Me, Travis, and Mechi grew up across the hall from each other in the apartments above their daddy's record store. I met Reece through Travis."

Now that I take a closer look at this cat, he does look kind of familiar. When I take away his neatly trimmed beard, reduce him by twenty pounds, and replace his deep waves with that little fucked up box cut that he used to wear, I know exactly who he is.

"You're Mr. McAllister's son right?"

"Yea that was my father. "he answers dropping his eyes in shame.

When we were younger, I remember us needing another man to go with us to the Southside Park where we were planning on playing a couple games of basketball and Travis knocking on Mr. McAllister's door.

"Can I help you?" the tall skinny man with glasses
opened the door and asked.

Travis said, "How you doing Mr. McAllister. We wanted to know could your son come out and play basketball with us?" He eyed us standing out in the hallway with a look of distaste.

"Jaye has more important things to do besides running around with a bunch of hoodlums getting into trouble." Before Travis could respond, he rudely slammed the door in his face. Mechi wanted to knock again and curse his ass out, but Travis and I stopped him. Later that day, while we were hanging out in front of the record store, Mr. McAllister and his son came out and climbed into their beat up Nissan Maximum. They walked past us as if we were invisible. I could tell that his son was embarrassed by the way he cast his eyes down in shame as he passed by. That and the longing backward look he gave us as his father drove off. Travis told me that only the two of them lived in the apartment across the hall together and he often heard the father yelling through the walls. I'd always wondered what that man's problem was. One thing was for sure; he definitely had issues. About a year later, Mr. McAllister committed suicide.

"So Jaye, do you make it a habit of taking advantage of yo ex neighbor's grieving widow?"

"Click!" Reece intervenes grabbing me by the arm. "Come're let me talk to you for a minute." She pulls me out of the room, through the mansion and doesn't stop until we're standing outside on the back patio by the pool. She spins to face me with one hand on her hip and pointing her finger in my face.

"First of all, Jaye didn't take advantage of me. If anything, I took advantage of him. He was a perfect gentleman. He helped me out when you were too busy and caught up with your revenge on Lafu, so don't you go judging him. Who do you think took me to my doctor appointments and Lamaze classes? And who do you think rushed me to the hospital when my water broke after Dena and I got to fighting? Jaye is a good guy so before you start jumping to conclusions, get your facts straight."

"If he's such a good guy and this all happened so innocently, why you been hiding it from me?" That seems to let all of the air out of her.

"I don't know...I guess..."She blows out a breath of frustration and runs a hand across her neat ponytail.

"I've been dreading this moment for years now."

"Years? How long have y'all been together?"

She pauses momentarily then looks bravely into my eyes.

"Jaye and I became an item not long before you went back to prison."

Ten whole years she's been keeping this from me. Instead of responding, I let my eyes travel the expanse of the fenced in pool area. The stained wood patio deck overlooking the Olympic sized pool surrounded by designer lounge chairs and tables complete with shade umbrellas. Being that it's late August, arguably the hottest month of the year, the ninety-eight degree weather has the sun shining brightly and shimmering off of the clear blue water of the pool.

Reece who is now sitting in one of the iron patio chairs says, "There's not a day that goes by that I don't think about...that I don't look at our son and remember the bond that I shared with my husband. I carry him with me every day. That's why I fought so hard against what was happening between me and Jaye. I felt so guilty when it first happened, like I was cheating on Travis. I still struggle with it even after all these years. Some days, I shut all the way down and lock Jaye out because Travis be on my heart so heavy. It's not fair to him having to compete with my past, but I can't help it. I've never betrayed Travis not one time throughout our whole relationship."

"Reece, Travis wouldn't have wanted you to spend the rest of your life alone. He would have wanted you to be happy. He would have wanted you to have a real man around his son."

"Jaye is a real man and TJ loves him."

"So why you been keeping him a secret then?"

"Because I thought you'd be mad at me." Her facial expression makes it apparent how important my approval is.

"I can't never be mad atchu for doing you. You're a grown woman. I'm just disappointed that you felt you couldn't talk to me about this. I thought we were tighter than that."

"You're Travis's best friend. I thought you would look at me differently if you saw me with another man."

I look at Reece and images of my late homeboy fill my mind, seeing his round face and that big Kool-Aid smile of his causes my own mouth to form a smile.

"The first day that I came over y'all house when I first got out and met you, Travis told me that you were his soulmate." Reece's worried expression softens into an emotional smile. "I couldn't believe it because as long as I've known him, Travis has been vowing to be a playa for life."

"Oh he still thought he was a playa. I had to put hands on a couple of females who couldn't get it through their head that Travis was married and off the market." I laugh thinking about the time that we all went out to a club in Memphis and Reece beat up some chick when she caught her kissing Travis on the dance floor.

"I just know that it had to take a special kind of woman to get my guy to the altar. The way he looked at you and talked about you, I knew that my homeboy was in love when he died. He died knowing that he was loved. That's the part that I'm gone always remember and hold on to."

"Aw Click, thank you so much." Reece stands giving me a hug.

"You just make sure he treats you right." I say giving her a tight squeeze along with my approval. "And let him know that if he hurts you, I'm gone be on his ass like back pockets."

"Duly noted." Jaye says from the doorway where he's been standing listening. He and I share a long moment of eye contact before he comes over to stand behind Reece.

She releases me and turns into Jaye's waiting embrace. One of her hands land across the center of his chest. The other hand in his where they interlock fingers. Jaye places a kiss on Reece's forehead. It's then that I notice the shiny engagement ring on her finger.

Seeing Reece standing there comfortable in Jaye's arms, I know that's where she wants to be, and I have no problem with that.

"Click!" Dena's alarmed voice reaches me moments before she appears in the patio doorway where Jaye stood not long ago. "Come quick! TJ and Cream are fighting and I can't break them up!"

CHAPTER 27

Click

    The huge round money dispenser hanging from the ceiling in the middle of the club releases a burst of one dollar bills that rain down all around me like large pieces of green confetti. The Migos club banger 'Handsome and Wealthy' thump through the speakers as big booty dancers shake their money-makers all in my face. The thongless dancer dry humping my lap suddenly stands up then drops down into the splits in front of me. Her skillful maneuver causes the carpet of dollar bills covering the glass floor to separate enough for me to see the baby sharks swimming lazily beneath the surface. Playboi really outdid himself. His new club, 'Playboi's Deluxe Palace' is the first club that I've ever heard of that has an underground aquarium built beneath the dance floor making it feel like you're partying on top of the ocean. My bachelor party has been going a little over an hour and seems to be turning up more and more by the minute. A floor to ceiling fountain filled with a constant flow of Ace of Spades has all of the fellas in attendance getting drunk for free and throwing money like crazy. Playboi and I sit at a special table that he had set up in the middle of the dance floor surrounded by strippers tossing it up.

    Another wave of one dollar bills eject from the money dispenser above adding to the money shower.

    I lean over towards Playboi's ear and asks, "How often does that thing go off?"

    "What thing?"

    I point up towards the dispenser.

    "Oh, it goes off about every five minutes."

    "Seems like a lot of money."

    "Not really. It only shoots out fifty dollars at a time." In my mind, I try to calculate how much fifty bucks every five minutes, for nine or ten hours amount to. "Five or six thousand a night. "Playboi says with a shrug solving the equation for me. "That's nothing when you pulling in twenty to thirty thousand a night." He looks at me and smiles flashing the two gold teeth on the bottom left side of his mouth.

    My phone vibrates in my pocket. I pull it out and see that it's Mechi calling.

    "Damn my nigga where you at? The party been jumping for over an hour now." I use one finger to plug my ear so that I can hear his response.

    "You ain't gone believe who I'm in traffic trailing behind right now."

    "Who?"

"Lil-Eighty nigga."

His answer causes me to sit up straight in my seat.

"Lil-Eighty?"

"Yea. I was on the interstate coming back from handling some business and just so happen to look over and see this nigga beside me in traffic."

"Did he see you?"

"Nah. I been on his ass for like ten minutes now."

"Where you at?"

"On I-40 heading west towards Little Rock."

"Aight, but don't kill him yet. See if you can get some answers out of him first. I'm bout to hop in the whip and head yo way so keep me posted on yo whereabouts."

"Bet."

The last I heard; Lil-Eighty had gotten sent to the state pen on a dope charge not long after I went away. I was pretty sure that he had been released, but no one had seen or heard from him since. I'd just assumed that he had relocated to another city and state.

I tap Playboi, who is turning up a bottle of Ace of Spades and watching the sexy chocolate and red bone freaks sixty-nining on the floor in front of him.

"Come take a ride with me." I say. Without waiting for him to answer, I get up and head out of the club.

A group of brothas are at the entrance trying to talk their way inside. I hear one of them say,

"Come on sweetie, we just tryna spend a little money and get our swerve on. We ain't gone start no trouble."

"Sorry guys it's a private party."

"So why you letting all these females walk in then?"

"It's a bachelor party so all females are welcomed."

"So any female can get in for free right now, but a brotha can't even pay his way in? That's sexist as hell."

"Sorry fellas, I don't make the rules."

I continue walking with Playboi coming out not far behind me.

"Playboi, wassup my nigga! Man tell ya girl to let us in."

"This a private bachelor party for my homeboy, y'all don't even know him."

"Come on man, this me Big Fitty. Me and you go way back. Back when yo uncles was still calling you Lil Stompa. I know you ain't gone play me like that."

Playboi lets out that sneaky laugh of his and says, "You lucky I fuck witchu Big Fitty." Then he tells the women in the entrance booth "Charge them a dollar a head." before walking off.

He climbs into the passenger side of the new Bugatti that Johnny Ray bought me as a wedding gift and asks, "How you gone leave yo own bachelor party? Where you going?"

"Something important came up." I say as I shift into reverse and back out of the parking space.

It's been years since I've thought about Lil-Eighty and his betrayal. I was content to just let the whole situation go as long as he never showed his face around here again. Now that he's resurfaced, there's no way that I can let him live. As I head towards the interstate, my mind travels back to a time and place when I had mad love for this cat, when Lil-Eighty was a part of my squad and always down to ride for the cause. Then without warning he flipped the script, went from being friend to foe, became the epitome of the same enemy that he once stood and faced with me. What bothers me the most is that to this day, I still don't know what made him switch up.

"Here, I forgot to give you this. "Playboi says handing me a sandwich bag full of Kush. "I noticed you been smoking that Babbage all night."

"Babbage? Man you trippin, this that Gorilla Glue. You don't know nothing about this" I say pulling out my personal stash although I know that what he just handed me is probably better than anything around.

Playboi did three years in prison and came home to reclaim his position in the game with a vengeance. Not only did he have a bigger and better version of his club built from the ground up, but he also flooded the streets with a new brand of Kush that made other brands that were around seem like Reggie. With a better brand at a cheaper price, it wasn't long before he absorbed all of the clientele.

Not long after I made it to the federal facility in
Forrest City, I had a run-in with a black female guard. She was a lieutenant who was known for being "Allstate ", a title that inmates give to the guards who do everything strictly by the books.

I was standing in the chow line, when the guard, whose name is Lieutenant Crawford, approached the line and demanded, "Who said that?" Everyone looked around at each other in confusion.

"Which one of you said that?"

Coming to the conclusion that I must have missed something because I hadn't heard anyone say anything out of the ordinary, I turned back around in line and continued to wait my turn. Imagine my surprise when Lieutenant Crawford and two other white male guards approached me.

"What's your name inmate?" she barked in my face.

"My name is Fevers."

"You got something to say Fevers?"

"If I had something to say I would have said it."

"Oh you wanna be a smart ass huh?"

"Nah. You asked me a question and I answered it."

"Well I tell you what inmate Fevers the smartass, turn around and catch the cuffs."

"Catch the cuffs for what? I ain't did nothing."

"Because she said so boy." One of the white guards said stepping up into my face.

It was bad enough that this black woman, who

obviously had a chip on her shoulder, had decided to pick me out of all the guys that were standing in line, but now this white guard had called me a boy; a word that's offensive to any man regardless of his race, statue, or position.

My first instinct was to check the white guard and tell him that his boy was between his legs and to refuse the handcuffs because I hadn't done anything wrong. I noticed the set jawline of both of the white guards and their body language. They were waiting for me to buck so that they could make an example out of me. Then my eyes went to Lieutenant Crawford and something about the way she was looking at me slowed me down and begged me not me not to do anything stupid. Knowing that I hadn't been at the prison for long and not wanting to start my bid off this way, I decided not to resist. I turned around and allowed myself to be restrained. They ruff cuffed me and threw me in the hole with no further explanation.

For the next few days, I sat there stewing on my predicament, wondering why I had been the unlucky one. On the afternoon of the third day, I received a disciplinary saying that I had been insolvent to the staff and disobeyed several direct orders. My anger went through the roof at being lied on. I wanted to hurt someone.

By the time Lieutenant Crawford entered my cell two weeks later, I had been to disciplinary court and sentenced to serve thirty days in the hole. The hole was actually a one man cell behind a door and a row of bars. The bars were set four feet inside the door leaving a space for the guard to come in and interact with the inmates and still be separated.

The thing about Lieutenant Crawford, although she was mean and Allstate as hell, she was also fine. Her crisp brown khaki uniform snugly embraced the dimensions of her coke bottle frame. I guessed her age to be somewhere from mid to late thirties. The paper sack brown complexion of her face barely held any traces of makeup yet had a youthful beauty about it. She stood inside the four foot space with the door closed behind her boldly staring at me. I didn't try to hide my angst at her presence. My eyes met hers with hostility. What she did next shocked me so bad that I had to blink several times to convince myself that I wasn't dreaming.

Her right hand went into her pants pocket at the same time that she brought the index finger of her left hand to her lips signaling me to stay quiet. When she pulled the small black phone out of her pocket and held it out to me, I only hesitated momentarily before I was on my feet taking it out of her hand. Next she began undoing the buttons of her neatly starched prison guard uniform. Underneath it, she wore an all-black t-shirt, which she untucked along with her khaki shirt. When she began unbuckling then unzipping her pants enough for me to see the white cotton of her panties, my nature responded. Lieutenant Crawford's eyes landed on the tent forming in the front of my pants and for the first time, I saw her smile.

"Now don't get too excited." she said as she lifted her shirt and began unwrapping some kind of saran wrap from around her mid-section. "This ain't that kind of party." I watched as she peeled a flat vacuum sealed package that was long enough to wrap around her body one and a half times and wide enough to reach from just beneath her breast down to the top of her sex.

Once she got it removed, she handed it through the bars to me and whispered, "Now make sure you don't try to open this up in here because that stuff is super loud. The cigarettes ain't that bad, but the weed had my whole house smelling. The best thing for you to do is just put it up and wait until you get out of here before you mess with it. For a minute, I thought you was gone mess everything up. I'm glad you kept your cool and cuffed up. Playboi's number is already programmed into the phone. He said for you to get at him as soon as you can. Now listen, this is the one and only time that you and I will talk face to face. I'll be getting atchu on my own time through my own people. Don't be coming up to me trying to talk and definitely don't be sending nobody at me. The first time you do, I'm cutting you off. You got it?" She was firm but not disrespectful, sultry but serious, sexy and about her business. She knew what she was doing and I couldn't do nothing but respect how she moved.

"Yea, I got it but damn, did you have to put me through all of this just to drop off a package?"

"You bet I did. Look, everybody saw what happened between you and I and as long as they think we got beef they won't think that I'm bringing you work. All you have to do now is play your role and I'll play mine." She began fixing her clothes but stopped short. "Oh, I almost forgot." Her hand went down the front of her underwear. With a wide legged stance, she squatted and pulled a long slim package wrapped in plastic out of her panties.

"Playboi told me to tell you that this is for your own personal use. It's way better than that other stuff." She gave a wink, finished fixing her clothes, and eased back out of the cell leaving me standing there smelling the intoxicating aroma of her pussy on the plastic.

Playboi had hooked me up once again. Even behind those walls he had managed to reach out and show me some love. From that day until the day of my release, I was known for keeping the best weed in the prison. When I finally did call and talk to him, I asked him how he managed to pull all of this together when he was still in prison himself. And of course his response was,

"I got a couple of connections."

As I drive down I-40 with murder on my mind, I look over into the passenger seat at Playboi and realize that he's the closest thing that I have to a brother since Travis got killed. Makes me wonder how the two of them would have gotten along if Travis were still alive.

The sound of my phone, which I've connected to the Bluetooth in my car, rings through the speakers.

"Mechi, what's good?" I answer.

His voice explodes inside the interior of the two seater causing me to have to adjust the volume.

"Yo Click, I got this pussy ass nigga!" I hear what sounds like a gun cracking against a skull followed by Lil-Eighty's pleas.

"Come on Mechi man, chill out. You ain't gotta do me like this!"

"Shut up bitch!" More licks followed by pleading. Adrenaline flows feverishly through my bloodstream knowing that I'm finally about to get my hands on this nigga after all these years.

Playboi, who still has no idea what's going on, looks over at me questioningly.

"What the fuck!?!"

"Mechi, where you at?"

"I'm in the Rock now. Meet me at Interstate Park. You a see my car."

"Shiid, I still got a ways to go before I make it to Little Rock. Man put that nigga on the phone."

A few seconds later, Mechi says, "He can hear you."

"Wassup Eighty, long time no holla."

His voice sounding distant and weak comes over the speakerphone.

"Click, man what's this all about?"

"Come on Eighty, we done always kept it funky with each other. You know what this shit about."

"I'm saying though, I know you was a lil upset with me about the play at the club, but I got caught up in some mo shit."

"Would have been nice if my guy would have at least came to the county and seen me and let me know something."

"Man you know shit was hot. I couldn't come up there."

"Kinda funny because Mechi stayed ten toes down through it all and he still managed to come up there. Ain't that right Mechi?"

"Damn right, real niggas do real shit. And busta niggas..." Another lick."...do busta shit!"

"Aah fuck man! Get this nigga up off me! Got my shit leakin everywhere!"

Playboi and I look at each other and share a laugh.

"You better hurry up and tell me something because Mechi sound like he having a field day on yo head."

"I mean what, you want me to tell you I'm sorry. I apologize for leaving y'all hangin and not comin to the county to see you but..."

"Nah nah nigga, I already know why you left us hanging and didn't come see me. I wanna know why you sent yo cousin Pipe G at me."

Silence from the other end of the line.

"Don't get quiet now. I been waiting over ten years to hear this. Or do you need Mechi to help you getcho tongue working again?"

"Nah, I'm good. I can talk."

"So let's hear it then."

More silence like he's getting his thoughts together. Finally, he begins letting it out.

"It all started around the time that Mechi went missing and everybody was talking about us killing the J.P. Posse. Right after we smoked those Omaha niggas. One of the fellas in my crew came to me and said that some bitch gave him a number that she wanted me to call. I just thought it was just another one of these freaks out here tryna get her back blown out, but then I saw the name Big Man written on the number that she gave me."

"Big Man? Who the fuck is Big Man?"

"I didn't know at the time, but I called anyway. Nigga knew all about me, knew who my mama was, where I grew up. He knew everything. Then he asked me if I wanted to make some money. A quarter million dollars. Shiid, I thought the nigga was joking. I laughed and asked him who I had to kill. He told me nobody yet and then hung up. A couple months went by with no word, so I just blew it off as some bullshit. Next thing I know, some fine ass bitch in a red Benz pulls up and drops me a hundred stacks and a new number. Told me Big Man wanted me to call him. That's when he started asking questions about you and Dena."

"About me and Dena? Why would some nigga that I don't even know wanna know about me and my woman?"

"I don't know, but he seemed almost obsessed with y'all. He wanted to know how often y'all be together, what cars y'all drive, and where y'all lay y'all head. Like he wanted me to keep tabs and report y'all every move."

"The fuck!?!" My mind swirls through the rolodex of my memory wondering what hidden enemy I have out there that I don't know about. Lil-Eighty said that this all began around the time that we killed the JP Posse, so maybe this was some kind of backlash from that. But what did Dena have to do with this?

"You mean to tell me that some cat you don't even know toss a couple bucks atchu and you sell me out just like that?"

"Not at first I didn't. I tried to curb dude by just making up shit to keep him going. I mean, I don't know the nigga. Plus he had already given me a hundred G's, so I wasn't fucked up. Next thing I know, some niggas snatched me outta my bed in the middle of the night. Had me out in the country, butt-naked, on my knees with a gun to my head. They put a phone to my ear, and it was Big Man. He told me that this was my one and only warning about playing with him. Next time he'd erase me from the face of the earth and investigators wouldn't even be able to find traces of my DNA."

"Why the fuck didn't you come to me Eighty? We was crew! If you would have told us that some nigga was putting the squeeze on you we would've handled it!"

"Man you don't get it. This muthafucka was watching me the whole time. He would call and tell me what I was wearing and exactly what I was doing at that moment."

"So who the fuck is this nigga?"

"After I got kidnapped, I started asking questions around the town trying to find out who Big Man was, but nobody knew nothin. Even when I put a price on it, I still couldn't come up with answers. That's when I figured that he had to be using a fake name. Next time he called, I asked him who he really was, and he said all I needed to know was that if I wanted the rest of my money then I had to kill both of y'all."

"Kill who, me and Dena?"

"Nah, he wanted me to kill you and Mechi."

"Hold up pussy ass nigga." Mechi jumps in. "How he know about me?"

"I told you this nigga be watching. He knew everything."

"See now I know you lying. I wasn't even on the scene back then. I was in rehab remember. Y'all didn't even know I was still alive."

"Exactly! How do you think I knew where to find you? What, you think I just popped up at the rehab out the blue?"

"Damn, I always wondered how you knew to come up there." Mechi says thoughtfully sounding convinced.

"I'm telling you man, this nigga ain't no average Joe. He playing on a whole different level of the game."

Now more than ever, I'm wondering who is this cat that was out there stalking and trying to kill me. Thoughts of Lafu, a man who was obsessed enough to plot, plan, and execute revenge on me ten years after he believed that I killed his brother flood my mind. Could this person who got Lil-Eighty to turn on me be the same man or somehow a part of the same conspiracy? This has to be in some way connected because there is no way that I had two separate hidden enemies at the exact same time for different reasons. I had done my share of dirt in the past, but nothing serious enough for anyone to still want revenge after all these years. Once thing that I know for sure; Lafu died in a twelfth floor condo in downtown Atlanta ten years ago. That means that whatever alternative scheme he had brewing in the background died with him.

Still I ask, "Did you ever find out who he was?"

"Yea. It was right after you got locked back up. I spotted the bitch in the red Benz who dropped the hundred stacks off to me. I knew it was her because I recognized the BOO DEAN plates."

"BOO DEAN plates?"

"Yea, the red Benz she drove had personalized BOODEAN plates on it. I caught her slippin and made her tell me who sent her to give me that money. Bitch tried to play hard at first, but when I saw that she had a baby with her, I told her that I would rock his lil ass to sleep if she didn't tell me what I wanted to know. She folded like a lawn chair, told me that the dude was her husband and he wouldn't rest until he got what was rightfully his."

"Fuck was she talking about what was rightfully his?" I asked confused.

"Some shit about yo girl trying to take his place and him being the real heir to the Dream Dynasty, Dean Dynasty or some shit like that."

It takes a second to register, but then I remember
watching the video in Dena's condo in downtown Atlanta that night where Johnny Ray told Dena that she had inherited Lafu's entire estate from her mother.

The Dean Dynasty.

Lafu's last name was Dean.

Boo Dean.

"Wait a minute, what did she say her husband's name was?"

"Barry Dean."

I look over to see the barrel of a forty-five automatic pointed at me.

Playboi says, "Yea nigga, you murdered my pops and yo bitch got what's mine. Both of y'all gotta die."

I don't know why it never dawned on me before. I knew from being in the county jail with him, that Playboi's government name was Barry Dean. For some reason, I didn't make the connection when I found out that Lafu's last name was Dean too. Maybe it was under the circumstances that I found out. Or maybe it was how smooth Playboi had played up under me, but never in a million years would I have guessed that Playboi is the son of the man that I went to prison for killing.

Playboi is Lafu's nephew.

Totally caught off guard, I react off of pure instinct by lunging for the gun at the same moment that I stomp down on the gas and cut the steering wheel hard to the right.

The flash of gunfire fills the interior of the Bugatti as we swerve off of the highway and the car begins to flip.....

Made in the USA
Columbia, SC
22 March 2025